Suite Fantasy

Suite Fantasy

JANICE MAYNARD

A SIGNET ECLIPSE BOOK

SIGNET ECLIPSE
Published by New American Library, a division of
Penguin Group (USA) Inc., 375 Hudson Street, New York, New York 10014, USA
Penguin Group (Canada), 90 Eglinton Avenue East, Suite 700, Toronto,
Ontario M4P 2Y3, Canada (a division of Pearson Penguin Canada Inc.)
Penguin Books Ltd., 80 Strand, London WC2R 0RL, England
Penguin Ireland, 25 St. Stephen's Green, Dublin 2,
Ireland (a division of Penguin Books Ltd.)
Penguin Group (Australia), 250 Camberwell Road, Camberwell, Victoria 3124,
Australia (a division of Pearson Australia Group Pty. Ltd.)
Penguin Books India Pvt. Ltd., 11 Community Centre, Panchsheel Park,
New Delhi—110 017, India
Penguin Group (NZ), cnr Airborne and Rosedale Roads, Albany,
Auckland 1310, New Zealand (a division of Pearson New Zealand Ltd.)
Penguin Books (South Africa) (Pty.) Ltd., 24 Sturdee Avenue,
Rosebank, Johannesburg 2196, South Africa

Penguin Books Ltd., Registered Offices: 80 Strand, London WC2R 0RL, England

First published by Signet Eclipse, an imprint of New American Library,
a division of Penguin Group (USA) Inc.

First Printing, January 2006
10 9 8 7 6 5 4 3 2 1

LIBRARY OF CONGRESS CATALOGING-IN-PUBLICATION DATA:

Maynard, Janice.
  Suite fantasy / by Janice Maynard.
     p.   cm.
ISBN 0-451-21750-0
1. Hotels—Fiction.   2. Erotic stories, American.   I. Title.

PS3613.A958S85 2006
813'.6—dc22   2005019599

Set in Berkeley

Printed in the United States of America

For Lori and Emily—two wise and wonderful women
who love life in general and romance in particular

Suite Seduction

CHAPTER ONE

*K*atie Spencer yawned and stretched, enjoying the feel of the cool, soft sheets against her bare flesh. Dylan lay beside her, snoring softly. She turned over and propped her head on her hand, watching him sleep. She really did love him . . . madly, passionately, deeply. The till death do us part sort of love that tied you up in knots and sometimes scared you silly. Though his heavy, dark lashes rested on his cheeks, she had no trouble visualizing his deep blue eyes. Those eyes should be licensed weapons. They could make a girl shuck her panties in record time, and although she had no particular desire to know about any of his previous relationships, she knew a man like Dylan Ward came by his experience the old-fashioned way.

They were introduced at a party by mutual friends. She had found him incredibly attractive, but after a recent messy breakup, she'd been in no mood for romance. But Dylan was persistent. She'd finally agreed to a date, and their courtship became the proverbial whirlwind from that moment on. After three months, Dylan was an integral part of her life.

He was sweet, sexy, and dependable. After dating a string of losers, Katie saw Dylan as the sunshine in her life. He was the reason she woke up smiling every morning. He adored her, cherished her. Which led to the unpleasant little niggle of doubt she was now experiencing . . . She was afraid that Dylan had put her up on some kind of pedestal. Not that it wasn't flattering, but heck . . . perfection was hard to live up to, and even though she was pretty proud of the woman she'd turned out to be, she was no saint, not by a long shot.

Maybe she was nuts to worry about this. What woman didn't want to be the princess in some man's life? Dylan treated her like fine china, wrapped her in cotton wool, protected her from the bad things in life. He was her knight in shining armor. It wasn't exactly a hardship.

But she had the unshakable notion that he was holding back sometimes when they made love. She suspected that behind his calm, even-keeled personality was a man who might be a little dangerous. That edge excited her, and Dylan was the first man she had ever trusted enough to want to shed her inhibitions and act out a few dangerous fantasies of her own.

She stroked his silky black hair and rubbed a hand across his back. He was all steely muscles beneath smooth, golden skin. He was tough, a prime specimen of a man at his physical peak. He owned his own construction company here in Atlanta, and despite the fact that he had a perfectly good office, more often than not he was out in the field wearing his hard hat and using the hands-on approach that had garnered him an impressive amount of respect and financial success.

She sighed and slid beneath the covers, spooning herself against his back. He radiated warmth. She closed her eyes and snuggled. She was working on an idea that might bring them even closer. It wasn't a *nice girl* plan at all . . . In fact, it was downright naughty. She smiled as she drifted off to sleep. Dylan Ward was going to see a whole new side of Katie Spencer.

It was a beautiful spring afternoon, the kind of day that made you forget the sweltering Atlanta summer. Dylan walked up the path to a doll-cottage-size white house and knocked gently before using his key and walking in. The smells of cinnamon and nutmeg enfolded him. He paused for a split second, sniffed the air appreciatively, and then went in search of his girlfriend.

He found her in the kitchen elbow deep in cookie dough. She looked up and smiled, her pleased expression catching a vulnerable spot in his heart and making his knees weak. God, he loved her.

She was pure sweet woman . . . nurturing, caring, and so damned beautiful she made his toes curl. Her baby-fine blond hair was pulled back in a ponytail, and she had tried to cover the smattering of freckles on her nose with powder. He thought the freckles were cute. Her big brown eyes mirrored her every emotion, and right now they were welcoming him home.

For the thousandth time he wondered how he had been lucky enough to find her before some other man snapped her up. She was fresh and open and unbelievably appealing. Sometimes he wanted her so much he couldn't breathe.

He stole a kiss and a piece of cookie dough. "How's my favorite day care director?"

She rubbed flour from her cheek and laughed. "It's ten after six on a Friday. The terrible two were the last ones to be picked up. I'm done with next week's snacks. I'm still in one piece and relatively sane. I'd say I'm doing pretty well."

He glanced at his watch. "I timed that just right."

She tucked the last tray of cookies in the oven and wiped her hands, leaning in for a longer kiss. His pulse kicked up a notch as her soft breasts pressed against his chest. She teased him with her tongue, and he groaned involuntarily. "Katie . . ." His hoarse whisper was half protest, half plea.

She nibbled his lower lip. "Why don't you hang around for a minute, and I'll let you try my goodies?"

He might have thought she was talking about cookies if her hand hadn't been roaming with wicked intent over the front of his jeans, teasing his fly with inventive fingertips. He gulped.

"I'm all dirty and sweaty, honey. Let me go home and clean up and I'll take you out to dinner."

She wrinkled her nose and sighed, but her smile was sunny. "Okay, but a man your age shouldn't pass up the opportunity for nooky."

His eyebrows rose. "Nooky?"

She grinned. "The airspace in this house is usually rated G. I have a hard time shifting gears. I assumed you could translate." She snuggled closer for another kiss, her arms sliding around his waist. "There's a new barbecue place out on Clairmont. Why don't we try it?"

He kissed her nose. "Sounds good. I'll pick you up in an hour."

Dylan watched Katie bite into a piece of corn on the cob and wondered glumly what kind of pervert got turned on by vegetables. She picked up part of her barbecue ribs and nibbled on them, laughing when some of the sauce dribbled down her chin. She tried to rescue it with her tongue, but failed. He reached across the table and used his thumb to clean her up. She smiled her thanks, and he moved restlessly in his chair as his groin tightened. His cock throbbed uncomfortably in the confining jeans he wore. Hell, he was headed for the funny farm if this kept up.

He was tired of hopping out of Katie's bed and scuttling home in the predawn hours. Her earliest charge was dropped off at six o'clock every morning, and the child's very conservative parents wouldn't take kindly to their son's caregiver having an overnight guest. Dylan thought the subterfuge was stupid, but he bowed to Katie's wishes. For now. He wanted her in *his* bed every night, all night. Naked, willing, at his mercy.

He swallowed hard. Damn. "Katie . . ." He fizzled to a halt, not sure what he was about to say.

She lifted an eyebrow, her eyes dancing. "Yes . . . you can have my last piece of ribs. I'm stuffed anyway."

He grinned reluctantly. "Well, thanks . . . and I'll take it. But that's not what I was going to say."

She cocked her head, smiling. "So serious . . . Should I be worried?"

"I'm tired of sneaking out of your house every morning."

Katie's smile slipped. He'd blurted it out with an appalling lack of finesse. She frowned. "I didn't know it bothered you so much."

He shrugged unhappily. "I don't like feeling as though our relationship is something to be ashamed of."

"But you know the Turners . . ."

"I know. I know . . . they wouldn't approve."

She took his hand, her expression urgent. "He's getting transferred in July. That's only a few more months. And then I won't have to open until eight. You leave for work at seven thirty . . . so no problem . . . right?"

Marry me, Katie. The words hovered on his lips, but he couldn't quite spit them out. He had to make up his mind. He'd nearly popped the question a dozen times, but he was afraid to lay his heart on the line until he knew for sure Katie was ready. He'd hinted once or twice, but she never let on that she was on the same page.

In the bedroom he'd handled her with kid gloves, afraid that she might be shocked if he made love to her the way he fantasized. He was a sensual man with strong appetites. He liked raunchy, elemental, unconventional sex. But he didn't want to lose her, and he knew she was coming off a bad breakup. Her exboyfriend had cheated on her, and Dylan suspected the whole experience had hurt her pride and shaken her confidence. He'd done his best to show her that she could trust him, but he still didn't know if it was too soon to show her how serious he was about the two of them and forever.

Katie finished her dinner and wondered about the scowl on Dylan's face. She sighed, wishing she understood him better. She was pretty sure he had a happily-ever-after agenda on his mind, but when he'd hinted as much on a couple of occasions, she'd managed to change the subject. In her heart, she wanted Dylan to be *the one,* but she didn't want to rush things.

Tonight she'd worn a sexy little sundress that tied between her breasts. Just enough skin showed to make it impossible to wear a bra. Dylan had struggled manfully not to stare, but she caught him more than once looking at her chest.

After the waiter dropped off the check, she took Dylan's hand across the table, gratified when he grasped hers in a crushing grip.

She licked her lips, stunned to see that her simple action made him tremble. She eyed him speculatively. "Dylan . . ."

He leaned forward, his eyes on her mouth. "Hmmm?"

She flexed her aching fingers, but he didn't let go. She tried to get his attention. "What would you think about going away this weekend?"

His gaze sharpened with interest. "I think it's a great idea." His voice lowered to a murmur. "I love the idea of being alone with you for two days, Katie," he said softly. "Concentrating on each other with no distractions . . . I'm your man."

Her stomach fluttered. "I was hoping you'd say that. I already made a reservation. I figured I could cancel if it didn't work out."

He nodded, still fixated on her lips. "I've been working too hard," he said hoarsely. "We both have."

She lost her nerve when it came to telling him about the hotel. Time for that later. Much later.

He dropped a wad of bills on the table and tugged her to her feet. He practically dragged her toward the exit.

Katie dug in her heels when they got outside, forcing him to stop. "Where are we going?"

He bent and kissed her hard, not at all like his usual, tender kisses. "To bed . . . now . . . Any objections?"

She took his hand and guided it to the laces nestled in her cleavage, smiling when he got the idea and tugged gently at the loose knot. Her breasts swelled. She gasped when his fingertips brushed her sensitive flesh. "No objections," she muttered. "Just hurry."

That Friday she almost lost her nerve. Dylan was leaving work midmorning so they could get on the road. He knew they were headed into the mountains near Asheville, North Carolina, but he probably thought she had booked them at a bed-and-breakfast.

How would he react when he found out about the Scimitar? The mysterious hotel was private, exclusive, and obscenely expensive. Her savings account had taken a big hit, but if she and Dylan reached a new understanding, it would be worth it. She refused to think about the alternative. Losing money was one thing. Losing Dylan would be devastating.

She was counting on the hotel's amenities to set the mood for the weekend. She didn't know much about the property other than the fact that it provided discreet, safe opportunities for consenting adults to indulge in playful fantasy scenarios. She had been required to sign several documents in which she promised not to reveal any specific information about the hotel and its location. All the cloak-and-dagger stuff made her a bit nervous, but she knew at least one person who had stayed there, so surely it was on the up-and-up.

Dylan, bless him, showed up exactly on time despite the fact that it was hard for him to break away from work. Another of his admirable qualities was that he made her feel like she came first in his life. He greeted her with a long, toe-curling kiss and then, grinning at her bemused expression, loaded their luggage into his forest green Explorer.

He had showered recently, and the citrusy scent of his aftershave tickled her nose. He wore a navy polo shirt that clung to his powerful shoulders and neatly pressed khakis that molded to his muscular thighs. He reached across the small space that separated them and took her hand, sparing one glance in her direction long enough to give her a quick smile. "I was worthless at work today. I didn't realize how hard I'd been pushing until I thought about escaping with you. This is going to be great."

She smiled. "I was so afraid that something was going to come up and we'd have to cancel."

He gave her a look that heated her cheeks. "Nothing short of a disaster could have stopped me," he said huskily. "Having you all to myself for a whole weekend sounds like heaven."

She cleared her throat and stared blindly out the window. It was now or never. "Dylan." His name came out as a squeak. She tried again. "Dylan." There . . . that sounded better.

He slanted her an amused grin. "Am I in trouble?"

Her throat was dry and her heart was pounding. "Of course not . . . but I thought you might want to know something about the hotel."

He chuckled, his eyes on the road. "Trust me, honey. With you there beside me, I won't even see the hotel."

Ha. That's what he thought. Doggedly, she tried again. "Well, actually . . . you might. I mean you will." She was stumbling over her words like an introvert at a nudist seminar. She sighed and went for broke. "It's a special, private hotel called the Scimitar," she confessed, watching his face carefully. "Where adults go to play, to act out fantasies."

They swerved wildly into the next lane as brief shock crossed his face. Dylan corrected the car's erratic path as a nearby horn blared rudely. "Fantasies?" he said, his voice choked.

She nodded slowly, stroking his thigh with one finger. "Games, role-playing . . . unusual costumes. All in a safe, protected environment with lots of luxury."

He was breathing hard. "You mean we would—"

She interrupted, her temperature spiking. "Whatever we want," she muttered. "That's the whole point. We can explore our wild side."

He pulled into a roadside rest stop and shut off the engine.

The air inside the car was thick with unspoken images. One of Dylan's fists drummed restlessly on the steering wheel. He stared out the windshield as though fascinated with the family of four trying to get their Saint Bernard back into their crowded van.

She swallowed hard. "Dylan, are you okay with this?"

He moved restlessly in his seat, his body language uneasy. "I'm not sure it's a good idea."

Her heart sank. "Why not?"

"It's going to be very difficult to drive the rest of the way with my boner bumping the steering wheel."

They stopped for a quick lunch on the road. Neither of them was a fan of fast food, so they bought bread, deli meat, and fruit for an impromptu picnic at a rest stop. It was a good idea in theory, but the picnic tables were all in the shade, and the sharp breeze was surprisingly cold.

Dylan pulled Katie into the shelter of his arm, cuddling her close, his large frame deflecting most of the wind. He managed to eat with one hand and enjoyed the feel of her slender body pressed close to his.

As they finished the modest meal, she produced a small plastic bag of homemade cookies from her jacket pocket. Dylan wolfed down four of the six and stuck his hand back into her pocket. "What else have you got in there?" His fingers tickled the tender skin below her rib cage, and she squirmed out of his grasp.

"There are people watching us," she said primly, with a pointed gaze at the elderly couple nearby.

Dylan grinned. "It's a good thing they don't know what we've got planned for this weekend. That old guy might have heart failure."

Katie pursed her lips. "Dr. Ruth says that senior sex can be very satisfying."

Dylan hooted. "Well, if that sweet old lady over there is anything like you, I suppose Dr. Ruth may be right."

From out of nowhere, a football thunked Dylan on the back of the head. He winced and scooped up the offending toy.

A scrawny boy, maybe nine or ten, came running up and then abruptly skidded to a halt as he got a good look at Dylan. His face paled, making his freckles stand out. "Uh, sorry, mister."

Dylan smiled at the kid. "No problem. Go long and I'll throw it back to you."

The boy grinned and jogged down the grass, turning with natural grace to catch Dylan's pass as it sailed toward him and then disappearing behind a tour bus.

Katie clapped her hands. "Very impressive, Dylan. You need a few kids of your own."

He cocked his head. "You offering?"

The flustered look on her face made him laugh again. "Right. I didn't think so. You'd better watch those provocative comments. A guy could get the wrong idea."

They continued north, arriving in the Asheville area by early afternoon. Katie consulted the map sent by the hotel and directed Dylan up a long, winding mountain road outside of town. Dense spring foliage shadowed the driveway, and despite the sunny day, she shivered. The moment of truth was fast approaching.

Although they passed not a single dwelling or structure of any kind, the road was well maintained. Finally, after what seemed like miles, they reached the top. There, amidst a grove of hardwood trees, stood the Scimitar. Katie stared at the large mountain stone building with its flag-decked turret and crenellated walls and felt her heart begin to race. It was a castle, a three-story medieval castle.

Dylan let out a long, low whistle. "That is one hell of a fortress. Sorry I left my suit of armor at home."

Katie shivered. "It's beautiful, but a little overwhelming."

He squeezed her hand. "Stick with me, fair maiden. I'll slay dragons for you if need be."

Flowering shrubs relieved the stark exterior, and a smiling bellman stood ready to relieve them of their luggage and park the car. Dylan stopped her before they went in and pulled her close for a kiss. They finally broke apart, looking at each other sheepishly. His grin was lopsided. "Come on. I don't think they expect their guests to make out in the driveway."

Inside the imposing high-ceilinged foyer, the theme of an ancient fortress continued. Woven rush mats covered the flagstone floor. The walls were decorated with a variety of period weapons that reminded her of the movie *Braveheart*. Overhead, suspended from a heavy iron chain, hung a gleaming, wickedly curved blade—the hotel's namesake.

A dignified older man dressed in unrelieved black welcomed them and directed them to the office. Since Katie had paid in advance, registration took only a matter of minutes. The pleasant desk clerk pressed a button and seconds later a handsome young man appeared, his open, friendly face as welcoming as the rest of the staff. The clerk handed them a copy of the paperwork. "This is Ron. He'll give you a tour of the suites and then show you to your room."

Ron wasted no time. He led them down a thickly carpeted hallway and around a corner to another wing. All along the corridor, doors stood open. Ron paused in front of the first. "This is the English schoolroom." Katie avoided looking at Dylan. Instead, she peeked inside and her jaw dropped. The room was authentic to the last detail, with a few added features. The riding crop and various Victorian costumes scattered around left little doubt that the curriculum in this particular schoolroom involved equal parts punishment and pleasure. She shivered, her nipples tightening in anticipation.

Next was the *Out of Africa* room, then the opium den, the jail cell, the elevator, the kitchen, the Chevy backseat. The list went on and on. Any scenario a couple might dream up was here for the taking, fully stocked and ready to explore.

When Katie finally sneaked a peek at Dylan's face, his expression gave nothing away. A tinge of red on his cheekbones was the only indication that he was affected by what they were viewing.

She was torn between avid curiosity about each of the suites and the need to gauge Dylan's mood. Was he as turned on as she was? Surely any red-blooded male wouldn't be able to resist the blatantly erotic mini playgrounds.

Finally the tour was complete, and Ron led them to their room. It was elegant, well appointed, and reassuringly normal, nary a handcuff or a silk scarf in sight. The carpet was thick cream and the bedspread, coffee, cream, and gold. An antique armoire housed a television, though she couldn't imagine anyone wanting to watch TV in this place. She watched Dylan tip the young man and close the door. Her hands were shaking and her stomach was doing flips.

Had she shocked him? She smiled brightly. "Pretty amazing, huh? I'm not sure what I was expecting, but this place is unbelievable. I was kind of embarrassed with Ron standing there, but it will be fun, don't you think?" She heard herself babbling but couldn't seem to stop. Dylan's silence was beginning to wear on her.

She went to him and slid her arms around his waist, unable to bear their physical separation a second longer. His arms tightened around her with reassuring force. Beneath her ear she heard and felt the steady thump of his heart. The jitters gripping her lessened a degree.

His chest rose and fell in a deep sigh. "You're one hell of a woman, Katie Spencer."

It sounded a lot like a compliment. She buried her nose in his chest. "So you're okay with all this?"

He pulled back, his face incredulous. "Are you kidding? The amazing woman in my life brings me to a sexual playground and wants to know if I'm okay with it?"

She buried her nose again. She was pretty sure she knew the answer, but she wanted to hear it out loud. "Yes . . . please."

He took her by the hand and they sat on the bed, his back against the headboard, Katie facing him, cross-legged. He smiled, an amazing flash of white teeth that managed to convey happiness, lust, and deep emotion. "I am better than okay. I'm damned stupendous. A little surprised, maybe . . . but definitely on board."

She winced. She was glad he had been honest enough to admit surprise. That was what they needed to work on. His seeing the real her.

She picked at a raveling thread in the bedspread, took a deep breath, and looked him straight in the eyes. "Here's the thing, Dylan. I love children. I like to cook. I'm probably going to be a darned good wife someday. When the time is right."

He grinned, but remained silent.

She leaned forward to emphasize her next point. "But there is more to me than that."

His smile faded, replaced by a frown of confusion. "I know," he said, his voice a tad defensive.

She tilted her head and smiled wryly. "Do you? Do you really? I get the feeling that when you look at me you see some kind of earth mother/Madonna. I'm not perfect, Dylan."

His eyes flickered, and she knew she'd hit a bull's-eye. He looked so darned guilty she wanted to kiss him, but the mushy stuff had to wait . . . at least for now. She sighed. "I want you to see the real me, Dylan. I enjoy sex with you. A lot. I think we're pretty amazing in that department."

His grin was smug, but he didn't interrupt.

She tapped his knee, smiling. "This weekend is about sex, obviously, but it's also about seeing each other in a new light. I want to know the Dylan nobody sees . . . and even though it's a little scary, I'm going to show you the Katie who's not all sweetness and light. Fair enough?"

Dylan nodded his head slowly, searching for the words to make her believe he was taking this seriously. It stung a bit to know she wasn't ready for a proposal and a ring. Every time he'd hinted in that direction, she'd headed him off. He'd done his damnedest to let her know he was in this for the long haul, but he would wait for her, however long it took. "Okay . . . I hear what you're saying. You're not perfect. I get it. But you have to understand that you're perfect for me. I can't get around that."

She smiled ruefully, shaking her head. "You are too darned charming for your own good."

He shrugged, almost grim faced. "I'm not kidding, Katie. You're everything I've ever wanted. Each time I look at you it feels like Christmas and my birthday rolled into one. That doesn't mean I expect you to never mess up. Lord knows you can't expect that from me. I know we'll fight. I know you may be moody sometimes, or I'll be grumpy. I know that one day in the future we may butt heads about finances or the kids or where to spend vacation. But that stuff is peripheral. It doesn't have a thing to do with how much I love you."

He reached over to collect one of the fat tears rolling slowly down her cheeks. "I didn't mean to make you cry, princess." He tugged her into his arms. "Tell me you love me."

Her face was buried somewhere in the vicinity of his armpit, but even muffled, her voice was strong. She sniffed. "Of course I love you, you idiot."

He grinned. "Flattery will get you everywhere."

She pulled back to look at him, her eyes dark. "Thank you for understanding," she whispered.

He touched her lips, his hand shaking. "No problem, angel," he said roughly. "But just so you know . . . there *will* be asking. When you're ready. Maybe a billboard in Times Square," he teased. "Or a message on the electronic screen at Turner Field."

Her smile was wobbly and her silence told him loud and clear that she wasn't touching that comment.

He sighed from deep in his chest and tucked her more comfortably into his embrace. "Would I sound incredibly insensitive if I told you I'm so horny I can't see straight?"

She laughed, her expression pleased. "Really?"

He began unbuttoning her blouse. "Really." He tugged down the cups of her bra to fondle her nipples. "Do you mind?"

Her breathing slowed and her head fell back, a flush spreading across her chest. "No," she whispered. "Not at all."

He undressed her rapidly, his hands clumsy with haste. Her skin was beautiful, very fair, almost translucent in places. He was always careful to be gentle with her, conscious of his size and strength. When she was completely nude, he flipped her to her stomach and rubbed his hands over her bottom.

He nestled his aching cock in the cleft between her butt cheeks, sliding it back and forth, feeling the delicious friction of skin on skin. Despite the seriousness of their conversation, his libido had taken in every detail of the suites, and the memories assaulted him now, making his need to go slow war with his drive for release.

Katie slid out from beneath him and turned to lie on her back, her lips pouting. "Why am I the only one undressed?"

He stood beside the bed and kicked off his shoes. He laughed hoarsely as Katie joined him and began stripping off his shirt and pants. Then she lay back and watched as he bounced on one foot and then the other to deal with his underwear and socks. All the while, her avid gaze raked him from head to toe, the tip of her tongue peeking from between her moist lips, making him crazy.

She giggled when he lost his balance and smacked his knee into the sturdy footboard. He cursed as pain radiated up his shin. She arched her back, making her breasts lift, the nipples pert. He felt the pain in his leg rise to meet the ache in his cock. His whole body trembled.

He knelt on the bed, bending to suck the tip of her nearest breast deep into his mouth. Katie moaned and grabbed his shoulders, her nails pressing into his skin. He switched to the other breast, his nose filled with the smell of her perfume, not her usual floral scent, but something heavier, more sensual.

Her hands left his shoulders and he gasped as he felt her squeeze his cock. She whispered a command. "Kneel over my face."

He obeyed, resting his hands on the headboard. He felt exposed, painfully vulnerable as her mouth roved with full access over his tight sacs. With one hand she stroked his shaft and with the other she lifted his testicles and raked her teeth gently across his balls. Fire shot from his scrotum to the base of his neck. He trembled so violently, the bed shook. Her voice was murmuring husky words, demands, compliments. He had passed the point of coherency.

He was a slave to the driving need racking his body. He straightened, prompting a protest from his tormentor. "Can't wait," he muttered, no longer capable of finesse. "Now, honey . . . now."

He spread her slender legs wide and slid one finger deep inside her to test her readiness. Slick wet heat enclosed him. He gripped her knees and centered the head of his penis at her entrance. With a Herculean effort he paused, searching her face, oddly in need of reassurance.

Her smile was wicked. "Forgotten the way in?"

He panted, looking down at her with glazed eyes. "No, ma'am. Just making sure you're with me."

She lifted her hips, forcing him a half inch into her hot, tight passage. "I'm right here," she whispered, her voice soft with promise.

He intended to go slowly, to show her tenderness. To cherish her. But his emotions were raw. He thrust deep in one nearly violent motion. He felt her vaginal muscles grip him, and his control frayed irrevocably. He pounded inside her again and again, some primitive need to claim her riding him hard. He wanted to make it last, to make this a healing statement of his love and devotion. But he was long past such delicate emotions.

Their conversation had stripped him to a layer of honesty, left him with his need for her exposed, his hunger unveiled. He heard her cry out as she peaked, and he thrust wildly one last time, allowing the hot rush of orgasm to close over him in a blinding wave.

When he was able to open his eyes minutes, maybe hours later, she was playing with his cock, gently cleansing it with a damp washcloth. His body's willingness to return to the fray was gratifying. Katie touched a particularly sensitive spot, and his shaft twitched and grew. She bent her head and took him in her mouth.

When her lips closed around him, his mind literally went blank. Every nerve cell in his body congregated in his throbbing dick. She licked and teased and nipped with uncanny knowledge. She was perfectly attuned to his slightest reaction, and he hardened by increments until he felt himself approaching the point of no return. Desperate to make this encounter last longer than the first, he pushed her away gently and rolled to his knees. He gulped in a couple of mouthfuls of much-needed oxygen.

"Why don't we take a cool shower?" he rasped, reaching for control.

She stared at him in amazement. "A shower? Now?"

"I'm on a hair trigger here, Katie. I want to be able to make things good for you. I need to slow down."

"I'll let you know if I have any complaints." She pushed him onto his back again and straddled him, succeeding only because she moved so quickly.

He felt her impale herself on his rigid penis, each wriggle of her limber body making black spots dance in front of his eyes. He counted to fifty and then started over again. She murmured with pleasure as her body accepted his, a perfect fit.

When she started to move, his skin tingled and his balls tightened, signaling his release. He cried out. "Slower, honey . . . please."

But Katie was a woman on a mission. She reached between their joined bodies to touch herself, and as he felt her fingers brush his shaft he groaned and arched his back, coming with a force that threatened to dislodge her. Katie hung on, pressing down as he thrust upward, crying out her own release and slumping forward in boneless exhaustion just as they both reached the end of the road.

CHAPTER TWO

*B*y the time Katie and Dylan woke up, both restaurants were closed. They laughed and ordered room service, pleasantly surprised with the quality of the food. Over two bottles of really excellent wine, they talked about anything and everything.

Katie was content . . . no, more than that, she was happy . . . and relieved. To her delight, Dylan treated her as he always had, with warm tenderness and affection, his mischief-filled blue eyes promising that the next round of sexual one-on-one was not far off.

They showered finally, but it was a warm shower, and Dylan behaved himself for the most part. He *did* demonstrate several creative uses for a bar of soap, but Katie was laughing too hard to take things any further.

Afterwards they snuggled beneath the covers. Dylan grumbled. "You realize that we missed our chance to sign up for one of those rooms this evening."

She stroked his hip, not too concerned about any fantasy other than the one at hand. "I think I want *you* to pick first. But surprise me, 'cause it makes me hot wondering which one you'll choose. We've got all day tomorrow and the next day. I can wait. Especially if you promise to entertain me here and now."

He murmured his agreement as his hand slid up her thigh beneath the covers and he zeroed in on her clitoris. She sighed deeply, her legs falling apart as waves of pleasure rolled through her abdomen and centered at the point where his hand was showing such creative genius.

He leaned down to kiss her, his lips warm and hard. He tasted like Chablis and toothpaste. She moved restlessly, realizing that his hand had gone still beneath the covers. She wiggled her hips.

Dylan laughed. "Demanding, are we?"

She gasped as she felt his erection brush her mound. "I need you."

He teased her with his cock, pretending to enter her and then moving away.

She hissed her frustration. "Sadist."

He laughed. "You can't possibly be that horny. I know what you've been doing all afternoon and part of the evening. I was there . . . remember?"

She grabbed a handful of hair at the back of his head and dragged him down for a desperate kiss. "You're making me crazy."

She wrapped her legs around his waist and clung, pressing him against her but unable to get him where she needed him.

He moved a scant inch until their bodies touched at the correct angle. "Is this what you want?" he asked innocently.

She bit his shoulder. "Dylan . . ." Her voice was hoarse and pleading.

His cock rubbed her intimately. "Say it, Katie. Tell me what you want." He was hanging by a thread, but he was determined to draw out the pleasure.

She glared at him, panting. "Screw me, Dylan Ward. Right this minute."

He shuddered, denying them both for one last second. "Well, why didn't you say so?" He shoved hard into her welcoming body and bit out a curse as the incredible pleasure swelled and crested. Making love to Katie was fast becoming an obsession. Before this weekend, she had been everything he ever wanted. But here . . . at the Scimitar . . . he was learning to want her in a whole new way.

The sexual excess of the afternoon enabled him to make this loving more prolonged. He stroked her slow and deep, using a rhythm that kept them both on the brink but denied them the final satisfaction. Her eyelids drooped. Her skin was flushed. Exhaustion etched shadows beneath her eyes. He wanted to screw her forever. He wanted to lock her away so no man could ever even look at her.

His possessive caveman thoughts scared him just the tiniest bit. Maybe Katie was right. Maybe he had looked at her from only one angle. And he had loved that woman. But now that she was forcing him to see her in a new light, he not only loved her . . . he . . . well . . . he wanted to devour her. He had always made it a point to rein in his physical reactions because of his size and strength. He never wanted to take the chance of hurting a woman, a delicate, fragile female.

But Katie seemed determined to push his buttons. Her sexual hunger fanned the flames of his own desire, and he was at the mercy of his own need. Her hands gripped his buttocks, her fingers clenching his flesh with surprising strength. He withdrew almost completely, wringing a cry from her that echoed his own anguish. He hovered there, just outside of paradise, testing his own control and hers.

She opened her eyes, their depths hazy and unfocused. He bent his head and kissed her, fighting back the urge to plunder and giving her every ounce of tenderness he could muster. "I love you, Katie."

He filled her again, his cock seeming to expand along with the wealth of emotions battering his chest. "I love you."

She whimpered and stiffened, caught up in her climax, perhaps unable to hear his words. He said them one more time and then he thrust his way home.

* * *

They had breakfast the next morning on the veranda, enjoying the beautiful spring morning and the unusual warmth of the sun after a succession of rainy weekends. The food was, once again, mouth watering. Smooth creamery butter on hot scones. Home-made jams and marmalades. Fresh-squeezed orange juice. Crisp rashers of bacon and plump, deep red strawberries.

Katie sat back with a sigh and rubbed her stomach. "We need to go for a walk, but I'm too stuffed to move."

Dylan smiled. "Maybe in a while."

She felt peace spread through her bones. Would life always seem so golden? The future so bright?

Dylan unwittingly dented her mood. He reached for her hand, his face serious, his voice soft and quiet. "I think we need to talk about Darren the doofus."

She grimaced. "Do we have to?"

"Were you in love with him, Katie? Is that why you took the breakup so hard? I haven't pushed you for many details. I figured it was your business and you'd tell me if you wanted me to know."

She tugged her hand away. "And now?" At some level she resented the fact that he was bringing Darren into their beautiful weekend.

Dylan's jaw firmed. "Now I'm tired of tiptoeing around the subject. Darren was an idiot."

She sighed. "I know that. And no . . . I wasn't in love with him. I liked him. I thought we had a lot in common."

"But?"

"But don't you see . . . *I* was the idiot. I was the one too dumb to see what kind of a guy he was. I knew his sister and his family, and they're all wonderful people. I assumed he was cut from the same cloth. But he wasn't at all like them, and I let my precon-ceived notions blind me to the truth for way too long. I think I *wanted* him to be a great guy so much that I was willing to over-look the warning signs."

They sat in silence, each lost in thought. They had never really discussed Darren in more than a superficial conversation. Perhaps it *was* time.

She took a sip of juice. His brow was furrowed in a slight frown, and she wondered what he was thinking. "Dylan?"

"Hmmm?"

"Do you understand what I'm saying?"

He looked at her, his expression serious. "You feel stupid for being misled. It happens to the best of us."

"To you?"

His lips quirked. "Well, maybe not in exactly the same way, but yes. Sure. I've been wrong about people."

He paused, and her stomach tightened at the look on his face. "He didn't have sex with other women because of you, Katie. You know that . . . right?"

She was silent. Intellectually, she knew what he was saying was valid. But it was hard to completely erase that little knot of hurt and humiliation buried in a deep corner of her psyche. She nibbled her lower lip, trying to work up the courage to give the whole embarrassing truth. Finally she sighed. "Darren didn't like me to be too aggressive in the bedroom. He said it was a turnoff. To be honest, he pretty much preferred the missionary position, and I never even had a chance to be the missionary, if you get my drift. Oral sex was no good either. He hated giving it, and if I took a turn, he'd lose his erection." She stopped short of describing what those experiences had done to her sexual confidence.

Dylan raked a hand through his hair, his expression disgruntled. "I've known dozens of guys like the doofus. They think their dicks are too small, and the only way they can prove their masculinity is by bed hopping, even after they find a great woman. If he felt threatened, it was because of his own insecurities . . . not because of anything you did or didn't do. I'd be willing to bet he hated losing you."

She chewed her lip. "His sister told me he was devastated. But

I couldn't forgive him. Maybe I should have tried. I don't know. I did feel bad about not at least letting him apologize."

Dylan scowled. "That's bullshit. You deserve a man who treasures you. I can't believe you even thought about forgiving him."

She lifted her chin and glared. "I never said I thought about forgiving him. I just felt guilty for dumping him so abruptly."

He smacked his forehead. "Lord deliver me from such convoluted logic."

She tossed a lemon wedge at him. "I'm done talking about the doofus. And clearly you don't know women very well."

He caught the fruit and chuckled. "Well, I'll admit, you *are* giving me an education I hadn't expected. He put his napkin on the table and pushed back his chair. "You ready to go back to the room?"

Katie wondered what Dylan had in mind. She hadn't seen him make any effort to sign up for a slot in one of the suites, but then again, he might have done it when she was washing her hair that morning. She had thought he might want to play some tennis or go for a walk. But as he led her back inside and through the hotel lobby, she realized he must be intent on indoor pursuits. Her pulse skipped a beat, and she smothered a grin. After all, a girl could play tennis anytime.

She was a bit turned around when they went down the hall. Although only three stories, the hotel sprawled on its mountaintop, and it was easy for the directionally impaired to get lost. But she could have sworn their room was the opposite direction.

"Dylan, isn't our room that way?" She pointed behind them.

He took her hand and kept walking, his expression bland. "I never said we were going to *our* room."

At that very moment they rounded a corner, and Katie recognized the corridor instantly. They had toured it from stem to stern with the delectable Ron. Her breathing quickened.

Dylan paused in front of suite number one, and Katie's heart lodged in her throat. It was the English schoolroom. She couldn't quite look at him, despite their conversation the day before. Her skin felt hot and tight, her whole body on fire.

He opened the door and scooted her through it, locking it with a loud click. And then the strangest thing happened. His face changed. His smile disappeared and a look of stern implacability took its place. She took a step backward and he noticed. His smile wasn't pleasant. With careful deliberation he picked up the cane and the riding crop, making sure her attention was on him as he did so. She couldn't have looked away if her life depended on it.

As she watched, he crossed the room to a cabinet, opened it, and stowed the two items out of sight. Then he turned and came to where she stood. She eyed him warily, totally at a loss to understand what was going on.

Dylan reached behind her and plucked a black, thigh length coat from the rack of costumes. He donned it along with a narrow black tie. Then he crossed his arms and stared at her. "You'll find, Miss Spencer," he said with a hint of menace in his voice, "that there are means other than corporal punishment to carry out the chastisement of the young."

Her mouth gaped. He frowned, looking her over with displeasure. His lip curled. "Your clothing leaves much to be desired." Once again he reached behind her, rapidly selecting a handful of items. He thrust them in her hands. "Step behind the screen and change."

Katie felt a curl of surprise in her stomach. Who was this man and what had he done with her gentle Dylan? She swallowed, her throat dry. A heavy pulse began to beat deep in her abdomen. "Dylan . . . are we just jumping right into this?"

He cut her off, his frown deepening. "Let's get a few things straight, Miss Spencer. While in this room you will speak only when spoken to. You will address me as 'headmaster' or 'sir.' You will carry out my instructions quickly and completely. Your marks and your behavior this term have been deplorable. Clearly, you are in need of guidance."

"But, Dylan . . ."

His nostrils flared. His voice was a low hiss. "Do you really want to add further transgressions to your list of offenses?"

She shook her head, mute, her knees shaking and heat pooling between her thighs. Who knew Dylan had such a talent for drama? But if he thought she would let him play all the cards, he had a few surprises coming.

She took the clothes and stepped behind the screen, her hands trembling as she removed her shirt and slacks. He had chosen a half dozen items in all. The underwear was provocative in the extreme. The lacy bloomers were crotchless, and the sheer batiste camisole must have been made for a nine-year-old. The narrow satin ribbon lacing up the front barely stretched to contain her breasts.

The blouse was severely plain . . . white cotton with a rounded collar. The pleated wool skirt covered her butt if she stood perfectly erect. The only things left were the lacy anklets and the back patent-leather Mary Janes. She stepped into the socks and shoes and glanced in the cheval glass, shivering. Her hair lay in soft curls against her shoulders. Appearing in front of Dylan like this excited her but rattled her nerves a bit as well. It might not have if it had been the Dylan she knew . . . but *this* Dylan . . . well . . . he was almost intimidating. Ridiculous, but true.

His voice snapped with irritation from very close by. "I don't have all day, Miss Spencer. Kindly present yourself."

She stepped out from behind the security of the screen with all the trepidation of a stripper performing at her first nightclub. She searched Dylan's face for any tiny indication that he might like her costume, but found none. His broad shoulders stretched the seams of the borrowed coat, and the expression in his usually sparkling blue eyes was hard and remote.

He had placed a ladder-back chair beside the wooden teacher's desk. He motioned almost insolently. "Climb up, Miss Spencer. Let's have a look at you."

She realized he meant for to step on top of the desk, which would put her butt precisely at his eye level. She hesitated a half second and then jumped when he barked at her. "Now, girl . . . You're wasting my time."

Her eyes narrowed and she poked a finger in his chest. "I could walk out of here if I wanted to, Headmaster. But I'm curious to see how far you will go. You don't scare me." She clambered awkwardly onto the chair and then the desk, hampered by the need to stand perfectly straight. The little navy-and-hunter skirt was rather breezy.

Dylan walked slowly around the desk, his lips pursed, his hands linked behind his back. She tried to stand perfectly still, but it was difficult, particularly when he was behind her. Suddenly he walked to the chalkboard and picked up a slender wooden pointer from the tray. It was far too small to be used for any kind of spanking, and besides, she sensed Dylan wasn't prepared to go that route.

She watched with trepidation to see what he might do. Her breathing was shallow and her skin was alternately hot and cold. She clasped her hands at her waist and waited, clenching her jaw to keep her teeth from chattering. She was experiencing the oddest mixture of apprehension and arousal.

Dylan stood in front of her. She could feel his breath on her stomach. His voice this time was soft and low. "Look straight ahead, Miss Spencer, preferably at the clock on the far wall. And spread your feet twelve inches."

It was torture not to look down at him. She obeyed with only the greatest effort. Determinedly, she focused on the timepiece on the far wall as she slid her feet apart, the soles of the shoes slick on the smooth desktop.

A long silence ensued. The only discernable sounds were the ticking of the clock and the sound of Dylan's breathing, heavy and rough. The uneven tenor of that breathing gave her the first inkling that perhaps he was as affected by their crazy little game as she was.

She shrieked as the tip of the pointer teased the lace edging of the bloomers and ruffled her most private curls.

But her involuntary cry made him angry. The pointer disappeared, and although she dared not look down, she could sense his mood. His voice was sleek with fury. "I said silence, Miss Spencer. Are you familiar with the concept?"

She pouted. "You're a bully, Headmaster. Is this the only way you ever get to touch a woman?" Between her legs she felt a trickle of moisture. She fancied she could detect the scent of her arousal in the quiet, heavy air.

He ignored her sarcasm. For long seconds nothing happened, and then the pointer resumed its desultory exploration, always chastely on top of cloth . . . never touching bare skin. This time she managed not to cry out. Her teeth sank deep into her bottom lip, and her fingernails cut little crescents into the palms of her hands.

The pointer grew bolder, circling one taut nipple at a time, leaving slight indentations in the thin fabric. Her head dropped back and her eyes closed. Her inner muscles clenched, searching for relief from the building tension.

His voice sounded again, this time contemplative . . . curious . . . as he continued his careful torment. "A number of your instructors have been only too happy to supply me with a litany of your sins, Miss Spencer. Insolence, laziness . . . flirtatiousness. Are you aware of these charges?"

She gave a brief nod, afraid to speak, almost incoherent as the wicked little pointer pushed her nearer and nearer to climax.

Dylan continued. "I've thought about various punishments . . . I always like the consequences to fit the crime." The tip hesitated once again near the opening of her bloomers, and she jerked. "I debated letting all the senior-level boys come in here and take a look at your nude body . . . That would be fair, don't you think, since you have enjoyed enraging their adolescent hormones?"

The pointer brushed her barely covered bottom and then returned to her aching mound.

"But then again, I could bring in all the senior girls for the same purpose. Seeing your humiliation would be a fitting recompense for the many times you've held yourself above them and degraded them with your insolent pride . . . So, do either of those two options appeal, Miss Spencer?"

She shook her head, intrigued by his creative suggestions. In her present position anything seemed possible. Dylan's interpretation of the fantasy was everything she could have asked for and more.

The pointer slid down her left thigh to the inside of her knee. She felt his lips brush the back of her leg. "But then again, I suppose I am more than capable of bringing a recalcitrant, haughty young woman to a better understanding of her place in the world. It would be my duty, after all . . . and my pleasure."

As he said the last word the pointer played with a lace seam. She flinched and without conscious volition her hands lowered to cover her crotch protectively. Suddenly he took one of her hands and nipped it lightly with his teeth. "I did not give you permission to move," he said, sucking one finger deep into his mouth. He thrust her hands back to their original position at her waist.

When she thought she could bear it no longer, he dispensed with the pointer. She heard the scrape of wood on flagstone as he dragged the chair in front of the desk. Sensing rather than seeing his movements, she was aware that he had settled himself more or less at her feet, though a short distance away.

He chuckled, but it was not the cheerful, teasing sound she knew. It was . . . threatening. "Remove your skirt."

She breathed a little easier. This wouldn't be so hard. She fumbled for the single fastener at her hip, releasing it and then stepping awkwardly out of the garment. The desktop was small, and she had no desire to fall. Despite the brevity of the skirt, she felt vulnerable without it.

"Toss it on the floor."

She obeyed.

"Now the blouse . . ."

She started to tackle the buttons, but he stopped her. "Wait . . . Rip the buttons as though you are overtaken with passion."

Her hands stilled. She would feel ridiculous.

"Perhaps you need my help." He stood suddenly and grasped the edges of the soft cotton in his large hands, wrenching the sides apart until tiny pearl buttons bounced to every corner of the room. His fingers brushed her aching nipples either by accident or by design. But then he sat again as though nothing out of the ordinary had happened.

She gulped in air, totally unnerved. But she summoned a bit of spunk. "You'll pay for that blouse, Headmaster. You're a brute."

For several long minutes there were no further instructions. She felt his gaze like a hot beam of light, stroking her barely covered body, assessing . . . wanting.

It was no novelty for Dylan to see her naked flesh, but this man . . . this headmaster . . . She cringed to know that his lustful stare was cataloging her most private parts. The laces of the camisole were stretched so far apart, only her nipples were concealed. The deep valley between her breasts, dewy with perspiration, was exposed to his view. And the curling hair between her legs was visible through the open center seam of the bloomers.

"Put your hands behind your neck."

She did so, aware that the movement lifted her breasts. She thought she heard him sigh. Then he stood once more, and when she chanced a lightning-fast glance out of the corner of her eye, she saw him retrieve a familiar object from his pants pocket . . . a Swiss Army knife he carried with him everywhere. The blade flicked open, and she felt the smooth noncutting edge of the blade press into her bosom. Before she could react, he had severed the laces, and the remainder of the garment fell away from her body like wisps of clouds in the wind.

Her nipples puckered and tightened. Without warning his fingers slipped through the gap in her only remaining garment and played with her damp, curling hair. She pressed against his hand, yearning for release. But the clever hand withdrew, and the headmaster laughed softly. "You are indeed more the wanton than the gently bred young lady. Perhaps your punishment will be more difficult than I had imagined."

Then his warm hands were at her hips, sliding the drawers down her legs and steadying her as she stepped free. She thought for one poignant second that he might give up the game and take her in his arms . . . She could almost feel his urgency. But apparently that was her own fevered imagination. Dylan resumed his assessment from his seat.

She had never contemplated the nuances of appearing nude for someone else's viewing pleasure. It gave one a feeling of desperate vulnerability.

But the man in charge was far from finished. He spoke once again, his voice almost bored. "Touch your nipples, Miss Spencer. I'm told you afforded that pleasure to more than one of your classmates."

The disdain in his voice stung. She determined then and there to make him covet what she had given to others for free . . . to the nice young man in her Latin class . . . to the strapping lad who was interested only in animal husbandry until she showed him how fascinating human mating could be. She blanked her mind to the present, becoming instead the young woman with loose morals.

She touched her breasts tentatively, carefully, pressing them together. Her nipples were sensitive to the point of pain. She encircled the tips and framed them in her fingers. "Like this, sir?" she asked, her voice deliberately provocative.

Apparently he had forgotten his dictum concerning silence.

She decided to see what he would do if she flouted his other command as well. Still caressing her breasts, she looked straight at him, her sultry smile insolent and taunting. "Am I doing it right, sir?"

Dylan nearly swallowed his tongue. His cock had been hard for so long he thought he might have permanent brain damage. Far more surprising than his own flair for playacting was his sweetheart's ability to become a little slut. Standing there before him clad in nothing but little-girl shoes and socks, she scared the hell out of him. He was trying his damnedest to stay a step ahead of her, but the headmaster was in danger of losing this round to the naughty ingenue.

He counted to ten and folded his arms across his chest, feigning boredom. "If you get that much enjoyment out of playing with your own tits, it's not much of a punishment. Turn around."

Her confident air slipped, but she obeyed. Now her delicious little butt was his for the taking. The sleek lines of her back and her supple, slender thighs made his mouth water. He forced himself to continue the game. "Bend at the waist and grasp your ankles."

She complied gracefully. *Now what, Ward?* His cock was beginning to wrestle control from him. He stood up, deciding he and his cock could compromise. He stepped closer and shoved his hands in his pockets to keep them out of mischief. Then, using nothing but his tongue, he traced a long, wet trail from one ankle up to her left butt cheek, across the divide to the other, and then down again. Now they were both trembling. He bit her buttocks one at a time, just hard enough to leave faint teeth marks.

It was a damned appealing picture. He reached for his headmaster persona. "Perhaps, Miss Spencer, I should leave you in this position until you collapse in a faint. Would that be a suitable punishment?"

She made an inarticulate murmur. He slid his finger between her legs. "How long would you last if I did this?" He stroked her gently, and then harder, stopping only when he sensed she was on the brink of orgasm. The word she said then was surely worthy of punishment.

He stepped to the other side of the desk, near her head. "Tired, Miss Spencer?"

She shot him an upside-down glare. He grinned evilly. "Beg me, sweetheart. Beg me for mercy."

She told him what he could do with his mercy. He shook his head sadly. "That's not a very nice thing to say."

She snorted. He laughed, enjoying himself more than he could ever have imagined. She was incredible. He reined in his impatience to screw her and continued the game.

"You may stand, Miss Spencer . . . and step down from the desk."

He stood prepared to steady her if she needed it, but she moved with all the grace of a queen, ignoring his outstretched hand with a sniff. When her feet were on firm ground, he glanced down and smiled at those silly little shoes. He was determined to leave them on, enjoying the contrast of nude, sensual woman and girlish footwear.

He debated rapidly. Her face was red, and her hair in disarray. He waved a hand toward the back of the room. "You may excuse yourself for a moment and freshen up. There are facilities behind that partition and other amenities."

She disappeared with comical haste. He assessed his next step. The hideous Victorian horsehair sofa presented some interesting possibilities.

When Katie returned, he instructed her to stretch out on the sofa, and he excused himself for a few personal moments as well. It was damned difficult to get his pants unzipped with his swollen cock throbbing like hell. He washed up and eased his eager dick back into confinement. Then he raided the small refrigerator for snacks and drinks. Katie's eyes were closed when he returned. He smothered his urge to comfort her. This little interlude was about something else entirely.

He tapped her shoulder. "Enough lounging, Miss Spencer. The sofa is mine from now on."

She scowled, but stood up, watching curiously as he arranged food and wine on a small table and then stretched out with his arms behind his head. He raised an eyebrow. "Get busy, girl. I need some sustenance."

She knelt at the table, her firm, round breasts swaying with mesmerizing beauty. "I'll feed you as long as you return the favor, Headmaster. You've made me very . . . hungry." He inhaled sharply and then nearly choked when she slid a grape between his lips. He chewed automatically. Her nipples were practically begging to be sucked.

She leaned back on her heels. "My turn." She parted her lips, the full curving smile glistening with shiny lip gloss. Her eyes dared him to refuse. He sat up and jerked a fat grape from the cluster, then stroked her bottom lip with his thumb as he pressed the fruit into her mouth. A soft sigh escaped her. She chewed slowly, never breaking eye contact. "Now I'm thirsty."

He took a sip from his wineglass and then held it to her mouth, placing the spot where his lips had touched directly against hers. She drained it in one gulp, her mannerisms reckless. He refilled the glass and offered it again, lecturing his libido all the while. They still had an hour in this room. He could and would hold out till the end.

After she drained half of the second glass, he stood up and tugged her to her feet, placing the wineglass on the table. He summoned a frown. "Why are you smiling, Miss Spencer? I don't believe you understand the seriousness of your situation."

Without warning, she sank to the sofa, sprawling in graceful abandon with her thighs apart. One foot, with its lacy anklet and shiny black shoe, rested on the carved, wooden back. Her cheeks were flushed. "If you want to keep your job, Headmaster, I suggest you pleasure me. Now. With your mouth."

He forced a sneer to his face. "Clearly, Miss Spencer, you are not influenced by traditional punishments. I'm forced to take alternate measures to correct some of your more outrageous behaviors. I'll accede to your request because it suits me to do so, but we are not finished here." He knelt and touched her thigh with the tip of his tongue. "Agreed?"

Her whole body shuddered. "Yes . . . yes . . ." He licked her hard, gripping her hips with strong hands. It didn't take long. She cried out, her head tossing wildly as she climaxed.

He gave her a mere minute to recover before he drew her to her feet, steadying her as she swayed. He drew her close. Her skin was soft and smooth everywhere he touched. His thick erection strained the cloth of his borrowed trousers. He kissed her hard, letting her feel everything he was feeling. Then he rested his forehead against hers. "Does it not embarrass you to be nude in front of me?"

Her fingernails raked his collarbone through his starched white shirt. She sighed. "I fear I have a fondness for you, Headmaster."

He lifted her chin and made her look him in the eyes. "Put your hands behind your back."

She obeyed, seeming dazed.

He shook his head sadly. "I'm sorry it has to come to this, but your lack of proper modesty leaves me no choice."

She stared at him with incomprehension. He grabbed a handful of soft blond curls. "On your knees, girl."

CHAPTER THREE

*H*e watched carefully to see if she would respond as Katie or as the schoolgirl. She fell to her knees, but her eyes widened dramatically and she shook her head violently from side to side despite his grip on her hair. "No, sir," she said, her voice agitated. "No, sir . . . That's wicked. I won't. You're a horrible man. I'm going to tell my parents. They will have you flogged."

He tugged the handful of curls just enough to make her wince. "I'm not really interested in your thoughts on the subject, Miss Spencer. And at any rate, it's a bit late to be worrying about wicked behavior, now, isn't it?

She stuck out her chin and pressed her lips together tightly, her face mutinous. She was the picture of righteous indignation, if one could overlook her spectacular nudity. Which he couldn't.

He released her hair and rocked back on his heels with a sigh. "I am trying to give you the benefit of the doubt, young woman, but you are not cooperating. Would you rather I take your untouched body?"

She blinked several times rapidly and then shook her head, soft curls tumbling around her lush breasts, her eyes downcast.

He lifted her chin with his finger. "You decide, Miss Spencer. You *will* be punished. One way or another."

Her silence was complete. He shrugged. "Well, if you won't or can't . . . I will. I certainly won't turn down the opportunity to initiate a fresh young virgin like yourself . . . After all, you are making this choice, not I."

He lowered her to the small Oriental rug, the only remotely soft surface in the entire room, and settled himself between her legs, still fully clothed. Her pupils were dilated, her breathing rapid. He pressed gently with his cock, letting her feel its length, its firmness. She flinched. He gave her one last chance. "Do you really want to be a fallen woman?"

Her lower lip trembled. "No . . ." she said, her whisper barely audible.

He lifted himself away from her and stood. She curled her knees to her chest, guarding her feminine charms. He snapped his fingers. "Come here immediately . . . as you were before."

She obeyed slowly, kneeling at his feet with her hands on her thighs. He ran his fingers through her hair. With his free hand, he reached into his breast pocket and extracted a navy silk cravat. He held it out to her. "Polish my boots, girl."

Her mouth dropped open in shock, but she took the scarf automatically. She stared at it blankly and then looked up at him, temper flaring in her expressive eyes. "Do you have any idea who I am?" she hissed. "My father is in parliament. I'm no common serving girl. Clean your own damn boots." She stuffed the piece of cloth into his pants pocket, her fingers brushing his rigid length.

His knee nudged her breast. "Profanity now, is it? And direct defiance? You should be ashamed."

She returned his stern look with a haughty stare. Though she still knelt at his feet, subservience was nowhere in her demeanor. Slowly, a naughty smile bloomed on her face. "I know what this is about," she said slowly. "You must have a little penis . . . and the only way you can get it hard is by bullying defenseless women. Admit it, Headmaster. You're a fraud."

His eyes narrowed, insulted on behalf of the character he was playing. "I assure you, impertinent miss, my masculinity is more than adequate. Or rather, I should say . . . bordering on the stupendous."

Her lips twitched as she tried not to smile. "Perhaps you've padded your breeches with a sock. Has any woman ever seen you unclothed? I'd wager not. And all on account of your unfortunate pencil dick." Her eyes widened dramatically. "Oh my," she said, as though having just stumbled on an incredible truth. "You're a virgin, Headmaster. I'm right, aren't I? A brutish untried man with nothing to entertain a woman."

He choked on the insulting taunt. "Women beg for my attention. And I'm too much for most of them."

She tilted her head to one side, her hands moving to grasp him just above his knees. "Prove it, then. Let me take you in my mouth."

He hadn't thought it was possible to get any harder. He was wrong. There was a buzzing in his head, and his heart was pounding so hard, he felt dizzy. He fumbled with the unfamiliar buttons at his fly and freed his aching dick. Her steady gaze made him nuts. His hands grasped her curls. "Open your mouth."

She complied, her lips pink and wet as they closed around his cock. He bit back a curse. He was no seventeen-year-old boy. He could control himself. Maybe. He guided her head with one hand, setting the rhythm.

She took him deep in her throat, her tongue stroking the underside of his shaft. This was no inexperienced schoolgirl, he thought hazily. He struggled to remember his part. "Wider," he demanded. "Take more of me . . . You're not trying."

She whimpered and let her teeth sink into him in warning. He almost grinned. Now he put both hands on her head, tunneling his fingers into her silky hair and rubbing her scalp. His body burned with the need for release. The urge to come in her mouth was almost unbearable.

At the last second he pulled away, his heart pounding in his chest, his whole body shaking. She leaned back and looked up at him, her face flushed. He reached out and tugged her nipple, twisting it gently but firmly. Her eyelids fluttered shut.

He stood up and took her with him, pressing the length of her slender body tightly against his, his hard length nestled against her belly. With one hand he reached between them and thrust between her legs. He held up his fingers, wet with her juices. "Clearly this punishment thing isn't working. I've managed only to arouse you, Miss Spencer. Isn't that the truth?"

She nodded, her tongue wetting his shirt as she made little forays around *his* nipple, stealing his breath and making his head swim.

He kissed her roughly, invading her mouth and plundering its depths. She wrapped her arms around his neck, trying to get closer.

He lifted her and groaned as her legs circled his waist. Rapidly he strode to the desk and set her on her feet. With his hands on her shoulders, he turned her around, lowered her facedown onto the desk, and spread her arms wide. The height of the desk wasn't exactly right, so he lifted her hips just enough to fit his cock into her tight sheath. When he surged deep inside her body, they both groaned in unison. He leaned over her back, careful not to crush her against the unforgiving hardness of the desk. He whispered in her ear, "Are you penitent, Miss Spencer?"

"Never," she panted.

He thrust several times in quick succession. "Now?"

"No." Her response was thready and weak.

He grasped her buttocks, pulled almost all the way out, and then surged forward, filling her completely. "Now?" he grunted, at the end of his control.

Her inner muscles squeezed him as she stiffened and cried out. "Yes," she moaned. "Yes, yes, yes."

"Damned straight," he muttered, and finally, with a rush of adrenaline and sheer, driving insanity, he let the red tide roll over him.

*   *   *

Aeons later Dylan opened one eye, blearily surveying his sur-roundings, vaguely surprised to find he was still alive. "Katie?"

"Hmmm?" Her voice was little more than a murmur.

He shifted his weight, not disconnecting their bodies, but al-lowing her room to breathe. He licked her shoulder. "I gotta tell you, hon. This schoolroom is great, but I'd give my last dollar for a bed right now."

She never moved. "We have a perfectly good room down the hall."

He nodded, trailing slow kisses partway down her spine. "Yeah. I know. But I'm pretty sure I lost all the feeling in my legs about a half hour ago."

With no small amount of regret, he eased out of her body and scooped her into his arms, carrying her to the ugly, but now surprisingly dear, sofa. They collapsed there in a jumble of arms and legs, their skin chilling slightly in the air-conditioning. Funny . . . he hadn't noticed the temperature before.

A slight pinging noise penetrated his haze of sexual well-being. "What's that?" he asked, only mildly curious.

Katie wiggled, pressing her breasts into his side. Unbelievably, his cock began to respond. She punched his arm. "It's the warn-ing bell. Our time's up."

She eluded his halfhearted attempt to pin her down and scrambled away, searching out her clothes and hurriedly begin-ning to dress. She frowned at his lack of concern. "Up, Ward, now. I don't want to be caught in the buff."

He stood up and stretched, pleased to note that her eyes lin-gered on him while she dressed. He retrieved his own clothes and put them on, sparing one last sentimental glance for his academic costume.

When they were both decent, he held out his hand, and she went to his arms instantly. He hugged her close. "You're an apt pupil, Miss Spencer," he whispered, his voice husky with emotion.

She smiled up at him, her eyes dreamy. "I appreciate your efforts to . . . reform me," she said, reaching down to cup him through his trousers.

He slapped her hand away. "Don't start that. I need solid food before you seduce me again."

"Seduce you?" she asked, her eyebrows raised. "I think we know who was the dirty old man in this scenario."

He pinched her butt as they left the room, both of them sparing one last glance at the austere setting. "I didn't notice you complaining."

This time they missed lunch. They opted for room service soup and sandwiches, which they ate in bed before curling up together for a long nap.

Later they cleaned up and decided to go all-out for dinner. The hotel boasted two restaurants, one casual and one extremely elegant. Dylan donned the tuxedo he'd brought, and Katie wore a new dress made of ice-blue silk sewn from bodice to hem with myriad tiny bugle beads in random patterns. The outfit was lined, but both layers of fabric were so thin that the dress outlined every dip and curve in her body. Dylan's hot gaze showed his approval.

Her hair was twisted in a loose knot on top of her head, leaving a few wispy tendrils to curl around her neck and face, and her lips were outlined with a light cherry gloss. It had been far too long since they'd last dressed up like this, she thought with a private smile. Dylan looked so adorably dark, rugged, and handsome, she almost hated to leave the room.

The restaurant was a masterpiece of soft lighting and soothing decor. All the tables were arranged with beautiful live ferns and other plants, ensuring the privacy of each and every couple. The waiters were attentive but as unobtrusive as possible, their quiet, efficient service barely disturbing the air of intimacy.

They dined on beef bourguignonne and baby carrots. Yet another bottle of fabulous wine accentuated the flavors of the various courses. Over coffee and biscotti, Dylan teased Katie about the afternoon. He laughed when she shushed him, looking around to see if anyone had overheard. "I can't believe you won't even talk about it," he said, shaking his head. "You didn't seem at a loss for words a few hours ago."

"That was different," she said, fanning her cheeks. "We were in the room. It was a game." Sex with Darren had been a mostly "lights out" affair. This openness with Dylan was wonderful, but she was still adjusting to the difference.

He leaned back in his chair, studying the beautiful picture she made. He smiled. "We're still the same people. That was *us* doing those things."

"I know," she hissed, glancing around to make sure no one could overhear them. "But it's different in the light of day."

"It's nine o'clock at night," he pointed out.

She rolled her eyes. "Whatever. And by the way . . . where did you get such a talent for improvisation?"

He shrugged modestly. "You inspired me." He watched, stunned, as she blushed from her breasts to her hairline, clearly remembering certain moments of their rendezvous. "Katie?"

Her chest rose and fell. "Hmmm?"

"Earth to Katie."

She came back to the present with an effort, her eyes slightly out of focus. Seeing her arousal made his cock swell and harden. He drained his wineglass, desperate to touch her. "Let's dance."

A small band situated adjacent to the tiny polished dance floor played a succession of romantic tunes. Every dance was a slow dance. That suited Dylan just fine. Katie was a tall woman, and when she wore heels, her height and his matched perfectly.

He rested his cheek against her hair, sliding his hand across her back. Her skin was like velvet, the bones fragile beneath his fingers. She was wearing her traditional scent, and the familiarity of it lodged in his psyche, making him content and aroused at the same time. She was still his precious Katie, despite the new things he had learned about her. He would always want to defend her, to cherish her.

If his need to protect ever conflicted with her need for independence, they could compromise, but he wasn't letting her go. He wanted so badly to make plans for the future, to put his ring on her finger for all the world to see. He only hoped she realized how much he was willing to invest in the relationship, how deeply he cared. She was everything to him.

It all came down to trust, and he knew in his heart that she was still wary about making a commitment as serious as marriage. Whatever it took, he had to prove to her that he was a man she could count on, that he was the man who would never let her down. Surely he'd be able to find a way.

He whispered in her ear. "Are you wondering what I am?"

She glanced up, confused. "What do you mean?"

He tipped his head, indicating the various couples on the dance floor. "Are you wondering what these other people were doing while we were in the schoolroom? Where they played?"

Katie glanced briefly at their fellow well-dressed guests and giggled. "They look so ordinary."

He snorted. "You mean like us? A pretty preschool teacher and a run-of-the-mill contractor?"

"I suppose. But I can't see that woman in the fuchsia suit cavorting in the backseat of a Chevy."

He laughed. "But isn't that the idea—ordinary people, extraordinary fantasies?"

She rubbed her cheek against his shoulder, her pink lips curving. "I guess you're right."

He lost track of time after that. Holding Katie in his arms was all he could handle at the moment. He felt drained, his emotions and his stamina depleted, and yet at the same time, quietly content.

When the lights flickered, signaling the restaurant was about to close, he kissed the top of her head and released her. They stepped outside for a few minutes to look at the sky. On this mountain, far from city lights, the stars seemed crowded together in the inky blackness, their numbers hard to comprehend. A brilliant, fiery meteor shot across the heavens, momentarily leaving behind a hazy vapor trail.

He slid his arm around her waist. "Are we supposed to make a wish? You go first."

Katie leaned her head against his shoulder. What she wanted more than anything was to know beyond the shadow of a doubt that she wasn't making another mistake. She wanted her confidence back. She wanted Dylan to be hers forever.

He brushed her cheek with his fingertips. "What did you wish for?" he murmured.

"Wishes are private," she said huskily.

He picked her up and swung her in a dizzy circle, smothering her shriek of laughter with a quick kiss. Then he lifted her, his arms extended toward the light-studded canopy of night. When he released her slowly, she savored the erotic friction as her body slid down his and back to earth.

"I love you," he whispered. "So very much."

She slid her arms around his waist. "I love you, too."

They made love again before sleeping that night. It was a slow, tender, gradual build to climax, but no less powerful than their frantic couplings earlier. Katie felt herself nearing the edge and wanted desperately to hold back, to savor the sweet and almost painful slide to completion. But Dylan knew her too well . . . knew the sensitive spots that made her body respond to his with quivering certainty.

In the drowsy aftermath, she pondered her one last hope for the weekend. Perhaps it was greedy to want more, especially when Dylan had given of himself so generously. But she was on a roll . . . exploring her naughty side and loving it.

She stroked his shoulder. "Dylan? Are you asleep?"

He grunted, burrowing deeper into his pillow. "I'm not now."

She grinned. Even when he was grumpy he was cute. She continued tracing patterns on the slopes of his muscular forearm. "Dylan," she murmured, "I've been thinking . . ."

"Sounds dangerous," he teased, his voice slurred with drowsiness.

She punched him. "Be nice."

He rolled to his back, tucking his arms behind his head. The only illumination came from a small lamp across the room, but she could see his lazy grin. "If I'm going to be awake, you might as well tell me."

"I've been thinking about which suite I should choose tomorrow."

He yawned. "Is this where I make a crass joke about women not being able to make up their minds? Can I go to sleep now?"

She straddled his waist. "I want you to be my prisoner in the jail cell."

She felt his whole body tense. "I don't think so, Katie."

The answer was swift and blunt. She winced, but pushed on. "Why not?"

His chest rose and fell. "Surely you've known me long enough to realize that I have some real control issues."

"I know you never let me drive, but I thought that was just a guy thing. It doesn't matter to me."

"Well, that's only the tip of the iceberg," he said, his tone thick with wry self-deprecation. "I make my crew nuts, sticking my nose in projects big and small every step of the way. I grill my accountant each spring and go over the books with him until I'm totally satisfied. I change my own oil. I mow my own grass. I built my own house. I trust myself and I don't like surprises. And if I'm completely honest . . . I'm kind of set in my ways. But I can try to change that, at least where you're concerned."

"But not the control thing?"

"Look, sweetheart. I am more than happy for you to run the show tomorrow. Take me to any other room. I swear you can boss me around as much as you want . . . and I'll obey . . . But the jail cell . . . I can't," he said, his voice adamant. "Or I won't." That was probably more honest. "I'm sorry, honey. I'm not into the whole bondage thing, *especially* if I'm the one being tied up. It creeps me out. Please pick something else. After all, be fair . . . I may have been in charge today, but I never used any kind of restraints on you, right?"

"True," she said, hoping her voice didn't reflect the disappointment she felt. They didn't have to check out until noon tomorrow, and she had already signed up for the jail cell. Her imagination had run wild with the possibilities. Something about having Dylan at her mercy appealed to the bad girl inside her. The naughty lover who often got pushed aside by the sweet Katie. She wanted to explore her darkest fantasies.

She scooted off his chest and lay beside him. A nasty thought occurred to her. What if Dylan was more like Darren than he realized? She frowned. "You're telling me that you're honestly bothered by the thought of being with me in the jail cell?"

He sat up, no longer looking sleepy at all. He frowned. "You sound like you don't believe me. I've never lied to you, Katie."

"I know that," she said slowly. "But what if deep down inside what really bothers you is the idea of your *perfect* Katie being your jailer?"

He stood up abruptly and began to pace. His magnificent nudity almost distracted her from their conversation. His face was a study in frustration, and he rubbed the heel of his hand across his forehead, his eyes shadowed. "When I got in trouble as a kid, my dad would punish me by locking me in my room. I developed claustrophobia. I've never been able to shake it. It's not exactly the thing a guy likes to admit."

"I see." She wanted desperately for Dylan to give them this chance to push the edge of what they knew about each other. But how could she insist when he had been so honest about his fears? "Okay," she sighed. "I'll choose another room."

He rejoined her on the bed, pulling her close. "I feel like I'm letting you down. I'm sorry, Katie."

She summoned a smile. "Don't be silly. We're here to play. I'm not letting you off the hook." She snuggled against Dylan as they drifted off to sleep, trying to banish the feeling that she had missed an important chance. She was probably making too much of the whole *bad Katie* fantasy. Dylan loved her. She needed to accept that and quit worrying about her own insecurities.

Katie's mind-blowing question totally obliterated any inclination Dylan felt to slumber. As he listened to the faint snuffling sounds she made in her sleep, he wondered how he could have handled that conversation differently. Here she was, his sensual little Katie, brave enough to push the limits of her comfort zone, and he-man Dylan Ward had to go and admit that he was afraid of letting a woman tie him up.

He tossed and turned in the darkness. A woman like Katie came along once in a lifetime. A man had to risk a lot for that kind of prize. But handcuffs . . . blindfolds? . . .

He tucked her back against his chest, cupping her breasts in his hands and relishing the feel of her bottom cradling his cock. Suddenly, like a blow to the gut, he saw his own duplicity. He'd sworn to himself that he would do whatever was necessary to gain Katie's trust, but at the first sign of difficulty, he'd bailed. He was a damned lily-livered chickenshit.

As he lay there wide-awake for what seemed like hours, he finally decided that phobia or no phobia, Dylan Ward would take his punishment like a man. And in the process, he'd prove to Katie that he was her partner for the long haul. No fear could possibly be worse than the fear of losing Katie. He would hold on to her, no matter what. Katie Spencer, in all her delightful personas, was his.

*   *   *

Katie woke not long after dawn, accustomed to rising early. Dylan slept heavily and deeply, his muscled arm pinning her to his side. She gently slipped free of his hold and went to the bathroom. After a quick shower, she dressed and began quietly tucking clothes and toiletries into her suitcase. Breakfast on the veranda again would be nice.

When he stirred, she sat on the edge of the bed and ruffled his hair. "I made some coffee in the little pot in the bathroom. You want some?"

He pulled her down into his arms and tugged the pins from her damp hair, grunting in satisfaction when it tumbled loose. He kissed her nose, her cheeks, and then her lips. "Good morning, princess."

She smiled, loving his rumpled, sleepy look. "Good morning to you, too."

She reached beneath the covers and stroked the silky length of his erect cock. "I bet you were a Boy Scout," she teased. "Always prepared."

He didn't return the smile. In fact, despite his affectionate actions, his face was closer to a frown than anything else. He turned her fully onto her back and held both of her wrists above her head, pinning them easily with one big hand. "We're going to do it," he said, his eyes dark and serious.

Her heart raced. "Do what?"

"The bondage thing."

His bleak pronouncement made her want to laugh. "Reeaally . . ." she said, drawing the word out mockingly. "What girl could resist such a sincere and enthusiastic invitation?"

"Don't mock me, Katie. I've made up my mind. We'll play out your little scenario."

The grim expression on his face was highly amusing. She brushed his cheek with her fingers. "We can have one of those code words," she promised. "You know . . . if you've had enough, you say the code word and I'll stop."

His lip curled. "I don't need a damned code word. I'm not a sissy."

She soothed him with a gentle, thorough, loving kiss. "I never thought you were. Not ever. But just in case . . . the code word is *chocolate*." She touched his cheek. "Thank you, Dylan. I've never been comfortable enough with anyone to try something like this. Trust me, sweetheart. I'll take care of you."

His eyes were dark. "I'm *not* like Darren, Katie, I swear. Having you in charge in the bedroom doesn't threaten me at all. In fact, it makes me damned hard. It's just this stupid phobia I have about being tied up. But I'll deal with it. You play your part and don't worry about me."

He was quiet all during breakfast, prompting her to choke repeatedly on peals of laughter as he chewed his food with all the dogged determination of a condemned man consuming his last meal.

Finally she couldn't take it anymore. She set down her juice glass with a thump that threatened to splinter the delicate crystal. "If you're going to be such a baby, just forget it. I'm not forcing you into anything. You're a big boy. Have the guts to say no if you don't want to do it."

He slouched in his chair. "I said I'll do it."

"And so charmingly, too."

"Hey . . . nothing says a prisoner has to be polite and amenable. Just consider me a hostile captive."

His outthrust jaw dared her to complain. Somewhere deep inside her a tiny flame of temper lit, fanned by the heat of a sudden, searing arousal. She stared him in the eyes, daring him to look away. "In that case, get your butt out of that chair, Ward. Time's a wastin'."

They stopped by their room for a brief moment and then made their way to the "entertainment" corridor. Katie unlocked the door to suite seven and motioned for Dylan to precede her. He entered, his feet practically dragging.

The room gave new meaning to the word stark. If the English schoolroom had been somewhat cold and lifeless, the ambience in the jail cell was downright brutal. For one thing, it was probably the smallest of the suites, measuring barely twelve feet square. Across the back of the room, walling off an area four-feet deep, was a set of entirely authentic iron bars, which enclosed the "cell." The only other furniture was a scarred table and chair over which hung an interrogation lamp. A rough wooden screen in the front corner concealed costumes and of course, handcuffs.

Katie nibbled her bottom lip. Being a dominatrix wasn't as easy in reality as it sounded on paper. She hadn't glanced at Dylan yet, but she did so now. He stood a few feet from her, his gaze downcast.

She unlocked the door of the cell. "Inside, Dylan." Her voice sounded more quavery than authoritative. She tried again. "Undress completely and shove your clothes through the bars."

When he passed through the door, she turned the key in the padlock and laid the key on the table. She didn't wait to see if he obeyed her second order. She disappeared behind the wooden screen and leaned against the bare concrete wall, her knees trembling and her heart racing. This wasn't going to work unless she became her character. In her mind, the idea of having Dylan at her mercy was interesting. But here and now . . . the reality threatened to overwhelm her.

She heard only silence from the other side of the room, and she wondered what she would do if he defied her orders. The thought of punishing him for his disobedience made her thighs clench and pulses of heat spread through her abdomen. Was this how Dylan felt in the schoolroom? Did he experience this hot, liquid arousal? She wanted to make him as crazy and as hungry as she'd been yesterday.

She took several deep breaths and studied her clothing choices. The options leaned more toward latex and leather than satin and silk. She picked up a black rubber bodysuit, and using the small mirror on the wall as her only guide, wriggled her way into it. The result was shocking.

She stared at her image for several long seconds and came close to calling off the whole thing. The outfit fit like a second skin, enclosing her like a swimsuit at the bottom, except for the generous slash in the crotch, which exposed the curling hair between her thighs. From there, the suit rose to her hips and above, where a series of wicked-looking metal studs made her waist look impossibly small.

Fanning out at her rib cage, the bodice became mere strips, exposing her nipples in a lewd fashion and then rejoining at the throat with a second circle of studs. Her back, legs, shoulders, and arms were bare. Despite the heavy latex, the brevity of the costume kept it from feeling too confining.

Next, she stepped into high-heeled black boots, their supple leather polished to a glossy sheen. Long, transparent mesh gloves covered her almost to the shoulder. She put up her hair and donned the last item, a black leather eye mask lined in lambs' wool. The soft fur tickled her cheeks.

When she looked in the mirror, she saw a stranger. A surprisingly voluptuous, wicked stranger. She flexed her fingers and tugged the top to cover a bit more of her breasts. When she could delay no longer, she stood at the edge of the screen without revealing herself and spoke firmly. "Are you nude?"

His voice was low but clear. "Yes."

"Face the back wall and close your eyes."

She peeked to make sure he was cooperating. Then she hurriedly collected all of his clothes and threw them behind the screen, pausing long enough to admire the picture he made. His arms hung loosely by his sides, and for some reason she noticed for the first time that he had no tan lines. Every inch of his taut sculpted body was a uniform, golden brown. Jealousy gnawed with unexpected force. Where in the hell did he sunbathe in the nude?

Unfortunately, that nagging question would have to wait. She lifted a black whip from a nail on the wall and wound it around her arm, leaving the tip to dangle artfully over her bare shoulder. After pulling the chair away from the table, she raised her right foot and propped it on the seat, making sure Dylan had a clear view of her open thighs.

Dylan breathed deeply. This wasn't so bad. He could handle it. He rested his hands against the bare concrete wall, wanting to turn around but not daring to incur Katie's displeasure right off the bat. He sensed her watching him, and it made his balls draw up against his body in an involuntary bid for protection. Would she really be capable of "punishing" him?

She was such a gentle creature, she couldn't bear to squash bugs. Watching her tender care with her little munchkins made his heart swell. She was so patient and loving. But somehow he doubted that those two characteristics were likely to be at the forefront this morning.

He looked down at his penis, realizing ruefully that the poor guy was not in top form. It hung shriveled and forlorn, probably wondering why the man who had taken such good care of him for thirty-three years had lost his mind.

He heard her say something, but he pretended not to hear. He wasn't ready yet. He needed a drink of water.

His fingers flexed, scraping the pads raw. His jaw locked. He was certifiable. He still couldn't believe he was going through with this.

His heart was beating so hard he could feel it jumping in his chest. What would she do first? Would she play with his balls? That wouldn't be too bad . . . and spanking . . . well, how much could it really hurt? Her hands were so small, and everyone knew women had no upper-body strength.

The plain, simple truth was, Katie could do to him or with him whatever she damn well pleased. He'd given her carte blanche. That was more than he'd granted anyone in his life . . . ever. The simple realization shocked him. What was he really afraid of? Having Katie tease and torment him would be exciting. And he could tough it out with the handcuffs. He'd conquered his claustrophobia enough to fly to Europe and back twice in the last few years.

But maybe Katie was right. Not about him needing her to be sweet Katie—that was nuts. But maybe he was more afraid of ceding control than he'd realized. He'd worried so much about getting her to trust him that he might possibly have ignored the fact that he had a few trust issues of his own.

She spoke again, from closer this time, her voice clipped, annoyed. "Turn around, Dylan. Face me."

He sucked it up like a man and obeyed, his hands covering his genitals protectively.

But then his jaw . . . and his hands . . . dropped. He swayed, dizzy enough to pass out cold given half a chance. "Sweet, holy hell."

CHAPTER FOUR

is response was reverent. If he lived to be a hundred, he'd never forget his first sight of Katie in that getup. She looked like a cross between Cher and a hooker with an attitude. Her lips were outlined in a deep, glossy red, and her eyes glittered behind the mask she wore, whether with excitement or anticipation, he wasn't sure.

Her nipples stood taut and firm, thrust into prominence by the tight latex straps of her costume. Between her legs, fluffy golden curls begged for his attention. Every centimeter of his body tightened in sheer, helpless arousal. His throat dried and his hands clenched into fists, desperate to touch her.

Seeing the whip curled around her shoulder gave him a moment's pause. Rationally he knew that this erotic, fascinating goddess of pain and punishment was the same sweet Katie who baked cookies and cuddled toddlers, but his brain was having a difficult time meshing the two realities.

She tossed her head, an arrogant, haughty motion that appeared entirely authentic. "Well," she said, challenge in every syllable, "what do you think?"

Beneath her confidence, he heard the tiny plea for reassurance. His smile bloomed, his misgivings buried under a wave of love and delight. He grabbed the bars in front of him and stepped as close as he could to his would-be tormentor. He shivered as her small pink tongue darted out to wet her lips, betraying her nerves. "You look like every man's secret fantasy," he said, his voice a husky whisper. "You're incredible, Katie."

Again the head toss. "Sweet talk won't spare you, Ward. They've reported your insolence, your refusal to behave like the other prisoners. I've been charged with carrying out your punishment. And you will call me 'mistress.'"

To deliberately provoke her, he reached down and stroked his fully erect cock, grinning as her eyes focused on the subtle motions of his hand. He spoke coaxingly. "You could forget your assignment, mistress . . . share this cot with me. I promise that my behavior will be . . ." His hand pumped faster. Was it his imagination or did her eyes glaze over behind her mask?

She swallowed and took her foot down from the chair. "Your behavior will be what?" she asked, her voice raspy.

"My behavior will be exemplary," he promised. "In every way."

She took a step forward, but as she did so, the whip slipped from her shoulder, uncurling in an untidy mess and nearly tripping her. It was enough to shock her back into character. Katie refurled the length of supple, plaited leather, her gloved fingers handling it like a lover, her smile unpleasant. "Your promises don't interest me. A man like you will say anything to get what he wants."

"I want you," he said, deadly serious.

"Perhaps in time . . . if you are truly penitent . . . and cooperative."

The impassive words . . . the implied threat . . . each reminded him why they were there. Katie wanted to play this game to the end.

He sucked in a deep breath, torn between heated excitement and anxiety. "I await your pleasure, mistress."

He saw the almost imperceptible movement of her body as she recognized his double entendre. Perhaps he was not so helpless after all. If he could maintain her desire at fever pitch, she might crumble at some point, might let him prove to her that he could be of more use to her as a lover than a prisoner.

But for now he had to play his part. He stepped back from the bars and sprawled on the cot, the coarse blanket scratching his behind. He propped up one knee and tucked his hands behind his head, feigning unconcern.

His cavalier attitude set her off. "Stand up this instant," she hissed. "I didn't give you permission to get comfortable."

He rose to his feet, sneering. "Comfortable? That piece of crap you people like to call a blanket feels like sandpaper. This whole place is a hellhole."

"What did you expect, Mr. Ward? A room at the Ritz?" She picked up the heavy metal key and inserted it into the padlock, releasing the mechanism with a twist of her hand. "Out here . . . now. Face away from me and put your hands on the bars above your head."

Dylan exited his little cell unwillingly, aware of the faint protection it had afforded him. He did as she asked and once again faced away from her . . . only this time on her side of the bars. He felt the brush of latex and leather at his back as she stepped closer. Moments later he smothered a curse as he realized she was tying his hands to the bars. It required every bit of effort not to knock her hands away.

For the briefest of seconds he felt the brush of her lips at the nape of his neck. "Katie . . ." He wasn't able to articulate his plea.

Her voice sounded close to his ear, her breath a tantalizing brush against his cheek. "Mistress," she said, tugging a lock of his hair roughly. "Don't forget my name again."

He nodded, mute. In every James Bond movie he had ever seen, from Connery to Moore or any of the others, good ole Jimmy had weathered being tied up and threatened by the wicked villains with a calm stiff upper lip and British panache. Now, feeling the cold concrete floor beneath his bare feet and at the mercy of an unpredictable, creative, wannabe bad girl, he took his proverbial hat off to 007. This whole captivity thing was a damned sight harder than it looked.

He braced himself, not sure what to expect.

Her first attack was swift and powerfully surprising. A slice of fire bit into his butt cheek as the whip flicked with careless precision. Shit!

He jerked his head around as far as he could, glaring, his arms straining. "That hurt, dammit."

Her smile was rife with satisfaction. "Good."

He sagged against the bars, his chest heaving with indignation. She was really going to do this. The whip sailed again, marking his other buttock, then the top of each thigh. The sharp stings spread heat down his legs and up to his groin. With incredulous amazement, he felt his penis respond.

Never in a million years could he have imagined himself in this situation. He steadied his arms and waited. She was incredibly gifted for a novice. She altered the placement of the strokes, making it impossible for him to anticipate. If he cringed in expectation of a deep blow, invariably she merely brushed his burning flesh. Just when he thought she was winding down, she gave him a lash hard enough to make him flinch. But even at the peak of her efforts, it was far from unbearable. He'd been hurt worse playing sports. His little tormentor simply didn't have the strength or the inclination to do any real damage.

He had no idea how much time had passed. His eyes were gritty, his ass hot and tingling. Finally he sensed her moving away. He thought he heard her drop the whip on the table, but he couldn't be sure.

Seconds later something brushed the back of his knee and he cried out, unable to help himself as he felt her tongue, wet and soft, licking the red marks on his butt. He groaned, his cock twitching painfully, his knees locking as the incredible sensation continued. Every sensitive inch of skin received the same careful attention. Her gloved hands clasped his hips as she silently tended to his wounds.

He found his voice, vaguely embarrassed by its weakness. "Is this part of the punishment?" He panted, his thighs quivering.

Her reply was muffled. "I have to keep the prisoner in good condition. At least long enough to carry out my mission."

"There's more?" The despair in his voice made him wince.

She stood up, rapidly releasing his arms from their ties and then handcuffing his wrists behind his back with smooth precision. She turned him to face her, her hands intentionally rough, her eyes holding his with a mesmerizing stare. "There's always more."

She sat in the chair, her legs outstretched in bawdy abandon, one finger crooked in his direction. "Come here and kneel."

He stumbled forward, relieved that she held nothing in her hands. He fell awkwardly to his knees, catching his breath as the unforgiving floor bruised him. Her scent swirled around him, hot . . . erotic . . . wickedly sensual.

She traced his nose with a gentle finger. "You've done well, so far. You've pleased me." She held his chin, her grip just shy of painful. "I hope that will continue to be the case."

He lowered his head, his heart racing like a freight train, his arms numb and tingling. Looking directly at her was a mistake. The sight of her dazzled him, like being blinded by an unwary glimpse at the sun. He had gone from simple arousal to something infinitely darker and less comfortable. His body was driving him, demanding completion, but his brain laughed cynically, knowing relief was far off, perhaps far from certain.

She jerked his hair in a painful grasp, pulling his head toward the lewd opening in her bodysuit. "Eat me," she said, imperious as a queen. "Make me come."

He buried his face between her legs, incoherent with desire. He devoured her with hungry openmouthed kisses, using the tip of his tongue to zero in on her pleasure point.

She writhed in the chair, her hands guiding his head, her keening cries echoing in the bare cell. She arched her back, nearly knocking him backwards as she came with a moan of joy.

Undeterred, he licked and sucked her sweet succulent folds until she pushed him away, her head lolling back in exhausted abandon.

He continued to kneel, still cataloging every nuance of her orgasm.

At long last, she stood. She helped him ease into a reclining position but did not offer to release him. She disappeared behind the screen, and he heard the faint trickle of water, smelled the fresh scent of soap.

He lay dazed on the cold, hard floor, his stiff erection an ever-present pain. He had slipped into some kind of sexual fourth dimension, unable to imagine what lay outside the door of this room, no longer capable of rational thought.

When she reappeared, every trace of sexual euphoria had disappeared from her face. Beneath the mask, her mouth seemed like that of a stranger. In total silence she helped him to his feet. She led him to the table and shoved him onto his back, pausing only long enough to open the handcuffs, reposition his arms above his head, and lock the cuffs once more . . . this time around the slender iron support beam in the center of the room.

The table was small, and his legs dangled awkwardly from the end. His arms stretched to the nearby pole with nothing to support them but the connection from handcuff to pole. It was damned uncomfortable.

Katie crossed her arms and looked at him with what appeared to be a dispassionate gaze. She circled the table twice, assessing . . . watching. He tried to take a deep breath, but his chest was constricted.

She flicked the head of his cock with a sharp fingernail. "I'm going to torture you now, Mr. Ward. If you climax without permission I will give you fifty lashes with the whip. Do you understand?"

He started to shake. His head bobbed once in a jerky motion she apparently took as consent.

She removed one of her gloves and trailed it from his collarbone to his groin, barely avoiding his swollen organ. She removed a second glove. As he watched in stunned fascination, she knotted the ends of the two, creating a length of sturdy black mesh. With a tiny smile teasing the corners of her mouth, she looped the fabric beneath his balls and up around the base of his penis, tying it in a firm knot.

He groaned, the sound reverberating from deep in his chest.

She paused, her head tilted to one side, her fingers brushing his thighs. "Did I hear you say 'chocolate,' Mr. Ward?"

"No." He grunted the word past the knot in his throat. "Take off the mask, mistress. I want to see your face."

She pinched each of his nipples, hard. "You are not in a position to make demands. My face is none of your concern." She leaned down and offered him her breast. "My costume is awry. Fix it."

He sucked hungrily at her nipple, then went for the other, barely in reach. The pieces of her costume taunted him, concealing the fullness of her ripe breasts. She laughed at his frustration. "You're distracting me. Lie still."

She reached for a blindfold. His body jerked violently. "No." Then a tad more conciliatory. "No, mistress. Let me see your beautiful body."

She paused, perhaps struck by the very real alarm he couldn't conceal. She kissed him softly, her lips moving on his with aching tenderness. For that brief second, she was his Katie.

But before he could savor the flash of reality, she was back in the game. She positioned the chair by the table, stepped onto it, and then carefully straddled his body. There was barely enough table on either side of his hips to support her knees. She lowered herself, brushing her moist heat back and forth against his penis.

He surged upward, trying to enter her. She laughed softly. "Forgotten already, my eager captive? No coming, remember?"

She allowed the tip of his penis to enter her passage the merest fraction, and his vision blurred, every ounce of his being concentrated on penetration. The studs at her waist pressed into his belly as she leaned forward. He tried to shove her mask up with his tongue.

She taunted him, reaching behind her back to tickle his balls. "You're rather clumsy aren't you, Mr. Ward?"

Helpless, suffocating with a deadly combination of lust and rage, he reached up and bit her lower lip.

She went completely still, the heat of her still nestled over his groin. She settled back on his thighs and rubbed her mouth with her hand, stripping off her mask and tossing it away.

He flinched, unable to meet her eyes.

Katie gazed down at her captive in shock. "You bit me."

Dylan, still avoiding her gaze, shrugged as much as a man could in his position. "You deserved it."

She felt a bubbling excitement in her chest, and she beamed at him. "You aren't looking at me like an earth mother/Madonna anymore."

That caught his attention. He grimaced. "Hell, no. You're some kind of man-eating vision from erotic hell, pardon the pun."

Despite his acerbic comment, he seemed curiously resigned to his fate.

She stroked his penis with both hands. "I have a hankering to use the whip again. I bet I can make you come."

He frowned. "Not without permission. I ain't stupid."

She circled the head of his cock with her fingers and squeezed. His eyes drifted shut, his face agonized. "Darlin', please."

Her thumbnail scraped him lightly. He shuddered. "Katie . . ."

She repositioned herself and took him deep. He gasped out a protest. She squeezed him with her inner muscles. His teeth clamped down on his lower lip. Sweat trickled down his temples.

She shook her head, smiling. "You really hate that whip, don't you?"

His only answer was a snarl.

She scooted off her deeply satisfying perch and climbed down from the table. She tugged away the mesh gloves, and with little ceremony, unlocked the handcuffs and massaged his chafed and reddened wrists. As she supported him, he struggled to a sitting position.

She felt a twinge of guilt as he flexed his arms and rolled his shoulders. He'd been a trooper. Even now, with his cock standing tall and hungry, his big, powerful body unrestrained . . . he stood passive . . . awaiting her command.

She regretted taking off her mask. The anonymity of the black leather made it easier to act like a bitch. Now that he could see her face, she felt self-conscious. She put her hands on her hips, lifted her leg, and used the sharp toe of her boot to nudge his balls. "Ready to say the magic word?"

She infused the taunt with as much sarcasm as she could summon, hoping if the truth were told, that he would cry uncle and put an end to their game. But Dylan Ward was made of sterner stuff.

His chin jutted forward. "I don't know what you mean, mistress."

Damn. She nibbled her lower lip, her mind racing. She lowered her foot. "Pick me up in your arms." After all, what was the point of having a captive if you couldn't get what you wanted?

He frowned slightly, but readily scooped her into a tight embrace.

She closed her eyes, enjoying the easy way he held her, the unmistakable strength. "Take me to your cell."

He crossed the short distance in three strides, his broad chest radiating heat. At the door, he paused.

She kept her eyes closed. "Remove the covers and put me on the cot."

He held her with one arm as he flipped back the rough blanket, revealing equally coarse sheets. Gently he lowered her and stepped back.

She took a deep breath. How did a dominatrix get screwed by

her slave and still remain in charge? She extended one leg toward the ceiling. "Remove my boots."

When his large warm hands touched her thighs, she nearly caved. Tormenting Dylan was the most exciting thing she had ever done. Despite her earlier orgasm, her body hummed with the need to feel him buried deep inside her, loving her, making her his.

Dylan struggled with the boots. They had no zipper, and her skin was damp with perspiration, making the leather cling to her skin. As he tugged at her ankles, grasping the stiletto heels, the ache between her thighs intensified. Finally he grunted with satisfaction as the last of the two tumbled to the floor.

She flexed her feet, relishing the feel of the cool air on her hot skin. She was ready to be done with the heavy bodysuit, but she curbed her impatience. Dylan had made love to her in the nude countless times, but how often in her life did a woman get to tempt the man she loved while wearing such a provocative costume?

Dylan knelt by the cot silent . . . watchful. Their time was winding down, and she had to come up with a fitting finale. She slipped a hand between her legs and began to play with herself. He went rigid. She turned her head to look at him, her cheek on the pillow, her eyes heavy-lidded with arousal.

She licked her lips, her hand still moving with desultory eroticism. "Shall my captive be punished by watching me come?"

His lips parted. His breathing labored as his eyes fixated on the gentle back-and-forth movements of her finger. "Let me do it, mistress," he muttered hoarsely.

She shook her head regretfully. "No. You'll be too busy. I'm giving you permission to ejaculate . . . now."

He stared at her, clearly confused.

She waved a hand. "Lean back against the bars . . . jerk off for me."

Protest hovered on his lips, and his eyes darkened with angry refusal. She raised an eyebrow. "It's your only guaranteed option for relief. I'd take it if I were you . . . and besides . . . I fancy watching you do it."

He visibly reined in his temper, the cords in his neck standing out. He went from his knees to his butt, settling back against the uncomfortable bars with outstretched legs, keeping eye contact all the while.

She nodded approvingly. "Good. Now hold yourself."

He slowly grasped his thick cock with his right hand, and she noticed the hand trembled.

She increased the friction and speed of her own self-stimulation. "You may begin," she said, forcing the words through dry lips.

As he pulled at his cock, using his left hand on his balls, she watched in fascination. He had been suspended in this state of arousal for almost three hours. His head fell back and his jaw clenched as he drew nearer to his peak. His hand worked quickly, pulling at his penis almost roughly.

Her body felt a matching urgency, but her hand slowed, unable to focus on Dylan and herself at the same time. He was magnificent, the sculpted contours of his chest glistening with sweat, his heavy thighs spread wide as he manipulated his beautiful, angry-looking erection.

She had thought they might come together. But instead, she became lost in his quest for pleasure, so enthralled she started to go to him, aching to join in that blinding reach for the stars.

She hesitated a moment too long. He came with a hoarse shout, his legs braced, his back arching as his seed shot out, landing to form a sticky, wet pool on the concrete floor. His chest heaved, his breathing labored.

Amazingly, his penis was still hard, twitching eagerly as though sensing her arousal. He opened his eyes, staring at her with fuzzy comprehension while reason slowly returned.

Before she could think of an appropriate response, he got to his feet, towering over her as she lay on the cot. His eyes were glittering with some unnamed emotion. His cheeks were flushed. Threat etched every line of his body.

Her heart pounded. He looked angry, aroused, and at the end of his rope. She trembled, trying to control the game one last time. She twisted her lips in a haughty sneer. "You're a careless, filthy man, spilling your come on the floor. Clean it up this instant."

The last word was swallowed in a gasp of surprise as he leaned down and bracketed her body with his sturdy arms. The expression on his face was neither tender nor romantic. He looked ready to commit murder.

He glared, fierce and intimidating. "Open your legs, mistress. It's payback time."

She pressed her knees tightly together in a pathetic show of defiance. His harsh frown deepened. He left her for perhaps three seconds, only long enough to retrieve the whip. She choked, shocked that her captive had forgotten his place, uncertain what to expect next. He flipped the length of the whip with careless authority, the ends wrapping around one of the far bars.

His gaze was hot. "Open your legs."

Her hands gripped the sides of the cot, but she obeyed. She fixated on the sight of a vengeful Dylan, not a gentle, soft emotion to be found.

He wrapped the bulk of the whip around his arm, holding only the last six inches of the slender leather strips that formed the end. He squatted, pushing her legs farther apart. The frayed leather tickled the achingly sensitive flesh at her core with diabolical precision. Her clitoris received the most attention, throbbing with increasing pleasure as the leather brushed it again and again.

Against her will, she began to writhe and moan, cursing and begging. The delicate strips continued their punishment, teasing but not satisfying. She needed relief. She needed him.

Abruptly the feathery strokes disappeared, and she arched,

ready to take him. She wanted Dylan inside her, Dylan's hard masculine perfection driving her to orgasm. She grabbed his wrist, her fingernails biting into his skin. "I want you," she panted. "All of you. I'm begging."

Hearing the frantic plea from his delicate but determined tormentor gave Dylan a jolt of hot, masculine satisfaction. He had enjoyed her twisted game of domination, but her reign of terror was over.

He smiled with his best evil leer. "Begging. I like that." He held her legs apart and bent as though ready to eat her. She wiggled in his firm hold, trying to pull away. "No. I want your cock."

He spread her knees another inch, wanting to strip the latex from her body, but physically and mentally unable to wait even a second longer.

"Finally," he groaned as he positioned himself. "Something we can agree on." He surged forward in one hard stroke. The exquisitely pleasurable sensation, coming as it did after hours of deprivation, took his breath away. The slightly rough edges of the latex slit scraped over the taut skin of his penis almost painfully. He had no plans to ever leave the sweet, tight warmth of her body. He could live here happily, her slender thighs clasped around his waist, forever.

He slid in and out in long deep strokes that gave each of them maximum stimulation. Thankfully, his recent orgasm had taken the edge off his lust. He was still in the grasp of a driving need to take Katie repeatedly, but at least he had regained a tenuous measure of control.

He sensed her nearing the edge and he pulled out abruptly, prompting the slender female beneath him to hiss and scratch in frustrated fury. He kissed her hard, smothering her unladylike curses and grinning all the while.

He jerked her to her feet and dragged her out of the cell, steadying her as she swayed. Before she could formulate a protest, he backed her against the cold steel bars and handcuffed her hands above her head. He unsnapped the studs at either side of her neck and peeled down the sweat-slicked rubber, exposing her lush, full breasts.

He scooped them into his hands, licking and sucking one at a time, tasting the faint flavor of salt and traces of perfume. She was his for the taking, helpless, vulnerable, totally at his mercy. He stepped back and stripped the rest of her costume down over her hips and legs, pulling it free.

The picture she made, hanging there in lewd abandon, hardened his resolve . . . among other things. He scooped up the discarded mesh gloves and ran them through his hands. Quickly, before she realized what he was doing, he tied each slender ankle to one of the iron bars, her feet spread wide apart.

He stepped back and studied the result of his efforts. Her skin glowed, soft and creamy in the unforgiving illumination of the cell's harsh lighting. Her hair tumbled in disarray, and at the top of her thighs, moisture glistened in her soft curls. He wanted to keep her locked here for eternity.

Her pupils were dilated. She seemed deep in a trance, her rib cage rising and falling with every breath. He kissed her tenderly, allowing no point of their bodies to touch except their lips. He knelt and gently probed her opening. She was wet and swollen. He placed his hands on her stomach and circled her navel with his tongue. She flinched, but remained locked in silence.

The logistics of his height and hers weren't a great match, but he was determined to take her this way. He bent his knees and probed for her opening. Awkwardly, he surged upward, lifting her to her toes, straining the cloth that held her firm. She gasped, sandwiched between the rigid bars and his weight.

His knees screamed in protest as he rammed her again and again, maintaining the up and in motion necessary to keep their bodies connected. Fortunately for Katie, the unorthodox position placed pressure where she needed it the most. He sensed her panting need and slowed his assault, wanting release as badly as she, but too wrapped up in the carnality of the moment to let it end.

His legs trembled. "Squeeze me, Katie. Make yourself come."

She whimpered in exhaustion, her head drooping forward. He felt the clasp of her most intimate muscles, but it was a weak grip, almost played out. He ground the base of his cock against her clit, impaling her to the hilt. She quivered and cried out. He repeated the motion a second time and she screamed, her body shaking and convulsing. Blindly, he surged upward again and again, succumbing to the blessed, inevitable conclusion.

His climax, when it came, was a punishment of its own, a moment of sheer physical pleasure so achingly perfect, it would haunt him for the rest of his life.

He slumped against her, his flaccid cock slipping free of her body. He felt her utter stillness and was racked with sudden alarm. Frantically, he released her arms and feet. He carried her to the cot and lay down with her, stroking the hair from her forehead, his thumb feathering over her cheekbone. Love swamped him, tightening his throat and bringing moisture to his eyes.

"Katie," he whispered. "Katie, my princess, my angel. Look at me, hon."

Her lashes lifted slowly and she smiled the lazy wicked smile of a diva dominatrix. "That's 'mistress' to you, buddy. And don't you forget it."

CHAPTER FIVE

he drive home was long and definitely anticlimactic. It started to rain just as they pulled away from the hotel, a hard driving torrent that turned the sky a sullen gray and wrapped the mountaintop in a veil of clouds. Katie glanced in the rearview mirror and saw the massive stone edifice through a curtain of misty raindrops. From this angle it looked gloomy and foreboding—or perhaps that was merely a reflection of her own uncertain mood.

They negotiated the twists and turns of the winding driveway and finally made their way back to the interstate. Dylan was quiet, lost in his thoughts. He smiled at her from time to time, but otherwise his concentration stayed on his driving and his own private reflections.

Katie huddled in her seat, chilled to the bone by the depressing weather and her even more depressing thoughts. She had a jacket in her suitcase, but she was reluctant to ask Dylan to stop the car. He seemed intent on getting them home.

They had exited the suite with only minutes to spare. After a quick lunch at the hotel's bistro, they checked out and loaded their luggage in the car. And all the while Dylan seemed different. She couldn't quite put her finger on the change, but it was there. He was his usual courteous, attentive self, but nevertheless, something was going on inside his head. She wasn't sure if she wanted to know what it was. Perhaps in this case ignorance was bliss.

She was suffering from a massive case of the sexual equivalent of buyer's remorse. The weekend had played out according to plan. Dylan certainly had seen her in a different light. But had she gone too far in her quest to explore the naughty Katie, in her need to assert her independence and have Dylan hand over the reins?

She grinned inwardly, despite her mental distress. Dylan had enjoyed the weekend—or at least parts of it, she amended, keenly aware that his participation in the jail cell had been under duress.

Had she shocked him? Was he even now pondering ways to ditch his wacko lover and find a woman more amenable, more interested in conventional pursuits?

Men were funny creatures. In an earlier era they kept one woman for amusement and another for hearth and home. Had she slipped from her pedestal? Suddenly the view from up there didn't seem so bad after all.

She sighed deeply, hoping he would ask her if she was okay, if she needed the heater turned on, if she needed to stop for a bathroom break. Any one of the simple gentlemanly actions she had grown to take for granted. But her partner in debauchery remained silent, his eyes on the road, his big, powerful hands locked around the steering wheel.

Looking at his hands was a mistake. She blushed, embarrassed by her own X-rated recollections. The memories alone were enough to keep her warm for years to come. But was that all she could expect?

She laid her hand on his thigh. He smiled absently, not really looking at her. "We'll be there soon, hon." When he turned a sharp curve, her hand slid away from his leg and she didn't have the courage to put it back.

Uncertainty bit hard. Had she realized the truth too late? At some point in the last forty-eight hours her brain finally admitted what her heart had known all along. Dylan Ward was a keeper. He loved her totally and unconditionally. What other man would have faced a very real phobia and embraced it, simply because it was important to her? He had done everything in his power to win her trust.

But she had given him nothing in return. As far as he was concerned, she was still unwilling to make the commitment he wanted.

She'd naively assumed he would make love to her at her house as he had done so many times in the past. Instead, he unloaded her and her luggage with unflattering haste, kissed her, and started to walk back to the car.

In desperation, she called out, "I can fix us a bite of supper."

He shook his head, smiling. "Thanks, but I can't stay. I have to pick up the dog, and I've got several calls to make about tomorrow's schedule, not to mention sifting through my messages. I'll call you."

She stood on the porch and watched him drive away, a leaden feeling in her stomach. He hadn't changed his mind about loving her. He wouldn't. Dylan Ward was the steadiest, most dependable, least flighty man she had ever known. She might have shocked the hell out of him, but he'd be back. Things were going to be okay. They had to be okay.

He called her every night that week, but he never darkened her door. The phone conversations were cordial but brief. He was swamped at work, and a series of crises demanded his attention. She tried to take his preoccupation at face value, but deep inside, she worried.

Dylan loved the cookie-making day care director. He'd enjoyed sex with the dominatrix, but most people given half a chance didn't choose sinfully rich chocolate as a steady diet. When they settled down for a satisfying meal they wanted meat and potatoes. Oh lord, she was beginning to sound like a bad episode of *Dr. Phil.* At this rate she'd be on Prozac by the time she was thirty.

By Friday at six she was at risk of sinking into what the Victorians fondly referred to as a decline. She wiped up an apple juice spill and tried not to remember the spill she'd commanded Dylan to clean up.

As she tossed toys into a storage cupboard, she picked up a plastic sheriff's badge and flashed back to a pair of shiny metal handcuffs. Her knees buckled, and she sank down on the sofa, her eyes burning with tears. Had she driven Dylan away? She could be what he wanted. The sweet, delicate woman . . . the amenable lover . . . the decent, law-abiding female.

But first he had to actually give her another chance.

When the doorbell rang at six thirty she sighed, picking up one last stuffed toy. Tommy Stevens couldn't sleep without his beloved teddy bear.

She opened the door and froze in shock, the small furry guy clutched between her breasts.

Dylan grinned. "Lucky bear."

She followed his glance and blushed, suddenly aware that the bear's nose was buried in her cleavage. She stepped back and invited Dylan in. He closed the door behind him and scooped her into a crushing hug, her feet dangling above the floor, her arms twined around his neck.

He kissed her passionately, deeply, as though they had been separated for months. Finally he let her stand, his hands roving over her back and hips, molding her to his body, letting her feel the hard length of him pressed against her belly.

He nuzzled her neck. "God, I've missed you this week."

Unexpectedly, her eyes filled with tears. "I know," she sniffed. "Me too." He was so warm and strong and familiar, her heart ached.

He bent his head, alarm in his gaze. "Katie, honey, what's wrong?" He pulled her to the sofa. "Are you okay?"

She curled into his arms, her sniffles developing into full-fledged sobs. "I thought you didn't want me anymore," she wailed, burrowing deeper.

She felt his shock in his sudden stillness, but she couldn't bear to look at him. He let her cry for a few minutes, holding her and stroking her hair.

When he eventually spoke, she could hear the smile in his voice. "I hate to be rude, Katie darlin', but that's just about the stupidest thing you've ever said to me. What on earth gave you that idea?"

She sat up, wiping her face with the back of her hand. "I haven't seen you all week," she said, hoping that single accusatory sentence didn't sound as whiny and pathetic as it felt.

He grimaced. "Well, there's a reason for that. I've been working like a crazy man, trying to get everything in order, 'cause I have plans for this weekend."

"Oh . . ." That sounded ominous. On the other hand, he wore ratty jeans and an old University of Georgia sweatshirt. How big could his plans be?

He tweaked her nose. "They include you, princess."

He cocked his head, studying her face, his eyes brimming with some kind of mischief. "Will you come with me . . . right now . . . no questions asked?"

She nodded slowly. "Of course."

He stretched, propping his legs on the coffee table. "I'll give you fifteen minutes to pack a bag . . . nothing fancy. Casual clothes only."

He picked up the television remote, seemingly confident that she would do as he asked.

She stood watching him for about sixty seconds before he looked up inquiringly. "Problem?"

"N-no," she stuttered, backing toward the bedroom. "I'm going."

In the car he pulled out his first surprise. He blindfolded her with a length of simple black cotton. When she tried to protest, he whispered in her ear, his deep voice cajoling, "Be a sport, Katie. I would think you'd be a little more cooperative in light of my recent stint as your captive." At that, he kissed her cheek and tightened the knot at the back of her head.

She subsided, shrinking into her seat in stunned silence. He didn't sound mad about last weekend. If anything, his reminder had been filled with sensual amusement. But the fact that he brought it up at all made her heart race.

He held her hand as they drove. She started out by memorizing the various turns and directions they took, but soon lost track. Besides, it was possible he was deliberately trying to confuse her.

When they stopped after a mere thirty minutes, it answered the question of whether or not they were going out of town. It was possible they were at his house. The length of time was correct, and the turns, at least the ones she could remember, matched the route.

She loved Dylan's house. She assumed they would live there after their wedding, keeping her much smaller place, at least in the short term, for use as her day care location. She had plans to sell the day care when she started having children of her own, but she hadn't told Dylan that, at least not yet.

He had designed and built his own house, a sprawling place of mountain stone and cedar. It was the perfect home in her estimation, large but not too large. Up-to-date but not so modern it had no charm. The rooms were spacious and welcoming, decorated with a comfortable, livable style that cried out for a family.

The couple of acres on which the house stood included a small pond, a wooded area, and a tennis court. The property was in one of Atlanta's older, more established neighborhoods.

He shut off the engine and helped her out of the car. When he led her carefully up what seemed to be a flagstone path, she was fairly certain her guess was right. She heard him unlock a door, and then he scooped her up in his arms and carried her over the threshold. Seconds later he deposited her in a deep, comfy armchair.

He caressed her cheek. "Don't move and don't peek. I need fifteen minutes. Promise?"

"I promise," she said, smiling.

He left her, and she concentrated on cataloging her surroundings with the four senses at her disposal. Unfortunately, the clues were few and far between. She could hear nothing but the ticking of a clock and what might be the hum of a refrigerator somewhere nearby. Beneath her fingers, the slightly rough fabric of the armchair gave no clues about its origin. The smells drifting on the air were faint . . . furniture polish, perhaps . . . Dylan's aftershave . . . chocolate baking? Since she wasn't prepared to go about licking her unknown surroundings, that was as far as she got.

Fortunately, Dylan was true to his word. He returned very quickly and helped her to her feet. With his hand beneath her elbow, she walked at his direction down what she thought was a hallway and into yet another room.

She felt his hands in her hair, and moments later the blindfold fell away. Her lips curved in a smile. They were in Dylan's bedroom, but as her gaze swept over the familiar surroundings, her mouth opened in shock. The room was lit with the glow of fifty or more candles, which were spread on every available surface. The forest-green comforter on the king-size bed had been folded back to reveal soft ivory sheets covered with a cloud of blush-pink rose petals.

On the bedside table sat an ice bucket chilling a bottle of champagne, alongside a plate of sandwiches neatly covered in plastic wrap.

She looked at him in amazement. "Dylan?"

He shrugged, his eyes wary. "We had such good luck with last weekend, I thought a repeat performance was in order."

He seemed to be waiting for a reaction from her, but she was speechless, unable to come up with a coherent comment.

He took her hand and led her to one of two closets on the far wall. He pulled the door back, revealing a narrow space completely empty except for garments on four hangers. They were each separated by several inches, as though to be completely in sight of the viewer. She touched the first one. It was a pure white negligee, delicate and sheer, bridal or virginal . . . take your pick.

The next item was a leather bodysuit similar to the one she wore at the Scimitar. Katie felt herself blush, and moved on rapidly. Next was a cream satin merry widow, outlined with delicate lace and tiny satin rosettes. The last hanger held a comfortable pair of lemon-yellow sweats.

Clearly, the items of clothing had been selected with care and hung in this empty closet for a purpose. She looked at Dylan, who stood in silence as she inspected the odd assortment of women's wear. "I don't understand."

He tugged her with him to the cushioned window seat overlooking the sloping backyard. In the embrasure he reclined and pulled her between his legs, her back against his chest. He hugged her close, his hands tucked beneath her breasts.

His breath fanned her cheek. "Last weekend was incredible, sweetheart, and I have to admit, you surprised the hell out of me. The things we did, the games we played . . . I walked around with an erection this whole damned week."

He paused and sighed. "Whether you're a naughty schoolgirl or an erotic female sadist . . . a sexy lover or an overworked mom . . . you're my heart. And that won't ever change."

The deep vein of sincerity in his voice made her tremble. She hadn't lost him . . . and it seemed their visit to the Scimitar had been a success after all.

She stroked his thigh, feeling the play of muscles beneath the layer of denim. "So," she said softly. "Tell me about these weekend plans of yours."

He chuckled. "Well, they involve your not leaving this room at least until tomorrow morning."

She turned to face him, tucking her legs beneath her. "I can live with that. What else?"

He glanced at the flower-covered sheets. "I have a hankering to play the big bad Viking deflowering his virgin bride."

The masculine anticipation in his voice sent a trickle of heat down her spine. She traced her fingernail down the center of his chest, caressing the soft cotton. Her hand drifted toward his fly, and he snatched it in one large palm, holding it away from his body.

He glared. "Not so fast, my horny little temptress. I think you've been in the driver's seat more than your share. This is my show. Any objections to that? Speak now or forever hold your peace."

She widened her eyes demurely and wet her lips with the tip of her tongue. "No, sir."

His cheeks flushed, and the big hand holding hers trembled. He focused his gaze on her mouth, his eyes glazing over. He swallowed. "Do you need food . . . drink . . . a bathroom?"

She shook her head. "No."

He started stripping off her clothes with more enthusiasm than finesse. She laughed helplessly, hopelessly in love with him. "I can do it," she said, giggling as he wrestled her dress over her head.

"No time," he muttered. He dragged her bra straps down her arms, cursing as he struggled with the tiny hooks at her back. Giving up, he snapped the small pieces of metal without compunction. Her panties and sandals were dispensed with on the way to the bed.

He tossed her in the center of the mattress, laughing huskily when clouds of rose petals billowed in the air. Before she had time to realize what he was doing, much less react, he retrieved two ugly neckties from under one of the pillows and proceeded to tie each of her wrists to the headboard.

She frowned up at him. "Is this really necessary? Where do you think I'm going to go?"

"Don't care," he panted, struggling with the slippery knot of a polyester monstrosity. "I like having you buck naked in my bed and completely helpless." The undisguised relish in his voice made her shiver. Perhaps she should have taken his Viking comment more seriously.

She wiggled her hips, testing the give in the fabric binding her wrists. There was none. "Dylan?"

"Hmmm?"

His face was already buried between her breasts, his tongue working its way toward one tightly budded nipple.

She persevered. "I really do love having garden-variety sex with you. It's not necessary to entertain me with this little scenario, really."

He lifted his head, his eyes hot and determined. "Don't care. This is entirely for me. You can lie there and take it."

Her jaw dropped. Dylan . . . rude and chauvinistic? Impossible. She choked, shivering as his teeth scraped her sensitive flesh.

He licked a trail to her belly button, clenching her hips in a bruising grip. As he tongued the little indentation, he slid his palms underneath her bottom and lifted her, sliding his mouth between her thighs. He tongued her clitoris, deftly, determinedly. The first tiny traces of orgasm rippled through her, but he stopped, leaving her dazed and throbbing.

He stood up, and she assumed it was to undress. Wrong. Instead, he reached under the bed and extracted a long beautiful peacock feather, brightly colored in blues and greens, with a slender pointed tip.

Her heart started to pound and her skin went clammy. She clenched her fingers around the ridiculous ties. "Dylan . . . stop right this minute. Listen to me. I didn't sign on for this."

He laughed, his dear face completely unrepentant. "Honey, when you locked me in that jail cell last weekend, you had no idea what you were starting. I've got a hell of a lot of catching up to do . . . and I had a really creative teacher."

He leaned over the bed slowly, his eyes on hers, his lips curling in a smile that made her stomach flip-flop. Apparently his docility in the jail cell came with a steep price tag. She'd created a monster.

She spoke rapidly, trying to distract him. "What about your Viking?"

He brushed the feather along her collarbone, making her jump. "He's waiting in the wings. We've got all night."

She whimpered as the feather circled first one breast and then the other.

"Close your eyes," he crooned. "Let me pleasure you."

Her eyelids drifted shut, not really wanting to cooperate, but unable to watch the slow, deliberate, erotic movements of the feather. The brushing sensation was light, almost imperceptible at times. Her stomach quivered with gooseflesh as Dylan traced her hip bones.

When the feather reached her aching center, she relaxed a bit. This wasn't so bad . . . more of a silky caress . . . pleasant, but not enough to drive her to climax.

Just as she was smugly congratulating herself on surviving the first wave of his sensual attack, he changed tactics. Instead of the delicate sweep of peacock feather, he used the tip.

Fiery pulses of heat shot from her vagina to her womb as the sharp, slender point gently scraped her most intimate flesh. Her back arched and her hips jerked as she tried to evade the unbearable stimulation.

Dylan, damn him, laughed. She panted, trembling as though in the grip of a fever. "I can't stand it," she whispered, her teeth clenched.

He increased the pressure incrementally. "Try harder," he demanded, his voice blunt. The lack of sympathy made her wince . . . or perhaps it was the shards of white-hot sensation.

She dug her heels into the mattress, her hands tugging vainly at the knots that held her captive. The sharp tip traced up and over her mound, combing through her curls. The tormenting quill stroked and raked and scored her swollen, weeping flesh with diabolical determination.

She felt her body racing for climax, and welcomed it, desperate for relief. Only orgasm would release her from Dylan's wicked little game. She closed her eyes, reaching, aching for completion.

And the feather went away.

She opened her eyes in shocked disbelief, but she was sluggish, drugged with sensual overload. The feather lay tossed aside on the rug, seemingly innocent. In that instant she remembered where she had seen it before . . . in a decorative urn in the foyer.

She didn't ask why he'd stopped. She knew. It was a carefully-thought-out plan born from a man made helpless by the woman he loved and now fully prepared to return the favor.

She lay motionless, her spirit weak and spent. She turned her head toward the window, vaguely surprised to see that darkness had fallen. The candles bathed the room in light, their shadows flickering on the ceiling, spreading odd silhouettes dancing across the bed.

A faint noise caught her attention. Dylan blew out most of the candles, plunging the room into semidarkness. He loomed over her, his silhouette threatening. His odd appearance puzzled her. And then comprehension dawned. He was wearing a Viking hat and some kind of furlike cloak.

He should have looked comical . . . even ridiculous. He did not. Her toes curled into the bed, her knees pressed together. He knelt at her side, his weight denting the mattress and rolling her toward him. But her bonds held firm.

He grunted, bending over her trembling body, letting his hairy costume brush her breasts. She caught her breath, shuddering from the tantalizing sensation.

He bared his teeth in the near darkness, his lips twisting in a leering smile. "You're a damned fine piece of bounty," he muttered, rubbing his big hands over her torso. "You probably don't speak my language. But a wife that don't talk too much isn't a bad thing, I'll wager."

He batted her clenched knees, more amused than angered by her tiny show of defiance. "Open those pretty white thighs, my girl. A man's woman is his for the taking. And I fancy taking you now."

Her sense of humor welled up from somewhere inside, determined to be his match. She pouted, refusing to obey his gruff command.

She expected him to pry her legs apart, force his way in. He did not.

Instead, he began to toy with her nipples, first softly, then with greater force. She moaned, helpless, as her arousal built again. He tugged and pinched and alternately soothed with his tongue, laughing softly as she began to twist and whimper, her skin hot and damp.

And without any kind of intent on her part, her legs opened instinctively, welcoming whatever comfort could be found.

Dylan's heavy body, made larger by the thick fur pelt, settled in the cradle of her thighs. She bucked in alarm, feeling the blunt head of his penis at her vulnerable opening. He bit her ear, his breath hot on her cheek. "Fight me, little captive. Make me work for it."

She went still, prepared to bargain. "Then untie me," she said. "Let us meet on equal ground."

He snarled some kind of response, but leaned to unfasten the awkward knots that bound her wrists. She stretched her arms, wincing as the blood flowed anew, prickles of discomfort running from shoulder to fingertip.

His weight pinned her to the bed. She raked her nails across his shoulders, laughing when he roared in protest. Again, the head of his cock prepared to invade her. She rolled to one side, shoving him with all her strength. Her puny efforts were futile, hopeless, only inflaming him, if the lengthening and swelling of his erection was any indication.

She tried to close her legs. He thrust his hand in the V of her thighs. "Give it up, princess," he growled. "Your treasures are mine."

He pressed forward, his cock lodging deeply in the welcoming heat of her body. She felt almost unbearably filled and stretched. She winnowed her hands through his hair, vaguely aware he had tossed his helmet aside at some point. Her breasts were crushed, her breathing hampered by the weight of his body.

He withdrew and thrust deeper. They both gasped. He rotated his hips, stimulating tissues that were plump and glistening with arousal.

She closed her eyes, imagining herself an innocent in the hands of a determined seducer. There was no pain, no fear, only the burning certainty that searing pleasure was just out of reach. He withdrew again, and she took him by surprise, twisting to one side and rolling from the bed onto the floor.

She raced for the door, but he caught her ankle, tumbling her to the plush carpet. He stripped off his only garment, leaving him spectacularly nude, his damp flesh gleaming in the soft candlelight. His eyes were dark, his lips curled in a smile that made her shake.

Holding only her foot, he dragged her closer, stilling the flailing of her free foot with his other hand. When she lay panting and still near his knees, he pulled her ankles apart and flipped her over.

As her hands scrambled for purchase, Dylan lifted her hips and entered her with such force they both collapsed in a heap. He raised her to her knees, careful to keep their bodies connected. Slowly, steadily, he began an assault.

Her breasts swung in counterpoint to his eager thrusts. She pushed back into his groin, meeting him at every stroke, her breathing as labored as his.

Suddenly he went still, his hands gripping her hips, his cock throbbing inside her. He leaned forward, forcing himself deeper. She dropped her head.

His teeth raked her spine, his mouth hot on her flesh. "Tell me you love me," he groaned, his massive body shaking.

"A woman doesn't have to love her captor," she whispered. "She has only to obey."

He laughed, the sound broken by harsh gasps for breath. "But this captor wants it all. He wants her heart as well as her honeyed sheath."

She lifted her head, wishing she could see his eyes. "You'll wait in vain, my lord Viking. No woman would love such an uncouth beast."

He slapped her butt cheek, then pressed a half inch deeper. "Wanna bet?" He reached beneath her and gently stroked her achingly sensitive clitoris. She whimpered, pressing into his hand.

He withdrew. "Say you love me."

"No. Never."

He widened his stance, forcing her legs apart at an awkward angle, their bodies locked in carnal embrace. He pushed on her back, forcing her breasts to brush the carpet. His finger stroked her clitoris a second time.

"Say it."

She cried out, tormentingly close to her climax.

She tried to force him to move, but his greater strength held her immobile. "Please, Dylan. Please. I'm almost there."

He started to withdraw and she screamed, bearing down on his cock with all her might, but he jerked away, separating their bodies. He flipped her to her back, holding her hands above her head.

His hair fell over his forehead. His chest was slick with sweat. He grinned, the sweet, impossibly sexy grin she knew and loved.

"One of us has to give, little girl, and Vikings never do."

She narrowed her eyes. "If I say it, you'll make me come?"

"Maybe . . . you've kind of tried my patience."

She said a bad word, broadening his grin.

"Shame on you."

With careful deliberation, he held his fingertip over her mound, brushing the hair but not giving the firm touch she needed.

She hissed, arching her back in wild frustration. "I love you, dammit. There, I said it."

He joined their bodies, sighing from deep within his chest. He stilled again, drawing one last tiny line in the sand. "Promise me we'll go back to the hotel at least once a year."

She arched her back, laughing breathlessly. "If you give me an orgasm, I swear I'll do just about anything."

He started to move. "Now that's an intriguing notion."

His words were clipped and terse, his breathing labored. Her legs wrapped around his back as he thrust again and again. She closed her eyes, loving him, stunned with the depth of her need.

Seconds later her body arched and she started to fall, a dizzying, scary plunge that ended as it began . . . in Dylan's arms.

Hours later . . . after sleep, a shower, and a very belated dinner, Dylan settled into the soft leather sofa in his den and tugged Katie onto his lap. She curled into his embrace, boneless . . . content. He was quiet, and she wished she knew what he was thinking.

But Dylan had faced a fear for her, making himself completely vulnerable. His love humbled her. It was her turn.

She slipped off his lap and sat beside him. He was smiling, but his eyes were wary, apparently sensing the fact that she had something of import on her mind. She cupped a hand to his cheek, feeling the faint stubble. "I love you, Dylan."

He captured her hand and kissed her palm. "And I love you, sweetheart."

Katie took a deep breath. "Will you marry me?"

Shock didn't begin to describe his expression. For several long seconds she wasn't even sure he breathed. He shook his head and rubbed a hand through his hair. "Marry you?" His voice was rough and choked.

She shrugged, her smile wry. "I'm asking because I realized I've been an insecure idiot, and I've wasted far too much time worrying about the past."

His eyes darkened to indigo. He touched her lips. "Don't criticize the woman I love." He got to his feet, startling her and raising her anxiety level. "Hold that thought, Katie."

When he returned, he grinned and sat back down. "Ask me again."

She narrowed her eyes, but decided it was in her best interests to cooperate. She slipped to the floor and positioned herself between his legs. With her hands clasped beneath her chin and her elbows propped on his knees, she tried again. "Dylan Ward, will you marry me?"

He sighed from deep in his chest. "Thank God you asked. Another two days and I wouldn't have been able to return this." He reached in his pants pocket and pulled out a small velvet box. While she watched with her heart pounding in her chest, he snapped it open and extracted a lovely diamond solitaire ring.

A small smile teased the corners of his mouth. "I really wanted that billboard in Times Square, you know. But hey . . . a guy has to compromise sometimes."

He slipped the ring on her finger, and she held her hand up to the light, admiring her new jewelry. Dylan nuzzled her neck and licked her collarbone.

"I haven't heard an answer," she said, her voice trembling. She shivered when he hit a sensitive spot. "You're just trying to torture me now, aren't you?"

He lifted his head slowly, studying her face with a half smile.

"You'll always be my fantasy, Katie love. I hope I have the stamina to be married to you."

She snuggled closer, her heart overflowing with gratitude and love. "Is that an affirmative?"

"Yes," her Viking answered, scooping her into his arms and heading back to the bedroom. "My answer is yes."

Suite Surrender

CHAPTER ONE

*S*helli Richards parted the lace curtains flanking the massive front doors and watched red taillights disappear down the driveway in the swirling snow. It was dusk, and the two vehicles were barely discernible in the gathering gloom. She breathed a sigh of relief, rubbing the back of her neck where bands of tension had tightened progressively since yesterday. The last two carloads of guests and employees were finally on their way down the mountain.

This evacuation was a first for her. She'd been manager of the Scimitar since it opened three years before, and this was the only instance where bad weather had forced a closing. The hotel didn't accept reservations from December 31st through the end of February for just that reason. At an altitude of over five thousand feet, and with only a winding, private mountain road leading to and from the valley below, the hotel was often inaccessible during the winter. The three down months were used for repairs and renovations, and surprisingly, the blacked-out dates seemed to make the Scimitar's clientele even more eager to schedule a visit during the season.

Not all the guests had been happy about leaving, despite the deteriorating weather conditions. She winced, thinking about the refunds she'd been obliged to give. This would affect the financial bottom line for months, but it couldn't be helped. The phone lines were already out because of the high winds, and even cell reception was spotty. It was only a matter of time until the electricity gave up the ghost as well, and although the hotel did have some backup generators, the power supply wouldn't be able to support a building full of people for an extended period.

What started as rain in the valley had quickly turned into something far more serious above three thousand feet. A strong low-pressure system had settled over western North Carolina, and the weather reports were starting to use the word "blizzard." With temperatures predicted to drop fifteen degrees by the following day, the outlook was bleak.

She wandered back to the office and found Tyler shutting down most of the computer systems. Tyler Strickland. Her assistant manager. Her tall, dark, and handsome coworker. For a man who embodied the TDH cliché, he was something out of the ordinary. At least in her experience. He was smart without being nerdy, strong without being a muscle-bound jock, and a decent, caring person without being a wimp. He was the real deal.

The object of her musings looked up with a tired grin. "You about ready to head out?"

She shook her head. "You go ahead. I need to stay. I feel responsible, especially without Jim here." Their caretaker was close to retirement, and she'd sent him home along with the rest.

Tyler shrugged, his expression resigned. "You're the boss, Shelli. I won't argue if that's what you feel like you should do. But if you're staying, I'm staying."

An entirely inappropriate burst of excitement jolted her stomach. Tyler was a natural at all that *I'm a tough guy looking after my woman* stuff. Not that he was her guy or she his woman. The only thing between them was a very boring boss/employee relationship. But a girl could dream, couldn't she?

She smiled gratefully. "Thanks, Tyler. I really wasn't looking forward to being up here by myself."

He bent over to unplug a couple of electrical cords, and she eyed his butt without apology. He'd already taken the time to change out of his suit into jeans and a long-sleeve tee. The shirt was olive green, and it brought out his moss-colored eyes. His curly black hair and golden skin shouted his Italian heritage. He'd told her once that the family name was really Strigliano, but his immigrant grandfather had Americanized it out of love for his newly adopted country.

He straightened and looked at her with a crooked smile. "You look kind of frazzled, Shelli. You okay?"

She felt her cheeks warm as she tried to come up with a reasonable explanation for her zoned-out statue imitation. "Um . . . I was just thinking about what we should eat for dinner."

His skeptical expression told her he wasn't buying her prevarication, but he didn't push. "I have a feeling we've got a smorgasbord to choose from. Chef Jacques was not at all happy about the food going to waste." He glanced out the window. "I'm going to do a quick walk around the building before it gets too dark. Just to make sure things are battened down. If you'll give me your keys, I'll put your car and mine in the shed. Lord knows when we'll be able to get them out again."

She looked down at his feet. "You brought boots this morning?"

He took her keys, his fingers brushing hers. "I keep them in my trunk, along with a heavy coat. That comes from growing up in Boston."

He disappeared, and she glanced restlessly around the nearly spotless reservation desk. The employees had done a great job of cleaning things up before they left. She almost wished for a little chaos that she could put in order, anything to keep her mind and her hands busy for a few hours. Her stomach was in knots as she contemplated spending a couple of days, maybe more, cooped up with Tyler Strickland.

He'd been her second in command for the last eighteen

months, and he was very good at his job. The guests loved him.
He had a deft touch at solving crises, and she had never once detected in him any dislike of working for a woman. She'd endured
her share of those uncomfortable situations in the last six years,
so it had been particularly nice to fall into an amicable working
relationship that was usually effortless.

In her mind, she and Tyler were the perfect match, speaking in
a purely business sense. Which made it even more hurtful that
he'd turned in his resignation four weeks ago. On the surface, it
was an entirely understandable career move. He was going to
work at the Grove Park Inn, a large and prestigious property in
nearby Asheville, North Carolina. Ostensibly it was a step up,
presumably with a nice pay increase. But at the Grove Park he
would be one of a bunch of assistant managers, a small fish in a
big pond. It was hard for her to believe that his work situation
would be as satisfying as what he did at the Scimitar.

Tyler had a lot of responsibility and autonomy in his present position. Not only that, but the clientele at the Scimitar was fascinating, in many cases world renowned. The hotel's astronomical
prices and guaranteed privacy protected their guests from any kind
of unwelcome tabloid publicity, so the Scimitar tended to attract
guests for whom it was extremely important to be anonymous.

Shelli and Tyler had met film stars, heads of state, and politi-
cians. It was an exciting job, and no two days were ever the same.
The pace was challenging, and it was a great place to work.

But obviously Tyler wasn't as enamored of their team as she
was. It was a depressingly *female* response to take his defection
personally. He had given her no concrete reason for the change,
nor should he have. It wasn't her business. But it hurt just the
same. He had two weeks left. Then she would inherit an assistant
from another property. Sometimes life sucked. With a loud sigh,
since there was no one around to hear her feeling sorry for herself, she headed for the kitchen to see what possibilities existed
for dinner.

* * *

Tyler bent his head into the icy wind and skirted the pool area, checking to make sure the groundskeepers had secured all the furniture. The wind-driven snow stung his cheeks and made his eyes water, but the cold didn't penetrate his heavily insulated parka. Perhaps because his libido and his heart rate were racing at abnormal speeds.

Snowbound with Shelli. It had the alliterative quality of a sappy, romantic chick flick. His pulse jerked as he thought about how long they might be stranded together. Plenty of opportunity to get to know each other as more than coworkers. Plenty of time to make some possibly not-so-wise moves on his part.

He'd worked at the Scimitar for a year and a half and had been in love with his boss for a big chunk of that time. He'd fallen and fallen hard. But it was an impossible situation and ultimately one that had led to his recent resignation. Seeing Shelli's face when he'd turned in his notice had been a kick in the gut. She'd tried to cover her reaction, but knowing her like he did, it was impossible not to see her hurt and confusion. And who could blame her? Their working relationship was damned near perfect.

But anything more personal was complicated. In Shelli's previous position she'd been accused of sexual harassment by a disgruntled male employee with an ax to grind against the company. Shelli had been cleared of all charges, but the gossip had followed her, and it was almost certainly a painful and humiliating experience. His heart ached when he thought about how she must have suffered. He'd walk over hot coals before he'd ever put her in any kind of compromising position. Or even make her worry for a nanosecond that his motives weren't pure.

But he'd reached the point where it was next to impossible to keep from showing her how he felt. He had two weeks of his notice left, and then . . . finally . . . he'd be free to ask her out. Free to pursue this woman who had stolen his heart. Free to explore an attraction that he hoped like hell was not one-sided.

He finished his circuit of the building and went in search of a broom. He had to brush the snow off the windshields of the two vehicles before he could move them. The amount of snow that had fallen in such a short time was a little unsettling, even for a guy who had lived a big part of his life in a northern climate.

He was sweating in his parka by the time he finished all his self-appointed chores, and darkness pressed in. He and Shelli could be in for a long, possibly dangerous isolation. Romance would be the last thing on his mind if the situation turned threatening. His job, at least on paper, might be securing the hotel, but in his heart, his only real responsibility was making sure Shelli was safe.

Shelli gazed at her handiwork with some trepidation. She'd set the stainless-steel worktable in the kitchen with cheerful place mats and delicate china. The utilitarian environment was supposed to offset the intimate picnic ambience. She would be mortified if Tyler picked up on any of her carefully supressed sentimentality. She was so very conscious that the clock was ticking, that her days with Tyler were drawing to a close.

She got teary-eyed just thinking about it, and she wondered whether he ever thought of her as more than a congenial col-league. Even if she weren't his boss, it wasn't likely. Men like Tyler had their pick of women. He probably dated the super-model types who graced the pages of magazines. Definitely not the curvy, could-stand-to-lose-fifteen-pounds females. And she fell firmly into that last camp. Regardless of trips to the gym and the occasional salad when she really wanted a steak, her body was more Botticelli than Flockhart.

She heated the clam chowder left from lunch and grilled some pork chops the chef had soaked in marinade that morning. There were salad greens washed and ready, along with the chef's private-recipe house dressing, so she set out bowls. She found some gourmet croissants in the huge freezer and popped them in the oven. The menu might be a little odd in terms of food combinations, but she wanted to use as much as possible of what was already prepared.

She smothered her overactive conscience and opened a bottle of excellent Australian chardonnay. Surely she and Tyler deserved a treat to reward their decision to ride out the storm.

She jumped and pressed a hand to her chest when Tyler appeared without warning. He was smiling. "Smells like heaven in here. Who knew you were so domestic?"

His teasing grin lit a warm glow in the pit of her stomach. She turned toward the stove, unsettled by his relaxed appearance. He looked wonderful in the suits he wore to work each day, but the casual clothes he donned now made him seem so much more approachable. "I hold my own," she said lightly. "But it helps to have a world-renowned chef do all the prep work. Are you hungry? It's almost ready."

He shrugged out of his wet coat and hung it over a chair. "Starved."

Together they served up the various dishes, then silence reigned as they devoured the gourmet food in the cavernous kitchen.

Tyler stopped chewing suddenly, his fork suspended in the air and an arrested expression on his face. "I just realized neither of us ate lunch today."

Shelli added some wine to each of their glasses. "Who had time?" she complained, remembering the controlled chaos. "This is the first time we've stopped since we got here this morning." The night manager had been more than happy to leave them to it, patently glad that he didn't have to deal with the unpopular decision to close down.

They finished their meal, and Tyler got up to rummage in the fridge for dessert. With a triumphant flourish, he held up a platter bearing a pristine, freshly baked coconut cake. It seemed a shame to cut it for just the two of them, but what the heck. No sense in letting it go to waste.

Afterwards, they elected not to use the industrial dishwasher. Instead, they worked side by side, Shelli washing and Tyler drying. Occasionally their hands brushed. Shelli felt light-headed, either from the wine or from being so close to Tyler, she couldn't tell which. Tyler with his shirtsleeves rolled up, his forearms bare, his long-fingered hands wet as they caressed the curve of a goblet . . .

Whoa, Shelli. Get a grip.

She wiped down the countertop and hung the dish towels up to dry. The kitchen was once again as spotless as Jacques had left it. She hovered uncertainly, suddenly uncomfortable. Now what?

Tyler glanced at his watch. "You want to watch a movie?"

She jumped at his suggestion. The large great room just off the lobby was furnished with a scattering of cozy conversation areas and several televisions. While Tyler selected a DVD, she looked out the window again. Even with a floodlight turned on, all she could see was the constant swirl of snowflakes.

"How about this one?"

He was standing behind her, and she actually felt his breath on the back of her neck. She turned around, looking at the case without actually seeing it. "Fine," she croaked, her knees trembling.

She followed him across the room and settled into a comfy armchair. Tyler settled on the adjacent sofa. The movie was one she hadn't seen. It was an action-adventure flick with a strong romantic element. Both stars had won Oscars, but she might as well have been watching a *Gilligan's Island* reunion special. She stared at the screen, unseeing . . . at least until the hero and heroine started having sex.

Shelli felt a hot blush roll from her collarbones to her hairline, but she couldn't look away from the action. Out of the corner of her eye, she could see that Tyler was completely relaxed. The woman moaned. Shelli's thighs clenched. The man thrust harder, nearing climax. Shelli's hands clamped down, white knuckled on the arms of the chair.

Finally, thankfully, after the obligatory car chase and a satisfy-ing ending, the credits rolled. She stood up, desperate to put some space between herself and the surprisingly silent Tyler. "I'm going to go round up my overnight case and see what clothes I have here."

She and Tyler both kept things in a little room off the office, never knowing when a situation might require them on site overnight. The small space contained a twin bed and a minis-cule bathroom. One of them could sleep there, but there was re-ally no need with a hotel full of empty rooms to choose from.

She gathered up a change of clothes and her cosmetics case. She found Tyler in the hallway. He was rotating his shoulders, and he looked exhausted.

He didn't quite meet her eyes. "I'm beat. I'm going to hit the hay. Why don't we use 101 and 102?" They were the two guest rooms closest to the office.

She nodded jerkily. "See you in the morning."

He touched her arm, making her skin tingle. His voice was rough with fatigue. "Make sure to unlock the connecting door. I want to be able to get to you if anything happens." This time their eyes made contact, his darkly concerned, hers soft with a yearning she hoped he couldn't read.

"I will." She nodded. "Good night."

While Tyler took his turn finding overnight gear, she wan-dered down to 101. The rooms were spotless. The housekeeping staff had been able to get most of the first floor cleaned before leaving. The other two floors were another story, but she'd worry about that later.

It was odd knowing that she and Tyler were the only two in-habitants of this large empty building. Odd and intimidating. The castlelike edifice with its sprawling layout and large square footage seemed almost menacing without its usual contingent of chattering guests.

She tossed her things on a chair and went into the luxurious bathroom to shower and brush her teeth. She washed her face and braided her long straight hair. During the day she kept it in a chignon, knowing it made her look older than she was. She found the formal style suited her position and helped her project an air of authority. But at night she slept with it loose or tied back in a ponytail or braid.

Her pj's consisted of a pair of soft plum-colored flannel pants and a long-sleeve pink T-shirt she'd gotten at a convention. The naughty slogan said "Hotel managers do it in every room." The suggestive sentiment made her think of Tyler. They could have sex three dozen times and never use the same bed twice.

Or they could never have sex at all. He could go to his new job and they'd never see each other again. She liked the first scenario, as improbable as it was, a whole lot better.

She didn't have any slippers, but she'd included a half-dozen pairs of thick socks in her emergency bag, knowing her tendency toward icy feet.

She flipped on the TV, hoping for an updated weather report, and unfortunately found out more than she wanted to know. Even down the mountain, the rain had changed to snow, and the entire region was under a blizzard warning. The local forecasters were referring to it as the "storm of the century" and were warning people to prepare for a long, dangerous situation and an almost certain loss of services.

She changed the channel to TV Land and tried to get into an episode of *Green Acres,* but it was no use. She was too conscious of Tyler in the next room. Was he taking a shower? Was his skin that same beautiful golden olive over his entire body? Was his chest hair as curly as what was on top of his head?

With a groan of frustration, she turned off the TV and the overhead light. She climbed into the large, comfortable king-size bed and shivered, burrowing into a warm cocoon of covers. Despite the steady hum from the heating unit, the sheets felt cold against her skin.

She clicked off the bedside lamp and immediately the sounds from outdoors seemed louder, almost threatening, in the dark. The wind howled and shrieked, and occasionally she heard something, presumably debris, clink and thump against the window glass.

For the first time she wondered if she had been foolhardy to stay behind. If anything happened to her and Tyler, it would be her fault. But it had seemed so irresponsible to leave the hotel completely unattended. Sebastian Tennant, the head of the Tennant Hotel empire, had been unavailable, and his assistant had urged Shelli to use her own judgment.

Fat lot of help that advice was. The ultimate in buck passing.

Well, it was too late now. The course was chosen, and she and Tyler would have to make the best of it.

She glanced at the green illuminated numbers on the alarm clock. Midnight. The witching hour. Time for all good girls to be asleep . . .

Tyler jerked off in the shower. He'd been celibate for months, having no interest whatsoever in any woman other than Shelli. He wasn't immune to the nuances of an intimate dinner and a wholly uncomfortable movie. Next time he would pick a G-rated cartoon if it came to that. Shelli had practically twisted her body into a knot while the onscreen lovers had been getting it on.

He had endured a long-lived erection himself. He'd known the movie was a shoot-'em-up, but he hadn't planned on the secondary love story. When it was over, Shelli had abandoned him with depressing speed, probably wondering if he was trying to take advantage of the situation to hit on her. He couldn't blame her. His movie choice would seem suspect, at best.

He closed his eyes and pictured the woman he loved, his hand moving slowly over his soap-slicked boner. She was everything he liked in a woman. Full-figured and enticingly female. Her breasts, though never crassly displayed, were enough to make a grown man whimper, and her curvy hips and long legs showed to advantage in the tailored skirts and high heels she favored.

Unlike his Mediterranean looks, her skin was pale and creamy smooth, a perfect foil for her vibrant red-gold hair. She had the look of a Celtic princess with her high forehead and regal carriage. It was one of his dearest wishes to see that hair unbound one day. His breath quickened as he imagined her riding him, her long silky tresses cocooning both of them in coital intimacy.

He felt her hot, tight sheath milk him, her plump breasts bouncing as she cried out in a ragged voice. He wanted to see how the fantasy ended, but his body betrayed him as he came forcefully, leaning his head against the shower wall as his orgasm drained him and left him weak.

But physical climax couldn't do a damned thing to relieve the ache in his heart. He dried off and wandered into the other room, tumbling into bed with an exhaustion that was as much mental as it was physical.

The power went off at two a.m. Shelli, a light sleeper, woke instantly, alerted by the sudden silence when the heating unit went dead. She reached for the small travel flashlight on the bedside table and looked at her watch. It would be several long hours until morning.

She knew it was her imagination, but already the air in the room seemed to be getting colder. She plumped her pillow and willed herself to go back to sleep. But the silence in the room was oppressive, and the lack of white noise magnified the malevolence of the buffeting winds outside.

After a sleepless hour, she got up and went to the bathroom. When she got back in bed she couldn't reclaim the warm spot she'd nestled in before. Even with her socks, her feet were freezing. And the total darkness was starting to get on her nerves. Except for Tyler, she was completely alone in this enormous, deserted, rambling building. She didn't believe in ghosts, but suddenly she was aware of an entire host of strange and inexplicable creaks and pops. What if an intruder broke in somehow, an ax-wielding serial killer with a penchant for redheaded victims?

It wasn't entirely far-fetched. That Olympic bomber guy eluded the Feds for months by hiding out in the North Carolina mountains. She and Tyler could be slaughtered in their beds, and it would be days before their bodies were discovered. A loud crash against the window made her yelp, her heart racing as adrenaline pumped through her veins.

Finally, in desperation, she slipped from beneath the covers and approached the connecting door. She stood in front of it for maybe thirty seconds before quietly opening it and its twin on the other side.

Tyler's room was as dark as hers. Big surprise. She choked back a nervous snort of laughter. She heard a rustle of bedcovers, and then his voice, a low, drowsy rumble that broke the silence. "Shelli?"

She nodded and then felt foolish. He couldn't see her. "Yeah."

"Is the power out?" He sounded endearingly sleepy and confused.

"Yeah." She cleared her throat. "It's a little creepy, don't you think?"

She could hear him moving in the bed, maybe sitting up. "I don't know. I guess. I was sleeping."

Guilt pinched hard. But she thought about returning to her lonely, cold, too-quiet room, and she ignored the remorse. For once, the dark was a friend, giving her the courage to say what she wanted to say. "Tyler . . ."

"What?"

She swallowed hard, wrapping her arms around her waist, fighting off a fit of trembling. "We may be stuck here for a long time."

"Possibly." His voice was impassive.

"I need to ask you a favor."

"Anything, Shelli."

She paused, struggling to find the right words. Thank God she couldn't see his face. She took a deep breath. "I don't want us to be boss and employee while we're stuck here. It's too weird and uncomfortable. Can we please just be a man and a woman?"

The weight of the silence increased tenfold. She couldn't even hear him breathing. Her stomach cramped. She'd embarrassed him. Oh, hell. She could never work again after this. She was his direct supervisor. It was called sexual harassment.

She closed her eyes, an entirely unnecessary move given the stygian gloom, and prayed for a hole to swallow her up. "Never mind," she said, her words jerky and forced. "Let's chalk this up to a bad dream."

Every nerve and muscle in Tyler's body tightened as he processed her mind-boggling request. Shelli wanted to think of him as a man and not an employee? Hell yes. Sign him up for that plan.

But he was struck dumb with surprise and a surge of testosterone that left him woozy. As he struggled to come up with an appropriate response, somewhere between shouting hallelujah and a gentlemanly affirmative, Shelli muttered a few words and turned to leave. His eyes were adjusting to the darkness and he could make out her silhouette in the doorway.

"Wait." He winced. His voice sounded like he'd swallowed gravel. He cleared his throat. "You surprised me, Shelli. But I like the idea. We'll be like fellow castaways, I guess. Man against nature and all that."

He deliberately tried to infuse his words with a teasing light-heartedness that was nothing at all like the hot, jubilant rush of excitement he was feeling.

She nodded, or at least he thought she did. She whispered the next request, but with the lack of noise from the heater, he heard her plainly. "Then may I ask you something else?" she said.

"Of course."

There was a heartbeat of hesitation and then she spoke again. "With the storm and this huge empty hotel . . . well . . . it's kind of creepy. And scary. And I can't sleep. And I'd like to stay in here with you. And if you ever tell anyone what a wuss I am, I'll smack you. It's a big bed, so don't think I'm throwing myself at you. We can put pillows down the middle . . ."

She finally trailed off, and it was everything he could do not to laugh out loud. He was charmed by her wry honesty and turned on by her artless request.

He sighed, reminding himself that he was an honorable man. He could not seduce his boss . . . or rather this *woman* simply because she was presenting an opportunity. He schooled his voice to a studied casualness. "Of course it's okay, Shelli. Why don't you grab your pillows and blanket and bedspread."

She disappeared momentarily and then returned, her arms full of what looked in the dark like a huge snowman. In her brief absence, he had pulled his covers to his side of the bed, leaving a huge space for her. He felt her bump the bed, and heard a muffled, ladylike curse. "You okay?"

Air brushed his bare skin as she fluffed her pile of covers and tucked them in. He grinned when she pointedly placed two pillows down an imaginary center line. She slipped into bed and wiggled around getting settled. Each innocent movement of her body made his harder. He smelled the fragrance of the hotel's signature shower gel, which shouldn't have been an aphrodisiac. He'd smelled that same scent on a hundred hotel guests and he hadn't had the slightest inclination to jump any of their bones. He turned on his side and faced her, straining to see her face in the dark. "Good night, Shelli."

"Good night." He could barely hear her reply.

He pulled the sheet around his shoulders and tried to think about anything but the woman next to him. Any moment now he expected to hear the sound of her steady breathing, reassuring him that she was asleep. Then and only then would he be able to coax himself into some shut-eye.

But apparently Shelli was as sleepless as he was. He had almost drifted off, when for the fifteenth time, she flounced from one side to the other, her frustrated movements rocking the mattress, despite its reputation for firmness.

He was tired. He was horny. And she was torturing him. On the sixteenth time, he lost his cool. "Damn it, Shelli. What's the matter?"

She went perfectly still, and he knew with a sick certainty that his outburst had hurt her feelings. He gentled his voice. "I'm sorry. You can't help it. Why aren't you asleep?"

Her voice was a tiny thread of sound. She sounded as wretched as he felt. "I'm cold."

His heart twisted. "I'll go see if I can get a generator going," he said, not relishing the task at whatever god-awful time of the night it was.

"No. We'll deal with that tomorrow. Would it bother you too much if I moved over there beside you to get warm?"

CHAPTER TWO

*H*e bit his tongue so hard he wouldn't have been surprised to taste blood in his mouth. "Uh . . ." His brain had ceased to function and he felt thickheaded. Thick somewhere else, too.

Shelli clearly interpreted his lack of coherent response in her own fashion. She sighed. "Look, Tyler . . . you're a gorgeous guy and I'm sure you have women trying to get into your bed all the time. But I swear . . . right now . . . I'm just cold. That's it. No ulterior motives."

He swallowed hard, latching on to the one promising piece of information she'd let slip. "Gorgeous?" He could almost feel her smile.

"Quit being coy. I've seen how our female guests look at you, and it doesn't seem to matter that they're not single."

"You're exaggerating."

"No, I'm not." Her voice grew exasperated. "You haven't answered my question."

He tried to find a tactful response and came up with nothing. "Shelli . . . I'm not wearing any clothes."

This time she was the one with the long silence.

"Shelli?" Part of him hoped she would abandon the snuggling

plan that was sure to turn him into a slobbering idiot. But another part of him, the guy who had been in love with her for months, would be crushed if she backed out now.

Her voice was more tentative this time. "Can't you wrap the sheet around you? You know . . . like a cocoon?"

He lifted his hips, maneuvered awkwardly, and twisted the sheet around his middle. "I feel like a damned caterpillar," he grumbled. "Okay, Shelli . . . your modesty is safe. Come on over."

She tossed her covers back and shimmied across the bed, bringing with her all sorts of warm, secret female scents. She stopped when she was about twelve inches away, clearly nervous about that last little bit.

He opened his arms, his heart pounding. "You're not going to get warm over there. Don't chicken out now."

After a split second's hesitation she scooted closer. He pulled her against him spoon fashion and spent a few seconds straightening out the covers until they were both wrapped in several layers. Even through her thin pajamas he could tell that her skin was chilled. He rubbed her arms, cuddling her close. He was rock hard, but beneath that helpless arousal was a deep contentment.

He yawned, settling an arm around her waist while carefully avoiding her breasts. She fit in his embrace perfectly. He exhaled. "Can you sleep now?"

She nodded, her head pillowed on his arm. "Yes . . . and thank you, Tyler. This is nice."

He wanted to tell her it was a hell of a lot more than nice, but he held his tongue. Mother Nature had given him a winning lottery ticket, and he was going to enjoy every minute of his good fortune. But for now, he'd settle for a few hours of uninterrupted sleep.

Shelli awoke disoriented but supremely comfortable, her head still pillowed on Tyler's arm. The light filling the room had a strange quality to it. Not sunlight, but a bright, grayish glow that felt unfamiliar. It took thirty seconds for her to process and re-member. The blizzard. The hotel. No power. Tyler's bed.

The source of her physical pleasure was wrapped around her, and an impressive erection nestled against her butt. She re-minded herself ruthlessly not to take it personally. Men had morning wood. It was a fact of life. But just for a moment she al-lowed herself the fantasy. Tyler rolling her to her back, parting her legs, entering her slowly until they both groaned with plea-sure . . .

Tyler groaned in her ear. "Shelli . . . can you move over? I can't feel my arm . . . shit." She scooted away from him and watched, wincing, as he suffered the pain of blood flow returning to his fingers, hand, and forearm. He massaged the skin, his face twisted in discomfort. Her head had held him trapped for hours.

She had imagined a slightly awkward, but nevertheless tender, morning after. The reality was somewhat less picturesque. She slipped out of bed, shivering at the contrast between the icy air and the warm covers she left behind. "I'm going to get dressed," she muttered.

Tyler banged a fist against his forehead and ran through a mental list of heartfelt curses. Waking up with Shelli had scared him spitless. He'd been within seconds of making love to her and to hell with the consequences. Assuming she had some level of attraction to him, and given their intimate and provocative situa-tion, it probably could have happened.

But some saner portion of his brain had prevailed. He'd faked the arm thing to get them both out of a dangerous situation. Well . . . it had worked. So why did he feel so crappy?

They met a half hour later in the kitchen. Tyler had his head buried in the fuse box, attempting to hook up one of the genera-tors so the refrigerator and freezer would keep the perishable food from spoiling.

Shelli eyed him dubiously. "I hate to offend your masculine dignity, but do you really know what you're doing?"

He straightened up and shook his head. "Your faith in me is astounding. Don't worry. My dad's a retired electrician, and he taught me all I need to know. I promise I won't burn down the hotel or kill us with carbon-monoxide poisoning."

She huddled deeper into her coat and shoved her hands in her pockets. "What about heat?"

He frowned. "I think we should try to tough it out as long as we can. We have three small generators, but I don't know enough about them to judge how long the fuel will last. If we can keep busy during the daytime, wear lots of layers, surely we can stay warm enough."

"You're thinking we might be here a long time, aren't you?"

He nodded slowly. "It's a possibility." He flicked the edge of a calendar hanging on the wall. "It's March the thirteenth . . . in the South, for crying out loud. I can't believe this."

She perched on a stool, watching him work. "I was a junior in high school during the blizzard of ninety-three. That was a March storm."

He flipped a breaker and listened for the humming of the fridge. Nothing happened. "Were you living here . . . in North Carolina?"

"No. Knoxville. We had almost fourteen inches. In the Smoky Mountains where it snowed two feet or more, tourists were stranded with nothing. Food had to be air dropped by helicopter. It was days before help could get to them."

He pointed across the room. "I found the radio and some batteries. Why don't you see if you can pick up a station?"

She inserted the batteries and twisted the dial, hearing mostly static. Finally she found a station that was strong enough to be audible. At the end of a Britney Spears song, the way too cheerful DJ summed up the weather situation. It was bad. The snow was supposed to end by midnight, but accumulation amounts were setting records across western North Carolina. The forecast lows for the next three days were in the upper twenties, and the day-time highs only in the mid-thirties. Skies would remain overcast, and without sunshine to aid in melting, the snow and ice would be around for a while. Motorists were being urged to stay home, and emergency and rescue personnel were struggling to keep up with the demands for assistance.

She turned off the radio. Hearing her worst fears justified was too depressing. She glanced at Tyler, still working on a confusing assortment of wires and fuses. "I'm sorry I got you into this," she said, her voice bleak. "It's all my fault. I should have made you leave with the others."

He lifted his head and frowned, a lock of his hair falling across his forehead. "Don't be crazy. You did what you thought was right. I made my own choice. We're not in any immediate dan-ger." Then he grinned.

"What?" When he smiled like that, her heart skipped a beat.

"You know what I would tell you if you weren't my boss? Same thing I would tell my older brother Tony. He's a lot like you . . . type A, overachiever, workaholic, never stops."

"Hey," she said. His summation hurt. Even if it was dead on. "I can relax." *Sometimes.* With a gun to her head.

He held up his hands. "I'm not criticizing. I think my brother is one of the most amazing people I know."

The unspoken comparison lingered in the air between them, and she felt her cheeks warm. Was Tyler saying he thought *she* was amazing? Then why was he so determined to jump ship?

She cleared her throat. "So let's hear it. I'm not your boss right now, remember? I'm just a woman. What's this advice?"

He stood up, stretched, and put his hands in his back pockets. His head cocked to one side, and if she hadn't known better, she'd have sworn the light in his eyes was deliberately flirtatious. His lips twitched in a smile. "Lighten up."

She smirked. "That's it? That's your big suggestion?"

He shrugged. "We might as well make the best of the situation. You were right to send all the guests home. But we're stuck here for the foreseeable future. We could look at it as a mini vacation."

"In case you haven't noticed, this isn't exactly Club Med. Our entertainment choices are limited."

Now there was no mistaking the naughty gleam as his gaze took in every inch of her bundled-up body. "Shame on you, miz manager. Surely you're forgetting our signature amenities. The pleasure suites?"

Shelli swallowed. She hadn't forgotten. How could she? The Scimitar was famous for its decadent playgrounds. She licked her lips, wondering where she had stashed her ChapStick. "I'm not sure it would be appropriate for us to . . . use . . . those rooms."

"Why not? I'm a man . . . you're a woman . . . It was your idea."

She frowned, suddenly suspicious. "You're pulling my chain, right?"

He laughed out loud. "Yeah. And you make it so damned easy it's almost not worth it." Still laughing, he squatted down again and turned his attention to the generator hookup.

Her heartbeat settled back into a normal rhythm, and she tried to ignore the disappointment that washed over her. She approached Tyler deliberately, determined to prove she was unaffected by his good-natured teasing. "Are you making any progress at all?"

Just as the words left her mouth, the freezer and refrigerator clicked on with a steady hum. The digital clock on the stove started blinking. Tyler looked up at her triumphantly. "Mission accomplished."

"How long do you think we can let them run?"

He stood up and wiped his hands on a rag. "I'm not sure. I guess we'll have to play it by ear. Keep an eye on the fuel."

"I wondered about putting some of the food outside. Chef Jacques has several large coolers."

"That's a great idea except for the animal factor. Those coolers would only keep the small critters out."

"We've been open over three years and we've seen signs of a bear only once. It can't be too much of a risk, can it?"

"With the snow so deep, food will be hard to find. Do you really want to take the chance of attracting a bear?"

"I guess not."

After a quick breakfast and even quicker cleanup, Tyler looked around the kitchen and then back at her, his eyebrows lifted. "Now what?"

She shivered and stood up. "Well, we can't just sit around all day. We'll turn into Popsicles. Housekeeping didn't get to clean the second and third floors. If you're game, we might as well get those rooms done."

He nodded. "Good idea. At least we'll stay warm."

They walked up the stairs to the second floor and took a cart from one of the utility closets. The hotel's thirty-six guest rooms were divided into two wings of three floors each, six rooms on each half floor. The central or middle block of the hotel housed reception, common rooms, the kitchen and dining room, a business center, and a workout facility. Though the purpose of the hotel was primarily pleasure, there were always those who had to stay fit and connected to the outside world.

The left and right wings angled away from the center in a wide V shape. At the rear of the central block, the corridor of fantasy suites, only a single story high, extended straight back. Atop that were a small putting green and a sunbathing area overlooking the pool. The fantasy suites would have to be cleaned as well, but she employed a trio of specialists who had been trained to disinfect and/or replace the props every time a room was used, and Shelli preferred to wait and let them do their job.

Tyler paused at the door of the first room. "Do you have a plan, or are we winging it?"

She picked up a spray bottle and a sponge. "I'll do the bathroom if you'll empty the garbage, dust, and strip the bed. Then when we're done, we can both put on the clean sheets."

He nodded and without speaking found a roll of garbage bags and a dust rag. Shelli spent about ten seconds wishing she and Tyler could magically whisk themselves away to the South of France. Hot sand, warm breezes, long sultry nights . . . She caught a glimpse of her dreamy-eyed expression in the bathroom mirror and shook her head. Fantasies were what the Scimitar provided for its guests. But the hotel was closed, and this was reality.

She really didn't mind cleaning. The manual labor had its own reward as she brought a shine to the marble countertops and floors. The bathrooms were large, elegant, and blatantly hedonistic. As she replaced the small bottles of toiletries, she imagined sharing the roomy whirlpool tub with Tyler. Sipping champagne by candlelight. Exchanging heated glances as the bubbles churned and foamed about them. Tyler setting down his glass . . . closing the space between them . . .

His cheerful voice intruded. "You done in there, Shelli? I put a stack of clean sheets out in the hall."

She used her fingertip to remove one last smudge from the mirror and sighed. The real Tyler obviously hadn't read Fantasy Tyler's romantic script. "I'm coming," she muttered.

Tyler tossed her one side of the fitted sheet, and she smoothed her two corners into place. He flipped out the top sheet and they each grabbed a side. Pillows fluffed, the cases on, blanket, bedspread, and shams in place. He glanced at his watch, smiling. "Four and a half minutes. Not bad. We make a good team."

She frowned. "Then why—" She shut her mouth, appalled. She couldn't ask him that. She didn't have the right to press him for reasons. He was leaving. And she would just have to deal with it.

He looked puzzled. "Why what?"

She shrugged, uneasy but determined to back away from a dangerous subject. "Why are we still on the first room?"

He took her challenge seriously and picked up the pace. They finished one wing and headed across to the other side. Two rooms later she cried uncle. She flopped down on the newly made bed and groaned. "Enough already. Jeez, you're a slave driver. I need lunch."

He grinned down at her with his hands on his hips. "Maybe you'll be thinking about a raise for housekeeping," he teased.

She closed her eyes and arched her aching back with a pained wince. "Maybe so."

Her eyes flew open when she felt his hand on her knee. Then he grabbed her hand and tugged. "On your feet, woman. Let's see a little commitment."

She let him help her stand up, mumbling under her breath what he could do with his commitment.

He merely smiled and sniffed her neck. "You smell like Windex."

She froze, feeling the whisper of his breath on her skin. "Is that good or bad?" She tried to joke, but her voice was tight. They were standing so close she could see the beat of a pulse at his throat.

He ran the back of his hand down her cheek. "Good," he said huskily. "On you, it's good."

His eyes had darkened, and inexplicably, arousal bloomed between them, hot and sweet. She knew she wasn't imagining that he felt it, too. They were both sweaty and rumpled. He had a smudge of dust on his cheek. She'd been cleaning toilets. His head lowered. Her lips parted. Her eyes drifted shut.

"Shelli?"

"Hmmm?" Fantasy Tyler was getting ready to make love to her. It was going to be amazing.

"Let's take a lunch break and then we'll finish this floor."

Her eyes flew open, stunned to see him walking away. Well, poopers. Those Windex people would be getting a letter from her. Talk about a letdown . . . She swallowed her disappointment and followed Tyler to the kitchen.

Tyler slathered spicy mustard on sourdough bread and stacked up several slices of honey-basted ham. If he couldn't satisfy his baser appetites, he might as well enjoy something. He bit into his thick sandwich, chewing without tasting. Shelli was a few feet away, heating up some soup.

Surely she hadn't been expecting him to kiss her. That dangerous thought had to be a figment of his overheated imagination. If he had followed his instincts and pressed his lips to hers, she would have smacked him. Right? The fact that he wasn't entirely sure of the answer to the question was beginning to make him crazy.

It was much easier to keep his distance when Shelli was dressed as Manager Shelli. The persona of the perfectly coiffed, immaculately attired woman he worked with every day warned a guy not to step out-of-bounds. But this Shelli with her snug, faded jeans, cherry red down jacket, and long flouncy ponytail looked like Cheerleader Shelli. And Tyler Strickland had always had a thing for cheerleaders.

She dropped a spoon and bent down to retrieve it. Tyler eyed her cute little bottom and zeroed in on a threadbare spot on her jeans just at the base of her left butt cheek. Was that a hint of pink? Pink satin panties? Lord help him.

He put down his half-eaten sandwich, his hands shaking. "I'm going to take a quick look outside," he said, snagging his coat from the chair where it had been drying overnight. "Be back in a minute."

He practically ran from the room, not breathing normally until he was through the front door and standing on the lawn, thigh deep in snow. His heart was racing and he felt dizzy. He loved Shelli. He wanted Shelli. He was quitting a damned great job so he could finally act on his feelings for Shelli. Now he was trapped alone with her for God knows how long. What was he going to do?

He was leaving in less than two weeks. Would it be so bad if he took the plunge and let her know how he felt? How she would respond was anybody's guess, but his self-control was wearing thinner hour by hour, and there was no way to tell how long they might be cut off from the outside world.

The landscape was almost unrecognizable. Familiar things were blobs crouching in the snow. A cardinal flew past him, it's scarlet plumage bright against the blinding white. His gut instincts had deserted him, and his plan of action was as undefined as the snow-covered landscape.

Two things he knew for sure. He loved Shelli. He needed to keep her safe. But after that . . . well . . . he was walking a tightrope without a net.

When he went back inside, half frozen and no more clear headed than before, he and Shelli got back to work. He'd picked up the radio from the kitchen, and he tinkered with it until he found an oldies station. Cranking up the volume, he was pleased when he saw Shelli smile. *One o'clock, two o'clock, three o'clock rock* . . . The silly familiar tune filled the room as they began to work. Through the bathroom door, he watched as her hips gave a little bump and sway to the music. His own toes were tapping. She finished what she was doing and joined him in fixing the bed.

Several hours later, as they worked on the last room, Chuck Berry sang "Johnny B. Goode." The Beach Boys ripped into "Surfin' Safari." And finally, just as the final sheet corner was tucked, the last wrinkle smoothed, the Platters eased into the plaintive notes of "Only You."

He didn't know what prompted his next impulsive move.

Without thinking, he held out his hand. "May I have this dance?"

She hesitated a half second before taking his hand. He could see the exhaustion on her face, in the weary curve of her shoulders. But she gripped his fingers and didn't protest when he pulled her into a loose embrace. He tucked her head against his shoulder and they moved slowly to the music.

His heart jerked in his chest as the poignant words surrounded them. Shelli was the only woman for him, and if she didn't feel the same way, then changing jobs would be the least of his worries. They danced in silence, their bodies in perfect accord. He held her a fraction closer, with only the utmost effort preventing himself from pressing her against him the way he wanted.

They fit together perfectly. His pulse raced and his erection throbbed between them, full and heavy. He hoped she didn't realize what was going on, but even so, he couldn't bear to release her.

The song wound to a close, and a commercial came on, offering new and used cars for closeout prices. It was almost obscenely jarring. Tyler and Shelli separated abruptly and without speaking began to replace the cleaning items they had taken from the cart.

They were both too tired to put much time or effort into fixing dinner. Instead, they took turns heating plates of leftovers in the microwave. By now it had been almost an hour since either of them had said anything. The silence was heavy.

Tyler shed his coat to wash the dishes and rolled up his sleeves. When the cleanup was complete, they stood awkwardly.

"Shelli . . ."

"Tyler . . ."

She smiled as they both spoke simultaneously. He gave a mock bow. "Ladies first."

"Aren't you cold?" she asked, stepping closer and laying a gentle hand on the icy flesh of his forearm.

He'd had enough. "Hell yes, I'm cold. Let's go to bed and get warm."

She released his arm with comic speed. Her eyes widened, and he cursed inwardly. He could make a joke, or he could try to ignore his gaffe. But it was as if his vocal cords had suddenly become paralyzed. Shelli had a deer-in-the-headlights look on her face, and her mouth opened and shut at least twice before anything audible actually came out.

She twisted her hands in front of her, an uncharacteristically nervous gesture for a woman who was usually confident and in control. "You mean now?"

He almost thought he detected a thread of excitement in her tentative question, but he gave himself a mental kick for wishful thinking. "Well . . ." He paused and cleared his throat. "We've worked hard today, and if we don't have to worry about lights, we can conserve fuel." God, did that sound as stupid out loud as it did in his head?

She nodded slowly. "I suppose you're right." She actually seemed to be giving his lame idea serious consideration.

Her teeth worried her lower lip. "Tyler . . ." Her cheeks were pink.

He reached for his coat and put it back on. Anything to avoid looking at her for a moment. "Yeah?"

She waited until he had no choice but to face her again. Her gaze met his bravely. "When you said . . . did you mean . . . ?" Her voice trailed off, but he understood what she was trying to say.

His smile felt lopsided. It was difficult to appear casual when every ounce of testosterone in his body was doing the tango. He spoke calmly with an effort. "We don't have a prayer of staying warm in separate bedrooms. Last night's arrangement worked for me. We have to be practical. Soldiers in the foxhole and all that."

She must have bought his entirely fake matter-of-fact tone.

Her body language went from guarded to relaxed, and she smiled, the first genuine smile he'd seen during this awkward and loaded conversation.

She patted his arm. "You're a sweetheart, Tyler. I can't think of anyone I'd rather be stranded with."

CHAPTER THREE

*T*he large hot-water heater for the kitchen also supplied the tiny bathroom just off the main office, so they were at least able to shower. They took turns, and then Shelli joined him in his room just as he was settling into bed.

The room was freezing. The blankets she had brought from her room the night before were still in a tumble at the foot of the bed. His heart gave a little jolt when he saw her in the doorway, and he spent an inordinate amount of time smoothing out the covers and waiting for her to move closer. Even if all she wanted was a warm body, he wasn't about to turn her away.

She turned off the flashlight and put it on the bedside table. Silently, she lifted the layers of sheets and blankets and spreads and scooted up against his side. They both sighed in unison.

Tyler played with a strand of her ponytail, hoping she wouldn't notice his fingers in her hair.

She lay beside him, quiet and still. He was tired, but not particularly sleepy. He could spend several days holding her like this, even if it was the purest kind of torture. Bit by bit, his whole body relaxed and settled in for the night. He had almost dozed off when she finally spoke.

Her voice was sleepy, as well. "Tell me about your family." She sounded drowsy but genuinely interested.

He stretched and shuddered when his feet hit an icy spot on the sheets. "I have two brothers. Tony's in real estate and Rico owns a restaurant in Boston. Gina and Angelica are next in line. Gina's an artist, and Angelica is just beginning to make a name for herself in bit parts on Broadway. Both of my parents are still living, and it's the great sorrow of their old age that none of us are married."

"You're the baby?"

"Yep. That's why I left Boston originally. My family is wonderful, but they can be a bit smothering. I needed to be on my own. Wanted to have the opportunity to make my own decisions. It was a good thing for me."

"Will you ever go back to Boston?"

"That will depend on the woman I marry, I guess. We'll make that choice together."

"Do you have a girlfriend?"

He smiled in the darkness. Was that jealousy in her voice? "Nope. I'm footloose and fancy-free. What about you?"

She wiggled closer, her hip touching his. "I'm an only child. My parents tried for years to have children and finally gave up, because they didn't want to go the fertility-drug route. Then one day when my mom was staring her fortieth birthday in the face, she decided she wanted to adopt. My dad agreed, and they brought me home a year later. They've been retired for a while now, and they live in Raleigh. I get to see them fairly often."

"And are they expecting grandchildren?"

She laughed. "Not anytime soon, I guess. I've put a lot of time and effort into my career, and it's paid off. When Mr. Tennant hired me, I was the youngest manager at any of his properties. I love my job, but I do want to get married, and I do want to have kids, maybe three or four. Being an only child was very lonely at times. I used to fantasize about having six brothers and sisters. I would have been very jealous of your family."

Tyler lay quietly, trying to read between the lines. He imagined bringing Shelli home to meet his parents and siblings. They would love her. And the thought of making lots of babies with her was a one-two punch to the gut . . . physically arousing and emotionally exhilarating.

He touched her arm. "Are you warm enough?" She was swaddled in multiple layers topped off with one of the hotels Egyptian-cotton terry robes.

"My nose is cold."

He reached out a hand, carefully locating her face in the dark. Yep, her little nose was noticeably cold. Like a cute snuggly puppy. He tugged her closer. "Turn your head toward my shoulder."

He felt her lips brush his arm just above the elbow, and he shivered.

She noticed immediately. "You're freezing, too," she whispered.

He cleared his throat. "I'm fine. Let's try to get some sleep." He slid an arm around her shoulders and tucked her more firmly against his side. She turned into his embrace trustingly, apparently unaware of the fact that the man she was plastered against wanted to spend the entire night doing something a tad more interesting than sleeping. But now was hardly the time to take advantage of Shelli. He couldn't seduce her when she trusted him to keep them warm and safe.

He closed his eyes and conjured up the image of a fat, wooly sheep, but he couldn't make the damn thing jump over a fence. It was going to be a hell of a long night.

Shelli woke up sometime in the wee hours of the morning. After the noisy storm the night before, the complete and total silence was eerie. Half of her was toasty warm, compliments of the way Tyler's big body was radiating heat. But the other half . . . where the blankets had slipped off . . . was freezing. That situation immediately took a backseat to a more pressing problem.

Tyler was holding her left breast.

They had spooned during the night, and his right hand had snaked under her layers, his warm fingers cupping gently around her naked flesh. It felt incredible. She swallowed hard, frantically trying to decide what to do. If he woke up, she'd be so embarrassed she'd never be able to face him again. It was bad enough that they were sleeping together.

She put her hand over his and tried to lift it. He murmured in his sleep, and his grasp tightened. His forefinger stroked over her nipple. Heat swept from her breast to her thighs. Sweet holy Hannah. Suddenly he nuzzled her neck, his mouth hot on her chilled skin. She felt the scrape of his teeth.

In desperation, she eased onto her back in preparation for slipping out of the bed. Tyler grunted and moved over her, settling between her legs and trapping her even more securely. For one insane second she contemplated seducing him. They could blame it on the blizzard. No one would have to know, and besides, Tyler was leaving. They wouldn't be hurting anyone.

Her rationalization combined with the darkness to weaken sense and reason. She felt the press of his erection against her abdomen. Her heart was beating so fast, she thought she might hyperventilate. She lifted her hips a half inch. Tyler didn't move. His scent enfolded her . . . warm male skin, shower soap. She was dizzy. What would it be like to have him awake and concentrating on her and her alone? Would he be gentle, or would he take her hard and fast?

She darted her tongue over the stubble on his chin. He muttered something unintelligible. She pressed a butterfly kiss to his lips. Her legs were trembling, spread wide by his big body. Even clothed, his masculinity was potent. She was shaking with the need to have him deep inside her.

She kissed him again, this time allowing her lips to linger, to feel the firm contours of his mouth. He tasted amazing. And then without warning . . . he kissed her back. His hips thrust against hers and his tongue found its way between her lips. She moaned. Every bone in her body turned to water. Her hands clung to his shoulders and she whimpered.

He kissed like no man she had ever known. His mouth devoured hers, hungry . . . demanding. She nipped his tongue with her teeth, shivering not from the cold, but from a passion unlike anything she had ever experienced.

He reacted when she bit him. His body stilled, and he spoke in a husky, puzzled groan. "Shelli?"

Hearing him say her name was a dash of cold water in the face. She went perfectly still, and she prayed fervently that he wouldn't wake up. Going from sheer physical pleasure to raw, gut-wrenching doubt was not fun. Memories of the horrific mess at her previous hotel flitted through her mind like nasty reminders. Finally, what seemed like aeons later, his breathing lapsed back into a steady, regular cadence, and she exhaled a sigh of relief.

She shook off the bad vibes. Tyler would never accuse her of anything. He would never hurt her in any way. Her moment of madness passed as quickly as it came. She was Tyler's boss. He was asleep, dead to the world. She wasn't so desperate that she had to trick men into having sex with her. But if she didn't get out from under him ASAP, her yearning body might take issue with her prim-and-proper conscience. Because Tyler Strickland was one potent temptation.

It took maybe five minutes, but she extricated herself inch by excruciating inch. Tyler's body was a dead weight. When she finally stood beside the bed, her skin was damp with exertion, despite the icy air. She pulled the nearest blanket around her shoulders and then stood quietly for a moment, just to make sure he was asleep. Silently, she opened the door and slipped into the hall.

With the tiny beam of the flashlight she had grabbed from the nightstand, she made her way to the kitchen. She'd never been particularly afraid of the dark, but she'd be the first to admit that wandering the halls of the Scimitar was much less menacing with Tyler at her side.

The generator was still hooked up to several appliances, so she turned on the stove and heated some milk for hot chocolate. When it was ready, she huddled over the cup, cherishing the tiny bit of steam and warm crockery every bit as much as the sweet, rich drink. Her fingers gripped the mug, savoring the feeling of warmth. She'd never take heat for granted again.

She left the pot of milk on low in case she wanted seconds, and wandered out into the foyer. She peeked through the curtains and saw the faintest hint of pink toward the eastern horizon. Standing there all by herself, in that darkest hour just before dawn, she felt a bone-deep loneliness. She was so tempted to let Tyler know how much she wanted him to stay. To tell him she was attracted to him. To ask if he wanted to explore a relationship.

He seemed to respond to her physically, but some men—many men—were easily aroused. Both she and Tyler were young and healthy and at a time in their lives when sex should be a natural, frequent occurrence. This enforced isolation merely accentuated those needs.

She usually knew when a man was interested in her, and Tyler had been giving some subtle signals. But what if she was wrong?

Could she risk it? She crossed into the lounge and set her empty cup on a low table, then curled up on one of the big, comfy sofas and tucked the blanket around her, a poor substitute for a man's arms.

Tyler found her there, her entire body covered except for the thick, silky hair falling over the arm of the sofa. He scooped her up in his arms, crooning softly when she muttered in her sleep. He'd awakened from the most amazing dream to find her gone. He waited a few minutes, thinking she was in the bathroom, but after that he began to worry. He followed the smell of chocolate to the kitchen and turned off the pot of milk that threatened to burn dry.

It took only a few more minutes to track her down. He cuddled her close as he walked down the hall, kissing the top of her head and wishing he had the right to carry her to bed like this every night. His chest ached with love.

It was barely six o'clock, still plenty of time for sleep, especially with their calendars conspicuously empty. He flipped back the covers and tucked her in, then slid in beside her. She nestled against him as naturally as if they had been sleeping together for years. He allowed himself one chaste kiss on her forehead before he closed his eyes and succumbed to sleep again.

Once breakfast was eaten and cleaned up, Shelli tried her cell phone for the umpteenth time and finally got a signal. After calling her parents and reassuring them that she was okay, she passed the phone over to Tyler . . . and then eavesdropped unashamedly while he talked to his dad. Even hearing only one end of the conversation, she could tell that the two men were close. Every time Tyler smiled and chuckled, her heart did a funny little jump in her chest. She loved the fact that his family was important to him.

He said his good-byes and handed her the phone, still grinning. "Dad thinks we should be out sledding."

She laughed. "Did you tell him we might end up in a snowdrift and never be seen again?"

"I did point that out." He shoved his hands in his back pockets and glanced at the clock. "You in the mood for a game of racquet ball? At least it would warm us up, and we could use the exercise, don't you think?"

She eyed him uneasily. Was that reference to getting warm a little loaded? His eyes were dark, and despite the teasing comment, he seemed rather . . . intense. Oh lord, was he actually awake last night?

She swallowed hard, her throat dry. "I'm game."

At the racquet ball court Tyler glanced down ruefully at his legs. "I don't think I've ever played in jeans before." He flipped Shelli's ponytail. "You're going to have to get rid of a few layers. You look like the Michelin man."

She shivered as she shed her top half down to her short-sleeve tee. "Let's get going," she said, rubbing her arms as gooseflesh popped out. "You could hang meat in here."

They played an easy game for a few minutes until their muscles loosened up. Then Tyler gave her an enquiring lift of the eyebrow. "You ready?"

She nodded. "Give me your best shot."

That offhand comment turned out to be her downfall. Tyler ran her all over the court. After one ball whizzed past her shoulder at roughly the speed of light, she dropped her racquet and leaned forward panting, her hands on her knees.

She gave him an upside-down glare. "You might show a little mercy here, Strickland. I am a girl, you know."

He assumed a very unconvincing look of innocence. "You think I'm being hard on you? I'm playing like I always do . . . to win." This time the tiny little evil grin slipped out.

She straightened and arched her back, groaning. "I think a gentleman would cut a lady some slack."

He snorted. "Have you ever in your life wanted special treatment because you're female?"

She picked up her racquet, grinning at him. "You do know me rather well, don't you?"

The look in his eyes was suddenly serious. "Not as well as I'd like to." The bald comment hung in the air.

Her throat closed up. Was he flirting with her? Her knees trembled, and it wasn't all because of exertion.

Tyler turned away, picking up his own racquet. "One more game, how 'bout it? Then I'll fix us some lunch if you want to clean up."

His demeanor had returned to its usual pleasant expression,

but in her mind, all she could hear were those seven words. *Not as well as I'd like to*. What did they mean? What did Tyler mean?

The ball came her way, and she managed to return it, forcing her attention back to the game. Tyler whooped when he scored a difficult point, and she wondered what he sounded like in the throes of orgasm. That unwise mental segue made her lose her concentration again, and Tyler snagged another victory.

She lifted a corner of her shirt and wiped her face. "Uncle," she said, leaning against the wall, her chest heaving. The air in the small, enclosed room had warmed up considerably.

Tyler curled an arm around her shoulders. "You play pretty good for a girl," he said, his tone loaded with patronizing male arrogance.

His big body loomed over her, making her feel remarkably fragile. She poked a finger in his abs, just for the pleasure of feeling all those firm muscles. "When I can breathe again, I'll make you pay for that comment."

He tugged her ponytail. She noticed that he seemed fascinated with it. "Promises, promises," he muttered.

They gathered up their excess clothing and stepped out into the icy corridor. He eyed her flushed face. "You go get cleaned up and I'll start lunch."

Shelli wasn't about to argue with that offer. She showered and washed her hair in record time. By the time she had slipped into her last clean set of underwear and rinsed out the rest, forty-five minutes had passed and her stomach was growling.

She wrapped her head in a towel and retrieved her brush and comb and hair dryer. She found Tyler in the kitchen, true to his word, stirring something that smelled fabulous. She joined him at the stove. "Your turn. I'll finish this and set the table," table being a relative term, since they were now accustomed to perching on stools at the stainless-steel prep station.

Tyler was faster than she was, and in twenty minutes they were digging into steaming bowls of vegetable soup and perfectly browned grilled-cheese sandwiches. His hair was damp, and despite the cold, he had rolled up the sleeves of his blue chambray shirt, revealing forearms lightly dusted with hair. As much as she had admired the old, professional Tyler, this new, casual look was definitely getting to her.

Although Tyler ate with enthusiasm, she couldn't help noticing that his face was unusually grim.

She pointed a spoon at him. "What's the matter?"

His mouth twisted. "We've used up all the fuel in the first generator and we're about a third of the way through the second, if I'm estimating correctly. I think we should turn off everything at night while we're sleeping and hope the freezer and refrigerator will stay cold enough to keep things from spoiling."

She nodded. That made sense. "We may be stranded for a while."

He wiped his mouth with a napkin. "Even with a four-wheel-drive vehicle, it will be difficult to get up here until a lot of this melts."

She nibbled her bottom lip. "Well, if the food goes bad, we can always live off of canned stuff. And we have all sorts of bottled drinks."

"I'm worried about the cold," he admitted. "Even in here with the little heat we're getting from the stove and oven, it's uncomfortable. And how many things can we think of doing to keep warm?"

Her face went bright red. She felt it happening and couldn't do a damned thing about it.

Tyler wasn't stupid. She could see the exact moment he read her mind. And she was shocked to see his cheekbones flush a ruddy color, as well.

She licked her lips, searching for a light, funny comment. Something about shoveling snow. Or doing aerobics. Nothing at all about touching and stroking and learning everything there was to know about another person's erogenous zones. Her mouth was so dry she couldn't force a syllable past her numb lips. Heat, entirely self-generated, pooled between her thighs and tightened her nipples. Thankfully, with the layered look she was sporting, Tyler wouldn't be able to tell.

But despite her couture armor, he knew exactly what she was thinking. He ran a hand through his hair, and she could swear the hand was shaking.

He didn't meet her eyes. "You need to dry your hair," he said in a rough voice. "Don't want you to catch pneumonia." He found an extension cord so she didn't have to huddle beside the stove.

Shelli unwound the towel and began combing out her damp hair. It was always a chore, but she liked it long and never contemplated cutting it. When the last of the tangles were gone, she turned on the hair dryer. It was difficult to lift her arm with the bulky clothing she had on.

Tyler stepped behind her, his hand on her shoulder. "Hand me that thing," he said gruffly. "I'll do it."

She surrendered the small appliance, shivering when she felt his fingers winnow through her hair and massage her scalp. It was an incredible sensation. He was gentle, and yet the feelings his touch inspired were not gentle at all. She felt hot and achy and very close to some imaginary line in the sand.

He rubbed one narrow strand of hair at a time, fluffing and separating and directing the deliciously warm air from one side of her head to the other.

Her head lolled on her shoulders as a delicious lethargy swept over her. "Maybe you were a gay hairdresser in another lifetime," she teased, her voice slurred.

Tyler winced inwardly. Not in this lifetime. Not when the woman he wanted more than his next breath sat docilely beneath his hands. Not when his brain cells were being depleted by a semipermanent erection. Not when he was contemplating going against his own personal code of honor and saying to hell with the last two weeks of his employment. Besides . . . weren't there extenuating circumstances? Wasn't he going above and beyond for the Scimitar? Putting himself in harm's way to protect a lousy building?

He cleared his throat. "You wouldn't want me with a pair of scissors in my hand," he joked. "I tried to give Gina a Mohawk when we were kids. My dad paddled my butt so hard, I couldn't sit down for a week."

"And poor Gina?"

"Well, let's just say that by the time Mom's hair salon finally evened up my hatchet job, Gina looked like a cute little boy angel."

Shelli shuddered theatrically. "Bless her heart. Maybe being an only child isn't always such a bad thing."

He ran his hands through her hair on the pretext of checking for damp spots. It was like liquid fire in his hands, the fiery red shot through with amber and taffy yellow. "It would be a crime if anyone ever cut this," he said softly, cupping her neck before he could stop himself.

He felt her go still. "Is it dry?" she asked, her voice hoarse.

What would she do if he lied? Would she sit there indefinitely, allowing him to touch her at will? He put the brakes on his dangerous thoughts and tossed the comb on the counter. "Yeah," he said reluctantly. "All done."

He watched with regret while she did that amazing thing women do, scooping and smoothing and twisting until her hair was once again neatly contained in a ponytail. He wondered if it would be PC to beg her to leave it loose. Probably not.

"C'mon," he said impulsively. "I've got an idea."

Shelli followed in his wake, shivering when they entered the icy stairwell and began climbing. They bypassed the third floor and kept going up, emerging at last in a narrow corridor that led to the only room on this level. Not much of a room really, just a small storage area that from the front of the building resembled a lookout tower. All in keeping with the castle theme.

Tyler took her hand and tugged her toward the window. He encircled her with his arms. In his embrace she felt safe and yet at the same time quiveringly aware that she stood at the edge of an emotional precipice.

They both fell silent, stunned by the view. As far as the eye could see, the world was white. Enormous firs bowed under their heavy blankets, and the black lacy skeletons of hardwoods trembled in the icy wind. In the distance, range after range of ancient mountains melted into one another, their contours shrouded in snow.

A few birds, the hardy ones who had not migrated south, twittered and flitted from tree to tree, no doubt wondering what had happened to all the early-spring goodies they'd been enjoying the week before.

Shelli sighed, moved by the power of the bleak but powerful landscape. "It's beautiful, isn't it?"

His breath brushed her cheek. "Truly amazing."

He reached around her to unlatch the mullioned casement windows and fling them wide. She shrieked as the bitter wind swept into the small area, stealing her breath and bringing the raw elements inside.

Tyler shoved a box of Christmas lights toward her feet. "Step here," he demanded, urging her up and then pressing against her back. He leaned forward, forcing her to do the same. She was laughing so hard that tears froze on her cheeks. He laced their fingers together and stretched out their arms.

"I'm the king of the world," he shouted.

His lips brushed her icy cheek. "Do it, Shelli."

Feeling slightly ridiculous but unwilling to let the moment pass, she inhaled and yelled, "I'm the queen of the world."

Their voices seemed to linger on the wind, echoing among the trees on this vast, isolated mountaintop. Tyler stepped back, their faces level. She searched his eyes, looking for answers. "You're a nut," she whispered, unable to mask the warm, almost sentimental affection she felt at the moment.

She leaned forward to kiss him, and then froze, appalled. Her mouth was open slightly. Tyler's chest rose and fell. His whole body was tensed . . . waiting.

She wanted to ask him to close the window, but the extreme temperature was the only thing keeping her sane. She touched his cheek. "Tyler . . ."

He seemed dazed, his eyes cloudy. "Hmmm?"

"Do you have feelings for me?" Saying it out loud made her breathless, almost faint. But she had to know.

His eyes glittered and his hands settled at her waist. "God, yes."

Her eyes widened. "Yes?"

He shook his head as though frustrated by her surprise. "Why the hell do you think I'm leaving?"

Tears welled in her eyes. "I didn't know what to think."

He muttered an apology and reached around her to shut the windows. The resulting silence was deafening.

She stuck out her chin. "You should have said something."

His rueful smile was crooked. "Shelli, you went through that nasty business with the sexual harassment thing. I didn't want to muddy the waters. I wanted to come to you without any ambiguity."

Her face softened, and she touched his cheek. "Thank you for caring. But I think it's too late for that. It's not realistic for us to lie beside each another night after night and not want to touch." Her words trailed off in a breathy little sigh.

He groaned and slid his arms all the way around her waist, resting his head on her shoulder. "I'd already decided that wasn't working anymore."

She stroked his hair tentatively, feeling the thick, springy waves. "What do you mean?" Was he tossing her out of his bed?

"I mean . . ." he said, pausing to nibble the side of her neck. "The hotel is getting colder every hour. And it would be stupid to use the generators for heat when we might need them for other things."

"So? What's your point?"

"There are fireplaces in the foyer and the lounge, but both places are too huge to close off for heat."

"I agree."

"So we have only one other *realistic* alternative."

She blinked, sure he was not about to suggest what she was thinking. "And that would be?"

He released her and stepped back, his arms folded across his chest. "We move to suite nine."

CHAPTER FOUR

helli felt a tingle of electricity snake down her spine. Her breathing grew shallow. Suite nine, the sultan's harem, perhaps the most decadent and luxurious of all the fantasy play rooms. Instead of a traditional bed, a huge double mattress rested on the floor atop an enormous, and quite literally priceless, Oriental rug. The bed was covered with genuine silk sheets, and multicolored silk hangings draped from the ceiling, giving the illusion of a tent.

A recessed track ran down the ceiling on either side of the narrow room, allowing heavy velvet curtains to be pulled, enclosing the occupants in opulent privacy. The resulting space extended from the ornate fireplace through a nest of plush, jewel-colored pillows, to the room's hedonistic centerpiece . . . the sultan's bed.

With the curtains pulled shut, it would be an easy matter for the fire to warm the relatively small space, even without electricity. It was an eminently practical solution to their sleeping situation. If you discounted the fact that every corner of the room screamed sex.

Familiarity was supposed to breed contempt. While it was true that she and Tyler knew each of the fantasy suites down to the last detail and checked them periodically for broken or missing props, given the right mood, they'd be bound to succumb to the ambience. Especially since she was in love with Tyler.

Wow. The realization hit her squarely between the eyes. Was she really that good at self-deception? She'd acknowledged to herself months ago that she had a pretty serious crush on her number-two guy. But Tyler had never once given her any indication that he felt anything toward her other than a friendly work-place camaraderie. At least not until the last forty-eight hours.

Was she exaggerating the strength of her own feelings? She and Tyler were trapped for the short-term in a weird and unprecedented situation. Proximity and isolation were dangerous cousins. Maybe the cold had frozen the portions of her brain that controlled rational thought. And how was it possible to be so damned cold and at the same time so damned hot? It was all Tyler's fault.

She licked her lips. "Do you think that's a good idea?"

He shrugged, his eyes hooded. "What do you mean?"

His body language issued a challenge. A challenge to admit the truth?

She stepped down from the box, avoiding his piercing gaze. "It won't be platonic if we sleep there."

Well, there you go. That put the cards squarely on the table.

He grinned slightly. "I imagine you're right."

She shoved her hands in her pockets, feeling off balance and jittery. "And you're okay with that?"

This time he laughed out loud. "Show me a man who wouldn't be."

That wasn't exactly what she wanted to hear. If she had sex with Tyler, she wanted it to be more than recreational sex or making the best of a difficult situation. And just because he admitted to having feelings for her . . . well, that covered a lot of ground. She should have made her initial question a heck of a lot more specific.

She hesitated, and Tyler took advantage of her momentary

silence to kiss her. Unlike the night before, this time she knew he was fully awake. It started out as a gentle, teasing kiss. Exploratory. Easy. Kind of a first-date kiss.

But that didn't last long. Tyler groaned from somewhere deep in his chest and lifted her, setting her on the window ledge and moving between her legs. His hands cupped her face, angling her head for better access. The cold glass at her back was in direct counterpoint to the blazing heat of Tyler's body in front of her.

He moved closer still and slid an arm around her back, crushing her breasts against his chest. His breathing was jerky, and she could swear his hands were trembling. She met his tongue with hers, dizzy with the taste of him. She wanted to strip off all her many layers and take him now, wrapping her legs around his waist and sliding down onto that wonderful erection.

But in spite of her complete and total immersion in the moment, her body wasn't immune to the circumstances. She shivered once, hard, and Tyler pulled back immediately, his face creased in concern. "God, I'm an idiot," he muttered. "We need to get you warm."

She fisted a hand in his hair, dragging his head toward hers for a kiss she needed more than air. "Warm enough," she whispered. "Kiss me, Tyler. Please."

It was insane. Exhilarating. She felt drunk with arousal, the hot, liquid stab of heat between her legs an insistent ache.

Tyler was kissing her like he'd never had a woman before, his raw hunger sending her higher.

She shivered once more, and Tyler cursed beneath his breath, releasing her and breathing hard. He ran a hand though his tousled hair, his unaccustomed agitation in stark contrast to the man whose usual calm demeanor was nowhere to be seen.

His jaw thrust forward. "I'll be damned if our first time is going to be like this. I'm not groping you through five layers, Shelli. I want to see you nude, all warm and silky and comfortable."

* * *

Who knew a woman could survive three hours of foreplay and not go up in smoke? Tyler led her down from the tower, holding her hand as they descended, and gave her one last quick kiss before disappearing outside. When she peeked through the window, she saw him using a wheelbarrow to move wood from the covered shed to the room where they would be spending the night.

She was torn between panic and exhilaration. Tyler wanted her. Even though she was dressed like a bag lady, he was interested in sex. With her.

She decided to inventory the linen closet, a mind-numbing task that helped settle her jumpy nerves. Later she worked on her laptop, hoping her battery would hold out a bit longer. Tyler paused beside her on one of his many trips back and forth and touched her cheek, his eyes guarded but kind. "Quit worrying, Shelli. The hotel will do fine. You're a great manager."

For some reason his sincere praise made her teary-eyed. She trapped his hand against her cheek. "How much longer are you going to be busy?"

He swallowed and looked away. "I'm almost done. I want our new quarters to be as snug as possible. We may be there for a while."

She giggled, and he actually flushed.

He cleared his throat. "If you'll excuse me, I'll go get the fire started."

He disappeared again and Shelli groaned. She wanted to smack him and attack him, and do anything else that would get him to quit being so darned responsible. It irked her that Tyler had the presence of mind to plan for the next few days when all she could think about was jumping his bones.

This was why she was lousy at romance. She simply didn't understand men. She'd had two . . . count them . . . two serious relationships. The first was with a classmate in her master's program. Right before graduation they had both applied for the same job.

She had naively assumed whoever came out on top would congratulate the other.

He dumped her when she landed the position. It made her mad enough to concentrate on her career and forget serious romance for a couple of years. But then she met Clive, a sweet-faced banker who didn't feel threatened by her success. But Clive had trouble adjusting to her nontraditional schedule. And Clive had a very serious *Leave It to Beaver* complex.

He'd have been delighted to see her vacuuming in pearls and a tiny-waisted dress while the babies—plural—napped. The relationship had been doomed from the start. Which proved her original point. Shelli Richards didn't know squat about men. Other than the fact they adored sex and were fixated on breasts.

Nah, that wasn't fair . . . she knew at least a few guys who were leg men. And some who actually had a brain large enough to think about something other than sex twenty-four seven.

But the sad truth was, she wasn't interested in Tyler's brain. At least not in the short-term. The fact that he was capable of carrying on an interesting conversation was rapidly taking a backseat to her obsessive need to see him naked.

She stared blankly at the computer screen.

Breathe . . . breathe . . .

She could share the sultan's harem with Tyler Strickland and not morph into a drooling sex-starved idiot.

And Arnold Schwarzenegger was elected governor of California for his political skills.

She sighed and decided the only way to speed up the evening's program was to help Tyler stock their new hangout. The only disadvantage to suite nine was that it was a good distance from the kitchen. Scimitar guests who chose to enjoy suite nine were provided with their choice of edible tidbits, everything from dates, figs, and pomegranates to sugared almonds and honeyed cakes, all in keeping with the Eastern theme.

Shelli decided drinks and mundane snacks would have to do.

She didn't think she and Tyler needed any further stimulation, although she couldn't quite shake the vision of his lithe, muscular body stretched out at her knees as she fed him from a cluster of grapes. She groaned and went to the window, peering out into the deepening darkness. Her flashlight was tucked into her coat pocket, and she wondered if Tyler had remembered to take one down the hall.

She changed into her pajamas and robe, not forgetting the two pairs of socks, and hefted the small cooler into her arms. Then she headed for the entertainment corridor with all the enthusiasm of a dental patient with a throbbing tooth.

The plastic was cool against her breasts. She stopped in front of the door with the brass numeral nine. Her palms were sweaty. She shifted the cooler to her left arm and reached down to twist the knob.

When Tyler left the kitchen, his guts and his gonads were in turmoil. Did Shelli want anything more than sex from him? Dared he risk putting his heart on his sleeve by letting her know how much he cared? With a rough curse, he scooped up a pile of kindling and began laying the all-important fire, a little-used but not forgotten skill from his Boy Scout days.

By the time he had a steady flame going, he'd shed his jacket, socks, and shoes, and was now wearing only a short-sleeved T-shirt and his oldest pair of jeans. He stared into the popping and crackling fire and searched for answers.

Was it wrong to let matters take their course? To have sex with Shelli and damn the consequences? Or was he honor bound to tell her the truth first? The easy thing to do would be to get her comfortable with him physically and then when they were intimate, sort of ease into his confession.

He lost his train of thought for a moment as his very creative imagination took over, entertaining him with images of Shelli naked and smiling in his arms. He cleared his throat and wiped the dampness from his forehead. Hell, he was in deep shit. Two weeks, just two damn weeks and he would have been free to do this the easy way.

A slow, deliberate courtship and then if he was lucky . . . the ultimate prize. But unfortunately, fate had forced his hand, and now he was about to gamble everything on one roll of the dice.

At a small sound, his head jerked around. Shelli stood in the doorway, swathed in clothing, clutching a small blue and white insulated cooler in her arms as though it were the modern-day equivalent of a chastity belt.

He leaped to his feet and took it from her, waiting until she scuttled into the room, then closed the door behind her. While she watched him with large, slightly apprehensive eyes, he reached for the heavy green velvet draperies and pulled them across the room. The matching set opposite them was already drawn. When he finished, he and Shelli were enclosed in a small, cozy love nest.

She smiled slightly. "Somehow, I thought there would be more women in a harem." She was clearly trying for a light-hearted note, but her posture was far less relaxed than her teasing comment suggested.

He shrugged, pleased in spite of the obstacles in his path, to be spending this time with her. "I'm told the sultan usually had a favorite. You fit the part."

She looked down at her bag-lady wardrobe. "Flattery will get you everywhere, Strickland."

They both laughed, and the immediate tension dissipated. Tyler returned his attention to the fire, hoping to give her a minute or two to adjust to their new surroundings. He used the iron poker to position the main logs at just the correct angle and then replaced the fire screen. The heavy iron guard was adorned with brass silhouettes of peacocks and doves.

He stood and wiped his hands. "You probably won't need that robe, Shelli. It's amazing how much heat this has generated."

He was talking about the fire. But her face said that *her* mind had gone down an entirely different path.

He smothered a grin of male satisfaction. It was damned gratifying to know she was so physically aware of him.

As he watched, she slowly shed the hotel robe. Her movements couldn't have been any more mesmerizing if she'd been a pole dancer wearing a thong and a boa. His cock lengthened and hardened, a condition that was becoming more and more familiar in the last three days. He glanced at his watch and almost groaned. It was only seven o'clock. No television, no movies, no distractions of any kind. Although the fire created quite a bit of illumination, he'd also lit the dozen or so candles that sat on the tiny, low tables around the edges of the room.

By candlelight, Shelli looked very young, almost vulnerable.

She opened a small, carved sandalwood cabinet near the bed. "We could read," she said brightly, holding up a leather-bound book.

He eyed her speculatively, wondering if she was baiting him. "Have you really forgotten what that book is?" he asked, not bothering to hide his skepticism.

She glanced down blankly at the cover and flipped it open.

Clearly she had.

Her face went bloodred and she tossed the book back into the cabinet so quickly, he winced for the valuable leather. That particular copy of the *Kama Sutra* had cost Sebastian Tennant a hefty sum.

Tyler took pity on her. He reached into his back pocket. "I grabbed a deck of cards from the lounge. You want to play rummy? Poker?"

Her relief was almost insulting. He looked at her feet. "Why don't you take off those socks? You'll love the feel of this rug beneath your feet." Again, Tennant had spared no expense. Instead of a less-pricey wool rug, he had selected a silk antique from Persia. It was pale green, the color of new moss in the spring, and it was ornately woven with brightly colored mythical birds and flowers.

Shelli bent over and pulled off her socks. Her feet were narrow and pale, with high arches and shell-pink toenails. He watched as she slid one bare foot backwards and forwards, a tiny smile blooming on her face.

"Amazing, isn't it?" he said quietly.

"It's so smooth and soft," she murmured, her eyes focused downward. "Sebastian has exquisite taste."

"Sebastian?" He'd seldom heard her use the man's first name, and unexpected jealousy bit hard. "I didn't know you were on such chummy terms."

She shrugged. "He's told me to call him that, but I usually prefer the more formal address. After all, he signs my paychecks."

They both froze when her careless comment registered. The inevitable level of awkwardness between them went from minimal to elephant in the room.

Tyler clenched his jaw and motioned for her to sit down. The pile of pillows was comfortable for lovemaking but a bit of a challenge for card playing. They finally settled and used one of the flatter, firmer pillows for a table. Shelli removed her sweatshirt. Now she was clad in only her sleep top and flannel pants.

He read the slogan across her breasts, enjoying the way the letters rose and fell with her breathing. "*Every* room?"

She glanced at her chest and a look of mortification brought another wave of color to her face. She wrinkled her nose. "I forgot I was wearing this. It was a convention freebie from a few years ago."

He let the moment pass and dealt the cards. They had decided on rummy, but Shelli had apparently forgotten to mention that she was a shark. After three hands she was up by two hundred and fifty points. He counted the cards he'd been stuck with and subtracted the penalty.

Her smug look was cute but maddening. Her thin shirt clung just enough for him to see her pert nipples. Since the room was plenty warm, those little beacons told him what he needed to know.

He tossed the cards aside in disgust. "I should have suggested strip poker. At least I'd have had a sporting chance."

Shelli gave him a measured look. "I didn't take you for a quitter."

He scowled, restless and itchy. There was too much damn stimulation in this room. "Cards aren't my forte," he grumbled.

She tipped her head to one side, her ponytail sliding across her shoulder. "Then what?"

"We could play dress up."

Shelli's mouth fell open. Tyler looked different somehow . . . more dangerous, not as laid-back. His sensual mouth was pressed in a straight line, his chin hard, his eyes dark and filled with heat. His biceps peeped from beneath the sleeves of his shirt, a shirt that strained across a broad, strong chest. He was leaning back on his hands, his long, jeans-clad legs stretched out in the welter of pillows.

"Dress up?"

He pointed to the ornate mahogany armoire. "Haven't you ever wanted to try on any of the costumes?"

She curled her knees to her chest and circled them with her arms to keep them from shaking. He didn't look like he was kidding. "Not really."

One eyebrow lifted, his emerald eyes taking on a naughty gleam. That beautiful mouth curled in definite mischief. "I dare you."

She huffed. "Don't be ridiculous. We'd freeze."

His eyes danced with amusement. "Try again, Shelli. That excuse won't fly. We're both toasty warm, and you know it."

The trembling moved to the pit of her stomach. "How exactly would we do this?" she whispered.

He shrugged, the epitome of male confidence. "I can slip behind the curtain to change. You stay here. I won't peek."

"You swear?"

His grin was pure bad boy. "I swear."

While she was still trying to decide how in the heck he had gotten the upper hand so quickly, Tyler stood and went to the armoire, selected a handful of items, and stepped outside their curtained paradise.

His voice floated through the cloth barrier. "Are you getting ready, Shelli?" She heard the rustle of fabric as he undressed. Her thighs clenched against a rush of honey-sweet anticipation and arousal.

Her voice, along with every other ultrasensitive inch of her body, trembled. "Not so fast. Give me a minute." She rifled through the assortment of houri outfits in the armoire, choosing what she hoped was the most modest.

And that wasn't saying much. She stripped off her clothes and eyed the costume with misgiving, then stepped into it. Damn those extra fifteen pounds. She wondered how long she could suck in her stomach and hold her breath. The transparent violet pants, à la *I Dream of Jeannie,* were comfortable, but not exactly designed to cover up much, and the crotch was suspiciously airy. She put them on anyway, and imagining Tyler's reaction made her lick her lips in anticipation. The top was little more than a strapless red velvet bra spangled with little gold beads that fluttered and caught the light when she moved. It barely covered her nipples.

Thank God there was no mirror.

Tyler shook the curtain. "What are you doing over there?" he said, clearly amused at her procrastination. "Weaving your own cloth?"

She tucked her utilitarian pajamas out of sight. "All set." The quaver in her voice was a dead giveaway, but maybe he wouldn't notice.

Tyler stepped through the curtain, and her heart stopped. He was huge and naked, well almost naked. His golden skin was bare from the top of his head to his big feet, except for a swath of white fabric wound between his legs and around his waist. Not a trace of civilized male remained.

She was afraid she might burst into nervous laughter, but then she noticed his eyes. They looked funny, kind of fuzzy and dazed, and she could see his Adam's apple rippling as he swallowed.

"Tyler? Are you okay?"

He wondered if this was what it felt like to be struck by lightning. He could hear her talking, but there was a ringing in his ears, and his palms and feet were tingling. The only unaffected appendage was his boner, and he hoped the folds of silky material covering his groin were concealing his physical state.

He licked his lips. "Ah, Shelli . . . ?"

She looked at him inquiringly, as innocent as a woman could look wearing gold spangles. "What, Tyler?"

"Will you take down your hair?"

She frowned. "I thought the ponytail sort of matched the outfit."

"Please," he said, his voice hoarse.

She shrugged, obviously puzzled, and reached up to unfasten whatever was holding her ponytail in place. When her arms lifted, her lush breasts nearly made a break for freedom. He was torn between cheering them on and watching her free the hair he had fantasized about for a year and a half.

She tossed a ribbonlike thing aside and shook her head from side to side, sliding her hands through her hair until it lay smoothly. One strand slid into her cleavage, clinging to the curve of her breast.

Although she looked calm, something about the set of her shoulders and the teeth mutilating her bottom lip told him it had taken a lot of courage for her to dress this way. For him.

His throat tightened. He crossed toward her, a tiny distance in reality, but a huge step in their relationship. He traced her cheekbones with his thumbs. Her pupils had expanded so far he could see only a faint ring of blue. Her skin was unblemished, warm creamy ivory. Her lips parted, the lower one trembling just a bit.

He bent his head. "I can't believe I've waited this long to kiss you again," he muttered, fully prepared to remedy that oversight.

She touched a finger to his mouth, halting him in his tracks. His heart sank. What did she think this costume thing meant?

But she was smiling, albeit faintly.

"What?" he demanded, feeling the hold he had on his emotions fraying by the minute.

She giggled, a light, happy sound that gave him hope. "I've been thinking."

He groaned inwardly. Crap. That was never good.

"These rooms are called fantasy suites, right?" she continued.

He nodded slowly.

"Well, it seems only right that we uphold the mission of the Scimitar and explore the fantasy. In this room. Now. Tonight." She paused uncertainly. "What do you think?"

He couldn't speak. He gathered her into his arms and bent his head. When their lips met, the ground beneath his feet moved. It was every wonderful feeling he had ever experienced in his lifetime all rolled into one. She tasted sweet, and hot, and surprisingly inexperienced.

She wasn't a bony stick like some women he'd dated, but even so, her curves were delicate, even fragile in his arms.

Her lips were moving on his, making his knees weak. His hands found the bare skin on her back and stayed there. He wasn't about to pounce on her like an animal, even if the idea did have a certain earthy appeal.

He could smell the smoke from the candles, but much more immediate was her fragrance—warm woman—and where her hand touched his face, the scent of dish soap. He had a sudden craving for lemons.

Her arms slid around his neck. Bountiful velvet-covered curves pressed his chest. He grabbed handfuls of her hair, wanting to bury his face in it, but reluctant to release her mouth.

He never knew that kissing alone could bring him so close to the edge. With a ragged sigh, he released her mouth and sucked in gulps of air, trying to curb the hunger that made him weak.

Her eyes were luminous in the candlelight, reflecting all sorts of feminine secrets. Her lips were wet from their kisses, her chin pink where his late-day stubble had marked her. He touched the spot with remorse. "I should have shaved."

She turned her head and kissed his fingers. "I don't think the sultan would worry about that."

"Well," he said slowly, looking down at her beauty, almost awestruck by the moment, "maybe no one in his harem was as perfect as you."

She leaned her forehead on his collarbone. "Don't make me cry," she muttered. "My skin gets blotchy."

He chuckled, wrapping his hand around a hank of hair and rubbing it on his face. "Well, we wouldn't want that." He held her tightly, wondering if she would change her mind about the line they had crossed. He hoped with every fiber of his being that she wouldn't. Shelli was decisive and confident, rarely second-guessing herself.

But it was one thing to make business decisions and another entirely to embark on a path as unknown as it was enticingly forbidden.

She stirred in his arms, putting enough distance between them to be able to tilt her head back and examine his face. He wondered what it revealed. Without her customary heels, she was half a foot shorter than he was. He liked it. The dainty and defenseless woman, the big tough man. Maybe that was politically incorrect, but hey, a guy was entitled to his fantasies.

Her stare was making him uncomfortable. He raised an eyebrow. "What? Do I have food on my chin?"

Her slender hands gripped his forearms, those luscious breasts perilously close to his chest. She smiled, a small tilt of the lips that was more Mona Lisa than Julia Roberts. "You're a very handsome man, Tyler Strickland. Maybe I just like looking at you." Her thumbs feathered over his biceps.

Her steady regard was flattering. He inhaled, puffing out his chest and making contact with velvet nirvana. His hands slid to her scantily clad hips, pulling her against his body. No way, now, could she miss his erection.

Her quick inhalation told him she was more than aware of his desire. She wiggled her hips, his erection rubbing against her silk-covered skin. A red haze obscured his vision. His brain ceded control to his body.

He dropped to his knees, pulling her with him. Still face-to-face with her, he bent his head and kissed her again. The first time wasn't a fluke, he thought hazily. How could such an innocent mating of lips make a man so dizzy?

He coaxed her into the nest of pillows. He wanted to spend hours paying homage to her body, and he hoped he'd be able to stay the course. He knelt beside her, barely touching her hip with his hand.

He sat back on his haunches. Now it was his turn to stare. Her hair, brought to life by the glowing fire, reflected a palette of red, gold, and bronze. It spilled across the tumbled pillows with natural abandon. Her legs, barely covered by the insubstantial fabric, were sleek and toned.

He chuckled when he touched her knee and she flinched. "Skittish, my little concubine?"

He saw movement in the slender column of her throat as she swallowed. "No. But I'm feeling a little nervous."

The raw honesty in her voice touched him. He leaned across her body, supporting his weight on one arm. "Relax," he muttered, kissing her again. Harder this time, pushed by an increasing hunger. "I'll take care of you."

Her mouth opened, inviting his tongue inside, returning the

kiss with enthusiasm. His free hand slipped between her legs, and he groaned his approval. The costume was made for a man's easy access.

He dragged his mouth from hers and sat up, feeling like a starving kid in a candy store. He parted her legs and saw the delicate fluff of auburn hair peeking from the open seam between her thighs. He touched her with a single finger, not her clitoris, just the damp curls.

Shelli moaned and squirmed.

He held her ankles and spread her legs a fraction wider. "Well," he said slowly, wishing like hell that his head would stop spinning, "I guess this answers the question of whether or not you're a true redhead."

CHAPTER FIVE

*H*er eyes shot sparks of azure fire. Somewhere he'd read that the hottest part of any flame was where the blue and white colors mingled. At this precise moment he believed it.

She thrust out her chin, looking regal and haughty, despite her vulnerable position. Her voice was low and taunting. "*Everything* about me is real, Strickland. One hundred percent."

He released her ankles and plumped her breasts with his hands. His thumbs toyed with strategically placed beads. She didn't have to convince *him*. Most men could tell the difference, and Tyler had always been a fan of breasts the way the Almighty had created them, whether large or small or any one of the many fascinating variations in between.

He smiled lazily. "So I see." He deliberately pushed the velvet below her nipples, exposing them to the air. They were a soft, rosy, bubblegum pink against her pale skin. He loved how they puckered with only the lightest stimulation. He gave each one a quick taste.

Shelli's eyes were closed, but her lips were parted and her breathing was rapid. He could have played with her tits all night, but other possibilities demanded his attention.

He pulled her by the hands until she was sitting, and then

reached around her to unfasten the velvet band. She sat docilely in his embrace. He bit gently at the sensitive flesh behind her ear. The cloth fell loose into his hands. He tossed it aside. Again, he pressed her to her back.

His hands were shaking. A hint of challenge in her eyes demanded that he play his part. He cleared his throat. "You are the jewel in my harem," he said softly. "Many men would pay a high price to steal you away from me."

She frowned slightly. "And you would sell me for gold?"

"Not for all the riches in the Orient," he murmured, extracting a silk scarf from the drawer in a nearby table and lifting her hands above her head. He tied her wrists together and then fastened them to a leg of the same table.

He picked up a multifaceted crystal jar. An ornate, script S was engraved in the sterling-silver lid. "I've always wanted to try this," he said, his heart pounding, his words half-serious.

She looked away from him, her cheeks flushed. "It's probably just cheap baby lotion with some perfume added," she muttered.

"Cynic," he accused, grinning. "Rumor has it that Sebastian Tennant procured this cream in Thailand. That it's wildly expensive and that it's a topical aphrodisiac. He's known for his love of the exotic."

She moved restlessly in her nest of pillows, curling into a fetal position. "No such cream exists. It's an urban legend."

He firmly but gently gripped her ankles and pulled her legs straight. "Don't turn your body away from me, my fair flower. Tonight you're mine." He told himself he was merely playing a game, but the intent in his statement came from some possessive place deep inside him.

He opened the jar and laid the cold metal lid on her stomach. Her belly contracted sharply, and goose bumps broke out on her silky skin. She shuddered, but remained silent, her dark blue eyes watching his every move. He held the heavy glass container to his nose and inhaled. If eroticism had a scent, this was it.

He left her for a moment and grabbed a bottle of water from the cooler, drinking thirstily, trying to keep his head.

He held the bottle in her direction and she nodded.

With one hand, he lifted her head a few inches and with the other, he poured water into her mouth. It dribbled down her chin and onto her throat. He capped the bottle and licked up his mess. Her skin was faintly salty. He thought he heard her murmur his name.

He moved the lid to the table. Then, holding the jar in one palm, he swirled his index finger in the thick perfumed cream. A pulse began to beat heavily low in his scrotum.

He sat cross-legged between her legs, draping them over his thighs. She lay before him like a sacrifice. He opened the harem pants as much as he could and spread a line of cream from Shelli's belly button down the left side of her abdomen and onto her most secret, delicate skin. His finger burned.

He repeated the procedure on the right side. Shelli's eyes were squeezed shut, the muscles in her arms straining. He dropped cream into the hair just above her sensitive, aching clit. She was begging now, her voice ragged.

He capped the jar and turned his attention to rubbing the cream into her body, eradicating every bit of evidence. Her beautiful skin was soft and resilient. He paid close attention to his pleasurable task, stroking and caressing every inch except for that one magical spot.

The heavy, foreign scent of the cream swirled about them. He used his thumbs to part her opening. She was moist and hot. He spread a tiny bit of cream inside. Shelli cried out, jerking at the bonds securing her hands. "Oh God . . . Tyler."

He was so hard, he felt ready to explode.

"Please . . ." she begged. "Please."

He found one last drop of cream and pushed it to a spot immediately below her clitoris, bearing down with his finger. For a moment he thought she would come without the direct touch she craved.

But apparently he had judged the edge just right.

She was trembling, her gaze wild, unfocused. With no small amount of regret he removed his hands from between her legs. Shocked, helpless frustration boiled in her expressive eyes.

Idly, he picked up a strand of her hair and used it to tickle the tips of her breasts. He was concentrating on his own breathing, trying to disguise his turmoil. He felt as close to being out of control as he had ever experienced in his life. In truth, the hunger driving him was a bit unnerving. He didn't want to hurt her.

She finally found her voice. "You are cruel to deny me my pleasure." Her eyes were narrowed. No forgiveness there.

He shrugged. "You're here for *my* enjoyment. Your feelings, physical or otherwise, are immaterial."

Shelli lay stunned, her breathing jerky. The skin between her thighs burned, almost unbearably sensitive. She was desperate for release, ready to bargain for anything that would give her respite from this gnawing, insistent ache.

She licked her lips. Tyler's eyes were hooded, his expressionless face hard. His broad chest was sheened with perspiration. The dark, curly hair dusting a path from his collarbones to his navel gave him a primitive, male beauty.

He wasn't moving at all. Her legs were still sprawled over his thighs, and she felt raw, exposed. Her voice was alarmingly weak. "Release me, master, and allow me to earn my pleasure by ensuring yours."

He stared at her, his eyes hot, his hair rumpled. "My appetite for pleasure is greater than the tides in the ocean. You may try to appease it, but it will return again and again, washing over you until you drown in its force."

His words made her shiver. "I was told when I came here that you had women too great to number who would service you at will. Where are these faceless females? Why do they not share the harem?"

He shrugged, supremely confident in his masculine power and arrogance. "I sent them away."

His words shook her. "But why? Will it not cause you to lose face among your people?"

He waved a hand. "They will understand. I have no need of pale imitations when I have the jewel beyond price in my palm." He held her knees, his eyes seeming to convey some deep message. "You have all the fire of the most brilliant diamond, the cool beauty of the pearl, the sensuality of the ruby, the serenity of the sapphire, the warm, steady glow of the emerald. What use are other women whose charms are no more enduring than paste stones?"

He stroked her inner thighs. "I want only you."

Her knees tightened. She would go mad if he tormented her again. Almost frantic, she begged without embarrassment. "Please, Tyler. Please let me go. I want to touch you."

A tiny grin broke through his stoic expression, for a brief second shattering the role he had embraced. "Well, sweetheart . . . what man can resist a plea like that?" He reached up and untied the knotted silk, his big torso looming over her. He grunted in satisfaction when the fabric bonds finally gave way.

She eluded him when he tried to scoop her up in his arms. "Excuse me for a moment." She escaped through the curtain. All of the fantasy suites had small bathroom facilities. She splashed water on her face and stared in the mirror. She looked like a wild woman, her hair mussed and tangled, her face free of makeup. And her eyes held an unfamiliar glitter. As though she was hovering on the edge of reason.

All fantasy aside, she was jumping in over her head and now she was torn between terror and exhilaration.

She dried her hands and stared at the reflection of her breasts. Knowing that he was looking at her like this made her pulse race. She cupped her breasts, imagining that her hands were his. His fingers were strong, the skin slightly rough. When he touched her nipples, she felt a jolt all the way down to her belly and beyond.

Though it had been only moments since he caressed her intimately, already she craved his firm, sure touch again.

With a half sob of incredulity, she felt the skin of her sex begin to throb and burn. She released her breasts and staggered back from the mirror, her legs threatening to collapse.

Tyler greeted her reappearance with a grunt of annoyance. "You took your own sweet time. I'm not getting any younger out here." He'd propped a mountain of pillows at the foot of the bed, and he lay sprawled out, the image of a hungry, promiscuous potentate.

She dropped to her knees beside him, her hands reaching for his waist. "How does this thing come undone?"

Surprisingly, he pushed her hands aside. He got to his feet and fumbled with the cloth until it fell away quite suddenly, leaving him wearing nothing but his wickedly sexy smile.

His penis was somewhat of a shock. If they awarded kingdoms by the size of a man's cock, then it was no surprise that he was a sultan. She felt a shiver of purely feminine apprehension.

She had nothing to feed him, no sweetmeats, no fruit . . . no fancy wines. And she had a hunch that girls who gave blow jobs on the first date might be considered a little slutty.

She put her hand on his calf, enjoying the feel of the hard muscle. "Why don't you relax, master, and let me pleasure you with the love cream."

He frowned, looking down his nose at her with arrogant incredulity. "You wish to put perfume on me?"

She tilted her head, looking up at him with a cajoling smile. "We're the only ones around. Who will know?" The testicles hovering so near her face were starting to hypnotize her. She'd feel a heck of a lot more confident if he would lie down, 'cause from this angle he was pretty darned intimidating.

After seeming to consider her proposition for several long seconds, he finally dropped to the tumble of cushions and got comfortable on his back, his thick, swollen erection demanding the lion's share of her attention.

He linked his hands behind his head. "You may proceed."

He closed his eyes as though he were settling down for a nap. His dismissive calm challenged her somewhat rusty erotic skills.

She retrieved the lotion. The jar was heavier than she had imagined. A soon as she opened the lid, the thick, lush scent triggered a renewal of her simmering arousal. But unfortunately, in this scenario, her needs would have to take a backseat to satisfying the sexy sultan.

She debated her plan of attack. She knew where she was *not* going to start, but that left miles of gorgeous male flesh to consider.

She scooped at least a tablespoon of cream into her palm. Then she lifted one of his feet, and began rubbing lotion into his arch. She kept her voice low and sultry as she touched him. "I've been trained in the erotic arts, Your Excellency. I know how to give you pleasure so pure and complete you will wish for the threshold of ecstasy to elude you time and again as you reach for the stars."

His eyelids flickered and a hissed exhale escaped his lips. His chest rose and fell, and he made a strangled sound when she pressed deeply into his calf muscle and gradually moved up his leg. She was slow and methodical. When she finished one strong, hairy leg, she started on the other. Each time as she neared the point where his torso and his lower limbs met, she came so close to his balls that she saw his belly muscles clench with anticipation.

Her technique was probably not endorsed by the best massage organizations, possibly because it wasn't the least bit relaxing. She was so hot, she wanted to rip off her pants, flimsy though they were, and demand he make love to her. But she resisted . . . barely.

She leaned near his ear, whispering in a low, taunting murmur. "How am I doing, my lord sultan? Do you like my touch?" She brushed his penis as if by accident, and he cursed, his face a mask of pained concentration.

After massaging every inch of his feet and calves and upper thighs, she warmed a dollop of cream between her hands and went to work on his chest. Sitting beside him was awkward, so she straddled his waist. His boner bumped her bottom from time to time, but she tried to ignore it.

She eventually coaxed him to his stomach and started in on his back. It was almost a sin to cover up all that sleek golden skin and rippling muscles beneath sophisticated suits. He should be out under the blazing sun in some vineyard, bare from the waist up. He would be sweating, working hard, when she brought him a glass of clear, sparkling water, wearing her thinnest tunic with no undergarments, eager to know his touch.

He would pause from his labors and drink, the muscles in his throat rippling as he tipped back his head, his classically handsome face caressed by the sun. He would take her by the hand to a nearby grove of olive trees.

Standing in a cool patch of shade they would kiss and then he would back her up against the rough bark of a tree trunk, lift her skirts, and impale her, driving again and again into her hot aching center until they both cried out, their shouts lingering on the hot summer breezes.

Her hands slowed to a stop on his back, her breathing heavy. She eased away from his body and retrieved a long narrow scarf. This time she straddled his ankles. Quickly, in case he protested, she pulled his hands to the small of his back and tied his wrists together. She reached for the *Kama Sutra*, opened it, and began to read aloud. The ancient words were explicit, carnal, evocative. She kept the cadence of her words even, mesmerizing.

She heard her captive moan, and between her thighs, moisture seeped. Although her mouth was dry and her heartbeat jerky, she kept reading. Occasionally she reached out and trailed a hand from his hip over his muscled buttocks. She touched him between his legs now and then, scraping a fingernail over his balls.

He began to jerk and pull at the restraint that kept his hands immobilized, muttering indecipherable words and phrases. She ground her pelvis into his legs, seeking relief from the almost unbearable tension that was a combination of her impromptu fantasy and the sensual stimulation from touching him.

Suddenly, he rose to his knees, tumbling her into the nest of pillows and causing her to drop the book. His eyes were wild, the skin pulled tight over his cheekbones. "Untie me this instant." The ragged command in his voice was entirely convincing.

She leaned forward and fumbled with the fabric at his back. His attempts to escape had tightened the knot so much she was barely able to get it free, particularly since her hands were clumsy.

When the scarf fell away, he rotated his shoulders, still resting on his knees. He dropped to the nest of pillows and pulled her into his arms, their legs tangled. His eyelids drooped. His cheeks were flushed.

He took her hand and deliberately placed it on his erection. "Did you not learn the last chapter of your instruction, little tease? You promise enchantment and yet you stop short."

Her fingers closed around him, testing the firm, pulsing flesh. "Pleasure deferred increases a man's ultimate ecstasy, sire," she protested, her voice faint and soft as she caressed his thick erection.

He closed his eyes on a little groan of pleasure. "I have increased to the point of pain, my dove."

She loved watching his face as her hand moved, tentatively at first and then, guided by his indistinct murmurs, more confidently.

But they were both too close to the edge for much of that. He clenched his jaw and shoved her hand away. "Enough."

He rolled to his knees, pulling her with him. "Stand up, desert rose."

She did as he commanded, but her knees were weak. He encircled her hips with his arms, his face pressed to her belly. Slowly, ever so gently, he pulled the silky harem pants down her legs and then balanced her as she stepped out of them. She felt his breath hot on her bare flesh.

His tongue found her navel and explored. His hands cupped her butt, squeezing and kneading.

Shelli inhaled sharply when his tongue moved lower.

Tyler wondered, in that portion of his brain that was still functioning, if a man's cock could explode from postponed gratification. He was surprised he had any blood left anywhere else in his body. He should be rushing this scenario to its inevitable conclusion, but he couldn't bear the thought of this erotic, perfect fantasy coming to an end.

And he couldn't ignore the tiny, nasty little voice inside his head that reminded him this might be a one-shot deal. So he was determined to make it last.

His hands gripped her hips as he spread her legs and tasted the soft skin of her inner thighs. He felt her hands knot in his hair and winced when she jerked involuntarily. He tongued her intimately and then held her close as she shattered in what he was determined would be the first of many orgasms.

While she was still recovering, he stood and scooped her into his arms. It was a kick in the chest to see her nude. In all his imaginings, she had been lovely, but the reality was far more than his feeble brain had been able to create.

He lowered her gently onto silk sheets that were the color of sunshine in the winter. The pale buttery color was a perfect foil for Shelli's hair. She watched him with a tiny smile. That small, self-satisfied tilt to her lips was making him nuts. She looked happy, but he wanted to hear the words.

He smoothed the hair from her face, needing to touch her. "Any regrets, Shelli? Second thoughts?"

She shook her head, her eyes clear and bright, her expression confident and serene. "Not a one. And you?"

Perhaps a hint of vulnerability there. He grinned. "Are you

kidding? This has been the best day of my life. How often does a guy get his own harem?"

She wrinkled her nose. "I'm not sure one woman equals a harem."

He trailed a finger from her chin down her throat to her breastbone. "I told you, Shelli. You're the only one I want." He grabbed a condom from the table and rolled it on without waiting for her help.

He moved between her legs, his heart pounding, his thought processes rapidly short-circuiting. The missionary position probably wasn't de rigueur in a harem fantasy, but he was man enough to enjoy the symbolic claiming.

He positioned his penis at her entrance and groaned in disbelief when her small hand pushed against his chest.

"Wait, Tyler." Her voice was breathless. "Tell me again why you're leaving the Scimitar. I want to know. Really." Her eyes were dark with confusion and turmoil, and perhaps even hope.

He smiled down at her, relieved she had finally asked. He'd wanted this moment to be free of hidden agendas, and here was his chance.

He took her hand from his chest and placed it on the pillow beside her head. He moved forward an inch.

Her lips parted.

His balls tightened.

He kissed her lips . . . softly, and then harder. "Because I love you, Shelli. And I wanted to be able to tell you so."

He entered her slowly, watching her face for every nuance of emotion. She was tight, and the sensation of being deep inside her was indescribable. His breath came in jerky gasps, and he closed his eyes, seeing yellow spots against the black. She was hot and wet. His scalp tingled.

He withdrew, drawing a cry of protest from her, and then plunged deeper still. They found a rhythm that was as natural as breathing. She wrapped her legs around his back and he slid his hands under her butt, lifting her into his thrusts.

He could feel his climax bearing down, and he willed it back. He reached a hand between them and touched her clitoris lightly. It was as though he had given her an electric shock. Her eyes went blank and her fingernails scored his shoulder as she came with a cry.

Her inner muscles clenched sharply, and he shouted his release with one last series of frantic thrusts. He slumped over her, exhausted, shattered. More at peace than he could ever remember.

Shelli awoke to a cool room, the fire having gone out sometime in the middle of the night. Tyler slept like a dead man, and no wonder. Her face heated as she did a quick mental replay. She would never again be able to walk past this particular room without remembering the sweet fantasy she and Tyler had enacted with such amazing success. He'd made the transition from trusted friend to inventive lover with all the flair of a true sultan.

And yet she still hadn't told him she loved him.

Her own motives were a bit murky. Perhaps she didn't know how they would manage this new relationship. Perhaps she didn't know her own heart.

Could they be happy working in separate but relatively close properties? Did they have a future together? She'd only begun to acknowledge to herself that she loved him, and now they were lovers.

Her face heated again. Wow. Tyler continued to surprise her.

He never stirred when she slipped out of bed and dressed once again in her own clothes. She left the room quietly, entering the frigid hallway with a shiver. In Room 101, she washed up as best she could with icy water, her teeth chattering and every inch of her skin covered in gooseflesh.

She felt a bit more like her old self once she had dressed in her multilayered wardrobe. She went to the kitchen and flipped on the generator. Minutes later, she had the coffeepot brewing.

While she waited, she peered outside, almost blinded by the

glare of the morning sun on snow and ice. After a cup of life-giving caffeine, she called Sebastian Tennant on her cell phone.

Tyler rolled over and reached for his bed partner. His fingers found soft pillows but no Shelli. He sat up and held a hand to his head. Shit. It wasn't a good sign when a man declared his love and the recipient vanished at first light.

He dressed slowly, wondering what Shelli was thinking. It wasn't conceit to know that last night had been amazing. He'd given and received pleasure, and it had been pretty damned spectacular.

But maybe Shelli was back to worrying about that boss/employee thing. Guilt twinged in his belly. He could have waited. He should have waited. But instead he allowed himself to be seduced by the prospect of having the woman he loved in a playful fantasy. He'd surrendered to his own lust.

He jogged to the kitchen, ruefully aware that things were bad when you could see your breath inside a building.

He found her sipping coffee and working the crossword puzzle from an old newspaper. Try as he might, he couldn't see any clues in her placid expression. Other than a hint of wariness in her eyes, she looked much as she always did.

He rubbed his stubbled chin, uncomfortable and reluctant to initiate the necessary conversation.

Shelli saved him the trouble. "The coffee's hot," she said, smiling. "You look like you could use a cup."

Despite the seriousness of the moment, his lips quirked. "It was a long night," he deadpanned.

Her lashes widened, and she choked on a sip of hot java.

After that, what could a man do but pat her on the back? Patting led to hugging, and hugging led to kissing . . .

They were both breathing heavily when he finally pulled away and poured his coffee. Their eyes met across the stainless-steel table.

She rubbed three fingers in the center of her forehead. "You first."

He antagonized her deliberately. "Chicken?"

She scowled on cue. "I'm not afraid of you, Tyler Strickland."

He lifted an eyebrow. "There was a moment last night when you looked a bit apprehensive. I believe you were tied up. Remember?"

Her cup hit the table with a clang. Her eyes narrowed. "That wasn't fear. That was horniness."

"Ah . . ." He took a long, satisfying drink. Between the hot liquid and their pointed banter, he was beginning to thaw out.

He pinned her with a glare. "You were gone when I woke up."

She took her cup to the sink, her back to him. "It seemed like a good plan at the time."

"You weren't interested in a little morning romp?"

She turned to face him. Surprisingly, her blush deepened. "Interested? Probably. But I needed some time to think."

"You women do an awful lot of that," he muttered.

She laughed, more amused than insulted. "There's a lot to be said for rational conversation, Tyler."

He picked up on her unspoken concern. "Especially when a lot of *irrational* behavior has recently transpired. Am I right?"

She shrugged uneasily. "I'm a little confused."

"Because I told you I loved you?" He stated the question calmly, but a dull ache set up in his chest.

Her smile was lopsided. "No. I love you, too."

He blinked, a roaring in his ears. A blow to the head couldn't have made him any loopier. Shelli loved him.

He dropped his cup to the counter, brown liquid slopping over the edge and nearly scalding his hand. She backed away from him, but he followed her, fighting back a smile. "Say it again."

She bit her lower lip, then sighed. "I love you."

He cupped her shoulders in his hands. Touching her resurrected an X-rated video in his brain. He swallowed hard. "You don't look entirely happy."

Her lip wobbled. "What are we going to do? I don't want you to leave the Scimitar."

He pulled her into his arms, tucking her close to his chest, holding her and saying a prayer of thanks that he hadn't ruined everything. "I'll be only thirty minutes away." He took a deep breath. "I want you, to be with you, Shelli, whatever it takes. Besides, we're assuming Tennant won't allow us to work together, and we haven't even asked him yet. You never know."

Her face brightened. "I hadn't thought of that."

"Of course, I'm not at all sure I can work with you and not get distracted . . . now that I've seen you naked."

She tried to smack him, and he captured her hand and kissed her fingers. "You knocked me for a loop the first day we met, Shelli, and I've never recovered. If it's a choice between working together or being free to love you and be with you every night, I know which one I'll choose."

Her eyes were bright with happy tears. "I guess I can always find another right-hand man."

"Or woman," he said, only half joking.

She grinned. "Jealous, are we?"

"I'll try to be civilized if it comes to that."

"I'll count on it."

He scooped her up and twirled her in a circle. "God, I love you. Let's go somewhere hot for our next fantasy."

He was unbuttoning her clothes as he spoke, his fingers clumsy. They didn't bother to undress all the way. He laid her on the end of the long countertop, ignoring her screech when the chilly metal surface made contact with bare skin.

He unzipped his jeans and shoved them down. The table was narrow, so getting on top of Shelli was a trick. That and the fact that she was laughing hard enough to make the whole damn thing shake.

He entered her gently, shocked anew by the biting pleasure. The frantic pace of the night before was unnecessary. He loved her with slow, steady thrusts, letting the heat build. And when they both tumbled into orgasm, he whispered her name.

When their breathing had steadied and he became conscious of their surroundings once again, he sighed. "It's a good thing Sebastian Tennant can't see us now."

Shock flitted across her face. "I forgot to tell you. He and I spoke on the phone earlier. The main roads have been cleared down in the valley. He's sending a snowplow and a four-wheel drive to rescue us." She sighed. "I suppose it was inevitable, but I'm kind of sad. It was a sweet fantasy while it lasted."

He kissed her cheek. "As far as I'm concerned, Shelli, it's just getting started." And later that morning . . . in an entirely different suite . . . he proved his point.

Suite
Revenge

CHAPTER ONE

Emily Drake smoothed the skirt of her tomato-red DKNY power suit and crossed her legs. Ten seconds later she uncrossed them, her grandmother's warning about varicose veins ringing in her ears. Emily wasn't really a "cross your legs at the ankle" kind of woman, but the alternative, feet flat on the floor, was darned uncomfortable. She peered at her feet and willed them to be still. They looked quite fetching, if she did say so herself. Black leather pumps, pointed toes, four-inch heels, just a hint of gold trim—enough to be stylish without sliding over the line into gaudy. Ferragamos, 75 percent off at Neiman Marcus in Atlanta. Business trips were great.

She sighed and fidgeted in her padded folding chair. She'd deliberately arrived early in order to get a front-row seat, but now she was paying for that privilege with a long, tedious wait. Patience wasn't normally her strong suit, and today, with so much at stake, her antsiness had increased tenfold.

She picked up her brochure and studied it, not that she hadn't memorized its contents, but she needed something to keep her hands occupied. It was either that or start biting her nails, a nasty habit she'd finally managed to break during her freshman year in college. Her roommate, Jenna, had been—and still was—the ultimate fashionista, and her stylish perfection in everything from undies to manicures had eventually shamed Emily into giving her own hands some TLC.

Jenna would be proud of Emily's look today. In fact, Emily would have loved Jenna to be sitting beside her for moral support. But then again, if this wild plan failed, Emily didn't want any more witnesses than necessary.

The front of the heavy vellum program was simple and elegant, its gold lettering done in flowing script. *The Knoxville Supporters of Children's Hospital proudly present our first annual Bachelors' Auction.* And in smaller type: *All proceeds will directly benefit the construction of the new pediatric oncology wing.* She flipped to page two, a shiny crimson fingernail sliding down the page to the one name that mattered. Bachelor #12—Luke Marshall. Pages three and four offered thumbnail bios of the eligible men. Luke's paragraph was at the very bottom of the last page.

She read it for the fifth time.

Luke Marshall is a native son of Knoxville. After graduating from the University of Tennessee with a degree in criminal justice, Mr. Marshall attended law school at Emory University in Atlanta. He worked for a number of years at the firm of Bentley and Kendrick in Atlanta, before returning to Knoxville and opening the doors of his own practice in 2000. Mr. Marshall enjoys hiking and snow skiing in his spare time. He is on the board of the Boys and Girls Club as well as the Knoxville Symphony.

Emily sighed. Too bad there weren't pictures. Instead, the organizers had settled for hanging twelve large posters around the room. The images of the dozen men were enough to make any female's heart go pitter-patter, but the only photo that stirred her blood and spiked her pulse was the one of Bachelor #12.

She didn't really need the larger than life image as a reminder. Though it had been five years since she'd last seen Luke Marshall face-to-face, she could describe him in intimate detail. Dark black hair with the hint of a wave if he waited too long between haircuts. Piercing gray eyes, always fiercely intelligent, glinting with humor on occasion. Broad shoulders, lean hips, a loose, rangy walk, and bronzed skin that tanned easily. The groove in his right cheek was almost, but not quite, a dimple. Luke Marshall was not whimsical enough to carry off a dimple. He was more of a "go ahead, make my day" sort of guy. Tough, focused, not the kind to put up with crap from anyone. A straight shooter. Emily winced, remembering with painful clarity her firsthand knowledge of that final characteristic.

Luke was a man's man, emulated by many, feared by some, respected by all. The other eleven bachelors paled in comparison.

Of course, she might be just the tiniest bit prejudiced. Emily Drake had been in love with Luke Marshall since she was fourteen. A decade and a half later, she was still unable to shake her aggravating, nonwavering fascination with the man who broke her heart.

It didn't help that her most recent memory of him involved the two of them dancing to a romantic string quartet in the lovely garden of a home on the banks of the Tennessee River. Five years ago her brother, Brad, had just married his ladylove, and Luke, as lifelong friend of the groom, had served as best man. Emily had been a bridesmaid, and despite the fact that she looked atrocious in lavender and pink, Luke had smiled and asked her to dance.

It was on that warm, delightful summer evening that she fully comprehended the extent of her problem. She had never, ever gotten over Luke Marshall.

A lady in silver sequins took the seat beside her. Emily thought the anorexic-looking woman's dress was a tad over the top, but as long as she was there to ogle only Bachelors #1 through #11, Emily had no beef with her.

Emily tried crossing her feet at the ankle and snagged her stocking on a rough screw in the chair leg. Muttering under her breath, she fished a bottle of clear polish from her purse and dotted the tiny tear. The woman in sequins looked down her nose, but Emily wasn't about to risk losing her coveted seat for a quick ladylike trip to the restroom. Let her stare.

She glanced at her watch. Six forty-five p.m. Only fifteen minutes to go. Her mouth was dry, and she could hear her heart beating in her ears. She flipped open her checkbook and verified the balance one last time. Two hefty deposits, her commissions on recent house sales, made the bottom line reassuringly sound. That, and her home-equity line at the bank, should be enough to pull off this coup. Luke Marshall wouldn't know what hit him.

She flipped open her compact and checked her lipstick. She was having a good-hair day, thank God. Her new ash-and-gold highlights made her boring brown hair a bit snazzier, though she was still getting used to the fact that Karla at the Hair Loft had cut the back far shorter than usual.

She glanced behind her casually, scanning the rapidly filling rows. She didn't really expect to recognize anyone. She'd lived in Nashville for the last six years, and though she still had many friends in Knoxville, they weren't likely to be attending an auction, testosterone laden or otherwise.

The one person she did know quite well was Luke's older sister, Pamela. Pamela was on the hospital's fund-raising board and was probably the only human in the world capable of convincing the very private Luke Marshall to strut his stuff in front of a roomful of women. Thankfully for Emily, Pamela was in the advanced stages of pregnancy and, per her doctor's orders, was home with her feet up. Which meant there would be no one to carry tales if this plan crashed and burned.

The house lights dimmed, and Emily's heart fluttered. Her palms were damp. She wiped them surreptitiously on her hips. She was vaguely aware that an emcee was doing the usual welcome shtick, but it was hard to hear over the buzzing in her ears. What had seemed like a good idea three weeks ago suddenly seemed the height of insanity.

Spotlights hit the catwalk extending into the middle of the

room. Pulsing, sensual music flowed from the enormous speakers flanking the stage. There was a moment's pregnant pause, and then Bachelor #1 strolled forward, his tux jacket tossed casually over his shoulder, suspended by a thumb. Even through his shirt you could see his abs. Impressive. He was a Tennessee football legend, Heisman Trophy winner, now a star in the world of pro football. He was tall and muscular, with that "aw shucks, ma'am" thing going on that Southern women loved. His lazy grin promised lots of fun for some lucky winner.

The bidding started out slowly and then escalated as the women in the audience got past their inhibitions and embraced the evening's dual purpose of philanthropy and entertainment. Strolling waiters handed out champagne flutes. Emily drained two and then stopped herself. A tipsy Emily wouldn't be a pretty sight, and she needed a clear head.

As the bidding slowed, the auctioneer cajoled the audience. Moments later, his voice boomed. "Sold . . . to the pretty lady in the blue dress for $5,600."

Emily sat back and sighed. Luke would go for far more than that.

Slowly, inevitably, the evening ground on. The next seven bachelors included a country-music star, a TV personality, a surgeon, a Marine, two well-known local businessmen, and a championship-winning pro bull rider. That raised a few eyebrows until the emcee explained that he was the mayor's brother, dragged in from Wyoming to help out.

At nine o'clock, the lights went up again for a brief intermission. Emily glanced at her watch. It was taking roughly fifteen minutes per bachelor. At this rate, she'd be able to qualify for an AARP card before the evening was over. She left her program to mark her seat and went to brave the line at the bathroom. After taking care of business, she grabbed a spot at the sink and dabbed her face with a cool, damp paper towel. The woman staring back at her from the mirror was almost a stranger. Her big brown eyes looked more scared than sensuous. She practiced pouting her lips. Great . . . now she resembled a rabid Pekingese. In heat.

Morose, hyped up on champagne and nerves, she returned to her seat. The room went dark for a second time, and the auction resumed. The next three guys were a blur. They could have been a Clooney, Pitt, Depp trifecta, and she wouldn't have batted an eye.

When the emcee finally announced Bachelor #12, Emily's tongue went thick, and she was pretty sure her hands were paralyzed. The bidding started off right away. She picked out at least three dominant voices, one behind her, one to the right, and the other sounding almost all the way in the back. She listened, dazed, as the bid bounced past four thousand and then rocketed to six. It slowed then, sliding upward in increments of $100. Several disappointed women dropped out at seven, leaving only a couple of determined bidders.

Emily listened, stunned, as the two other women doggedly upped the price. Evidently they got cold feet around the eight thousand mark. They began inching forward by measly fifties. There was a distinct lull at $8500. The large room had fallen silent, caught up in the drama of the moment. One of the women stood up, the one nearest Emily. Her voice trembled slightly as she called out, "Eight thousand, five hundred, and seventy-five dollars."

Even the auctioneer fell silent for a split second. Emily leaped to her feet, "carpe diem"-ing for all she was worth. Her legs were steady and hands dry. Miraculously, her tongue and her lips cooperated as she enunciated loudly, but with elegant diction, "Ten thousand dollars."

Luke Marshall was having a pisser of a day. He'd lost a heartbreaking child-custody case earlier that morning. One of his favorite stocks had tanked after an SEC investigation was announced, and now he was about to be purchased lock, stock, and barrel by a wealthy nutcase. He kept his casual smile with difficulty. The damned spotlights were blinding him. He couldn't even see the end of the catwalk, and he hoped like hell he wasn't about to go tumbling into the audience.

The collective perfumed aroma of several hundred women hovered in the air, and the estrogen levels in the large darkened space were off the charts. That last outrageous bid had plunged the room into shocked silence. The skin on the back of his neck tightened as he wondered what kind of wacko dropped ten grand for a couple of platonic dates.

The auctioneer recovered from his momentary paralysis. "Do I hear ten five . . . ten one?"

The silence deepened. Luke's stomach dropped and not in that good way you get on the crest of a roller coaster. The two women who had doggedly warred back and forth remained silent. Only the last bid stood, from the oddly familiar voice. It puzzled him, that flash of recognition. Adrienne? Nah . . . she'd rather feed him to the wolves. Their breakup hadn't been pretty.

Then who? He liked a mystery as much as the next guy, but under these circumstances, he was wishing he'd gotten engaged the day before—or broken both legs. Anything to get out of this stupid situation unscathed.

The auctioneer's pause went on for five minutes. Or at least that's how it seemed. Luke resisted the urge to loosen his collar. Waiting backstage had been excruciating. At least half of the bachelors were extroverts having the time of their lives. Luke couldn't relate. This was worse than showing up in court in your underwear. Not that he'd ever done that. At least not in reality. All during law school and several years after, he'd suffered through that nightmare with aggravating regularity.

He was ready to blurt out an extremely inappropriate and hostile comment when the blessed words finally rang out . . . "Sold . . . to the lady in red . . . for ten thousand dollars."

Emily hovered near the stage with her eleven counterparts, all of whom were eager to go back and meet their newly purchased booty, pardon the pun. She rehearsed her prepared speech in her head. It didn't sound insane, did it? Thinking about the check she had just written made her knees weak, so she concentrated on Luke instead. Bad idea. Thinking about Luke only set her nerves on edge again. She had to be out of her mind.

One of the event coordinators ushered the group of benevolent ladies to a nicely furnished room nearby. A buffet table to one side held a generous assortment of hors d'oeuvres. Bachelors queued at an open bar.

But Emily had eyes for only one man—the one leaning against a support beam, his expression equal parts wary and impatient. He didn't see her at first because she was lingering at the back of the group. She squared her shoulders and took a deep breath. Showtime.

She crossed the room rapidly and stopped in front of him. "Hello, Luke," she said with a cool, sophisticated smile that she'd copied from Angelina Jolie. "Long time no see. You look very handsome."

His eyes had widened fractionally when he recognized her, and she could swear a thread of relief momentarily darkened his blue eyes. But then his usual analytical thought processes must have kicked in, because she could see the curious, puzzled calculation in his steady gaze.

His hands were shoved in his pockets, and his bow tie hung loose, his shirt collar open to reveal a hint of dark chest hair. His voice was low and gravelly. "Hello, Emily. Quite a surprise. What on earth prompted this?"

Well, that was cutting to the chase. She shrugged casually, this time a move she'd learned from Sharon Stone. Late-night cable channels came in very handy sometimes. "I heard your name. It's for a good cause. Kind of a lark, I guess you could say. I always donated to the hospital when I lived in Knoxville. So I owed them a few back payments. No big deal." Her grin was meant to be three parts friendly and one part flirtatious. She had no idea if she was pulling it off. She'd always been lousy at fractions.

His lips twitched, amusement dancing in his eyes. "I'm flattered."

She tugged at the end of his tie, drawing it loose and tucking it in his breast pocket. "You would have brought in top dollar, even without my bid."

His cheekbones darkened in an endearing flush. She took pity on him. "I'm starved. Let's grab something before the food's all gone."

They filled their plates, snagged a tiny round table, and chatted lazily over shrimp cocktail, baked Brie, and fresh fruit. It was like old times, and they reminisced without apology. Emily felt her defenses wavering and shored them up. No time to abandon the plan now.

Luke wiped his mouth and settled back in his chair. "How are Brad and Stacy getting along?"

"You'd probably know better than me. The last time I was home was for Mother's Day weekend. At that point they were bickering over how to decorate the new sunroom addition and whether or not they could afford a membership to the country club."

Luke shook his head. "I never thought I'd see the day when my macho buddy, Brad, got henpecked. And liked it."

Emily frowned. "Just because you're anti-marriage doesn't mean the rest of the world is."

"Hey," he said, holding up his hands with a frown. "Innocent until proven guilty. Who said I'm anti-marriage?"

"The facts speak for themselves," she said primly. "You're thirty-three years old, and you've never even been engaged."

"I've concentrated on my career."

"You live in a condo, not a house."

"I don't have time for yard work."

"You date exotic women."

He choked out a laugh. "Define exotic."

"You know . . . big boobs, blond hair . . ."

"Chelsea was a circuit-court judge."

"What about Tammy?"

She had him there. Everyone knew that Tammy had done a spread in *Penthouse* as a college coed. He shrugged, his smile cooling. "That was more of a recreational relationship."

"Oh, is *that* what they're calling it now . . ."

He unfastened another button on his shirt. No fair. Didn't he know he was distracting her from the subject at hand? She focused on her shrimp, taking a big bite and wiping cocktail sauce from her chin.

He handed her a clean napkin. "You seem to know a lot about my dating life. Been discussing me with Brad?"

"Nonsense. It's usually Mom who tells me your latest sexcapades. She follows the society column in the paper religiously, and your name crops up surprisingly often. I'm not criticizing. I'm merely pointing out how you are clearly anti-marriage. At least Brad has matured enough to want the important things in life."

"And what would those be?" he asked, his eyes narrowed.

She smiled gently. "Monogamy. Children. A deep, loving, reciprocal relationship."

"And you would know about these things because . . . ?"

"I'm way younger than you," she said blithely. "I've got plenty of time."

His brows drew together, and she got a serious jolt of satisfaction from the knowledge that she had ticked him off.

Luke took a long slug of his imported beer. "Four years is nothing."

"That's not what you used to think."

Luke had stepped into the trap without the slightest hint of warning. Shit. So that's what this was all about. "Emily," he said, drawing on his vastly depleted store of patience, "you were a kid. I was getting ready to go off to college. What did you expect me to do . . . give you a ring? God, it was embarrassing enough that Brad knew what was going on. He razzed me like crazy."

"You hurt my feelings," she said quietly. "I was in love with you. You broke my heart."

"You were fourteen," he said a little too loudly, then lowered his voice when curious heads turned in their direction. "You had a crush."

"It was very real to me," she said with dignity.

He propped his elbows on the table and dropped his head on his hands. "So that's what this is all about? Settling an old score?"

"Of course not."

He looked up at her. "Then what, Emily? What do you want from me?"

She felt her confidence in her outlandish scheme waver. He seemed genuinely perplexed, and she wasn't sure she had a suitable answer to give him.

She glanced at her watch. "It's late, and Mom and Dad will be wondering where I am. I haven't visited them enough in the last few months." She paused. "I want to finish this discussion, but how about dinner tomorrow night?"

His face cleared, and he grinned. "Sure, but this won't be your ten-grand date. I'll take you to Club LeConte. My treat."

She started to protest, and he held up a hand. "No argument. I have a feeling that my bottom line is a bit better than yours at the moment."

It was her turn to flush. Ten thousand dollars. What had she been thinking?

"Okay," she said, not meeting his teasing gaze. "I'll take you up on that."

Dressing for a date that wasn't quite a date required a considerable amount of serious thought. Last night she'd wanted to project the image of a confident businesswoman, someone who could afford to shell out ten grand without blinking. Okay, she'd blinked, but she'd also seen something in Luke's silvery gray eyes that bolstered her confidence. He'd looked at her the way men look at attractive women. And she had liked it. A lot.

But tonight was the second phase of her plan. She needed feminine allure and a healthy dose of sex appeal. Pheromones . . . gut level sensuality. She glanced in the mirror and adjusted the narrow rhinestone straps of her black silk cocktail dress. Luke Marshall was in big trouble.

Luke dictated a few notes into a recorder and lapsed into silence, turning his desk chair to face the window. He might as well have stayed home today. All he'd been able to think about was why Emily Drake, beautiful, sexy, volatile Emily Drake, had spent ten thousand dollars to win a date with a guy who'd have been happy to take her out if she had only asked.

He'd known Emily since she was an infant. He vividly remembered his four-year-old self commiserating with his buddy Brad about the squalling addition to the Drake household. Both boys had been in turn fascinated and disgusted with the tiny baby who drew such attention just by opening her mouth.

Over the years, the fascination and disgust factors had changed in direct proportion to the boys' ages. At eight, they had enjoyed showing little Emily all sorts of ways to get into trouble. At twelve, they'd been way too cool to want an eight-year-old tagging along. At eighteen, Luke's adolescent self had been shamefully aware of his own fascination with pretty little Emily. She'd been getting ready to enter high school. He'd been preparing for college.

When she made it clear that she had a crush on him, he'd been flattered and then worried. Emily was unusually mature for her age, both physically and emotionally, and he'd found himself spending more time in her company than was wise. She was a good listener, and he'd been comfortable enough with her to share his fledgling dreams and hopes for the future. What he hadn't realized until it was almost too late was that Emily saw him as boyfriend material.

When they nearly kissed one hot summer afternoon, he panicked and lashed out. His sarcastic, unnecessarily cruel rejection had wiped the happy, uncomplicated smile from her face and replaced it with dark-eyed misery. Though he'd tried, he'd never been entirely able to erase that disastrous day from his memory.

Over the years they'd seen each other from time to time: Thanksgiving, Christmas, when he and Brad had graduated from UT, a few weeks later when he and his parents joined the Drakes for Emily's high school graduation. After that, the times in between "Emily sightings" had stretched out longer and longer. He'd missed her college graduation only because he'd been in the hospital recovering from an emergency appendectomy. Brad said she'd gotten teary when she heard he wasn't coming. He'd felt like a worm for disappointing her, but he'd been helpless to do anything about it. He wasn't Superman.

When they danced at Brad's wedding, he'd been stunned at the beautiful young woman she had become. Poised, obviously happy with her life. He'd tasted the bitterness of regret that day and told himself that the insistent hum of sexual attraction deep in his gut was a mixture of nostalgia and a healthy male's response to a gorgeous woman. He'd almost convinced himself, too.

But he had been dating Chelsea at the time, and Emily had recently moved to Nashville. The timing was all wrong, and he'd let her slip away again.

Now Emily herself had initiated a meeting, a very intriguing meeting. The rules of the auction had been communicated to each of the bachelors in advance. The winning bidder won at least two dates with the man of her choice, one an outing planned by the woman and a second date planned by the bachelor.

Luke wondered if he could convince her to slip away with him for a weekend at the beach. He had a rental property north of

Charleston that was cozy and right on the water. His groin tight-ened as he contemplated fun in the sun with Emily Drake. All that creamy skin would need lots of sunscreen. A gentleman needed to look out for his lady's well-being, even if it meant spending hours rubbing cream on all those places she couldn't reach . . . and if she returned the favor . . .

The pleasant fantasy ground to a nasty halt when his secretary tapped on his door. "Mr. Marshall, your three o'clock is here."

Emily pasted a smile on her face and tamped down the urge to scream. She knew Luke and her parents were close, but did they really have to chat for an hour? If she'd stayed at a hotel, things would have been infinitely easier. But her mother would have had a hissy fit, not understanding one iota her daughter's need for pri-vacy. And as a result, Emily's nerves were jumping all over the place.

"Um, Luke, don't we have reservations?"

Luke glanced at his watch and jumped to his feet. "Sorry, Emily . . . Yeah. We'd better go."

After a round of good-byes, they were finally in Luke's car. It was a hybrid SUV, just the kind of vehicle to appeal to him, Emily thought with a private smile. Luke had always demonstrated an overdeveloped sense of responsibility, but he did love his luxury items.

The restaurant, on an upper floor of a downtown building overlooking the city, was elegant and intimate, despite being booked almost to capacity. An attentive host showed them to a corner table behind a wall of ferns, where it was cozy and quiet.

Luke consulted her and then ordered for both of them, includ-ing a bottle of wine. The steward poured two glasses and excused himself.

Emily smiled. "Mom and Dad were tickled pink to see you. They love you like one of their own, you know."

Luke leaned back in his chair and grinned. "We had some great times at your house . . . throwing footballs till our arms ached so we could be quarterbacks someday. Working on Eagle Scout projects . . ."

"Looking at *Penthouse* magazines in the back of the garage."

"You knew about that?"

"I'll have you know I was insecure about my chest for years because of you and your girlie magazines."

He tilted his head, his eyes lingering on her modest cleavage. His intimate smile made her stomach do flip-flops. "Those women had nothing on you, Emily . . . Maybe when you were twelve, but certainly not now."

Though he wasn't wearing a tux tonight, he looked equally fabulous in a dark suit. "Smooth-tongued lawyers," she said, shaking her head. "Do they teach you that stuff in law school?"

He chuckled. "I'm being sincere. You are one beautiful woman, Emily Drake."

Her grin was wry. "Then I guess I should say thank you."

By the time they finished dessert, darkness had fallen. The lights of the city blinked and sparkled like stars. Emily sighed inwardly. As much as she loved living in Nashville, she missed home. Brad and Stacy would be having babies before too long. She wanted to be around for that.

But she'd been gone for six years, and she wondered if she could bear watching Luke date a string of fascinating women. At the moment he was free of entanglements. Otherwise he would never have participated in the auction. She knew him that well. But a man like Luke wouldn't be without female companionship for long. Perhaps if her plan worked, she could put behind her, once and for all, this silly, inconvenient crush she had on her brother's best friend.

Luke drained his wineglass. "Okay, Emily. We've exhausted all the family gossip, both yours and mine. We've rehashed old times. I've told you about my job and you've done the same. So out with it . . . Why the grand gesture? What on earth prompted you to spend ten thousand dollars at a bachelor auction? What do you want from me? I've spent the better part of the last twenty-four hours trying to figure it out, and I've come up with zip. My curiosity is killing me.'"

She shifted a small pile of bread crumbs with her knife. The expression on his face was amusement, but she detected a layer of the same wariness she had first noticed last night.

She put down the knife and reached across the table, taking his hands. He looked a bit surprised, but he twined his fingers with hers. She glanced around to make sure no waiter was in earshot. Leaning forward and lowering her voice, she whispered her request. "I want you to have sex with me, Luke."

CHAPTER TWO

*L*uke prided himself on his unflappability in the court-room. He'd faced down hostile criminals and skeptical judges without blinking. But at the moment there was a loud buzzing in his ears, and the dinner he'd recently consumed was rolling in his stomach like the deck of the Titanic.

He swallowed and smiled weakly, wondering if he looked as shocked as he felt. Not that he hadn't been propositioned by a beautiful woman before. He had . . . on several occasions. But those situations were totally different. Those women weren't little Emily. He had to stop thinking of her that way. She was all grown up. And then some. That dress she was wearing clung to her slim feminine curves in a way that made a man's thoughts go straight to the bedroom.

He'd tried not to notice. This was Brad's little sister, after all. But her short fluffy hair was all waves and curls, and except for a few loose tendrils, the nape of her neck was bare, practically begging for a man's lips.

He glanced at her wine goblet, trying to remember exactly how many glasses she'd consumed.

She sat back and released his hands, her lips curved in a faint smile, a hint of challenge in her warm brown eyes. "I'm not drunk, Luke."

He managed a rough laugh. "I never said you were."

She inhaled and exhaled, and the small diamond solitaire she wore on a slender gold chain caught the light in a flash of colored sparks. The delicate stone hung suspended at the beginning of her cleavage. Sex with Emily Drake . . . Hot, sweaty, incredible sex with Emily Drake . . .

"Why?" he stuttered. Every ounce of polished self-possession he'd ever claimed to have had disappeared without a trace. He was stunned.

And for the first time, she seemed a bit uneasy, too. She scanned the room, her delicate features in profile as she avoided looking at him. He took the hint, lifting a hand to summon the waiter with their check.

After dropping a handful of twenties on the table, he pressed again. "Why, Emily? This is no time to clam up. You can't drop a bomb like that without some explanation."

She winced. "Could we go somewhere more private?"

He sighed, knowing he'd have to wait a while longer to satisfy his curiosity. "Sure. How about the river walk?"

Silence reigned during the short time it took them to drive the half mile down the hill and park the car. One of the more popular restaurants on the river was extremely crowded, so they spent several minutes finding a parking space. But the river walk itself was fairly empty, just the occasional jogger and one young couple pushing a fancy European-style baby carriage.

They strolled in silence for a bit. The colored lights from the bridges above reflected in the dark, murky water. A gentle breeze carried a whiff of dead fish, and Luke laughed when Emily wrinkled her nose.

They walked shoulder to shoulder, but not touching. Finally, he lost patience and ushered her toward an iron bench. He spread his jacket in case the seat was damp and after she was seated, joined her.

He tapped her knee, resisting the temptation to stroke it.

"Okay, Emily. Enough mysterious silence. I think I deserve an answer to my question. Why do you want to have sex with me?"

She smiled, her eyes hard to read in the dim light. "Isn't that a silly question? You're handsome and successful, Luke Marshall. What woman wouldn't want to have sex with you?"

He almost smiled but held back, not wanting to encourage her stall tactics. "Quit blowing smoke up my ass. Tell me the truth."

She nibbled her thumbnail for half a second before muttering something indecipherable and clasping her two hands tightly in her lap. "It's not that big a deal, really."

"Then you should be able to tell me." His brain had assessed and discarded all sorts of possibilities, but none held up under cross-examination. The only remotely plausible scenario he'd come up with was that she'd discovered she was a lesbian and she wanted his sperm to make a baby.

He'd be flattered about the sperm thing if he weren't crushed by the idea that she didn't like men . . . or rather him. He blurted it out with an appalling lack of forethought. "Are you a lesbian, Emily?"

She choked, and he had to slap her on the back until she could breathe again. It wasn't dark enough to conceal the heated combination of shock and insult on her face. "A lesbian?" Her voice went up several octaves.

He shrugged uneasily. "I thought you might want my sperm. You know . . . for a baby."

Her eyes narrowed. "I'm sure you have impressive . . . sperm, Luke. But no . . . thanks."

"Then what?" He was genuinely perplexed.

She hissed in annoyance at his apparent obtuseness. With an incredibly sexy, feminine grace, she kicked off her strappy sandals and propped her feet on the railing that separated the river walk from the tumble of brush below them that led to the water's edge. She was bare legged, and the sleek lines of her calves entranced him. He imagined those legs wrapped around his waist.

She sighed, her face toward the river. The lift of her chin drew attention to the curve of her throat. "It's really very simple."

He waited for her to continue.

After a couple of seconds fraught with his own rampant curiosity and her almost palpable nervousness, she finally spoke. "Ever since I had that stupid crush on you, I've done this weird thing where I compare the men I'm with to that old you I used to know. I think it started when you rejected me so horribly, and it marked me somehow. Maybe left me in some kind of adolescent time warp. I know that no man could possibly be as perfect as the "Luke" memories I've harbored over the years. I was simply hung up on a teenage girl's fantasy. But I can't seem to get past it, and I'm tired of finding nice guys who don't measure up to this impossible yardstick."

"And sex with me is your solution?"

She half turned to face him, her expression eager. "Exactly. Maybe part of the problem is that I wanted you because I couldn't have you. But if we have sex, you won't be unattainable anymore. And the sex is bound to be normal. You know . . . not violins and fireworks. My psyche will once and for all get the message that Luke Marshall is a guy like every other guy, and I'll finally be free of you. I'll have closure."

Luke leaned forward, his elbows on his knees, his head in his hands. He had to admit that all the other times he'd been propositioned were a hell of a lot better on his ego than this one. Emily didn't want to go to bed with him because he was some kind of superstud bachelor. She wanted ho-hum sex. To prove a point. To break the curse. To make it possible for her to hook up with another guy.

He didn't know whether to laugh or cry. His masculine pride was pretty much in the toilet. "Let me get this straight. You think that because you've cherished some silly memory of me, that if we have bad sex, you'll be able to move on."

She patted his shoulder. "It doesn't have to be bad sex, Luke. Just . . . you know . . . average."

His anger began to boil, and he sat up. "And what did the ten thousand dollars have to do with all this?"

She hesitated. "Well, I was afraid if I asked you outright, you might refuse. I thought if you knew I had spent all that money to have a date with you, you might feel an obligation to help me."

Surprisingly, he wanted to laugh. It was pretty naive to reveal your trump card so easily. Especially to a man trained to spot weakness. He kept his voice deliberately even. "The only obligation I have is to accompany you on two platonic dates. The rules were clear about that." She deserved to sweat for a moment. She'd certainly turned his world upside down in the last twenty-four hours.

Her face crumpled. "But, Luke, surely this isn't so much to ask. We've known each other forever. And when it's over, I'll be back in Nashville. There won't be any awkward encounters."

God. She was really serious. She actually believed the nonsense she was spouting. He ran a hand through his hair, frustrated and surprisingly horny. He was male, after all. It was hard for a guy to have a theoretical discussion about sex and not respond to the idea on some visceral level.

His silence must have worried her, because she started talking—chattering actually. "Don't say no right off, Luke. Sleep on the idea, at least. I know I sprang it on you out of nowhere. I'm driving back to Nashville in the morning, but you can call me anytime. My cell phone is almost always on and I—"

He interrupted her, not caring that it was rude. "What if we find each other repulsive in bed?"

Her jaw dropped and she let out a little gasp. Her eyes widened. "Repulsive? Why would you say that? We wouldn't . . . would we? Would you?"

He had the strangest notion that he'd hurt her feelings, and his conscience pricked. Why was he being such an asshole?

He slid his right arm behind her shoulders along the top of the bench, not quite touching all that alluring bare skin. "Perhaps we should test the waters," he said huskily. And then Luke

Marshall—analytical, careful, never impulsive Luke Marshall—took a gamble.

Emily's heart stopped when Luke's firm, warm lips touched hers. In the distance an angel choir started singing the "Hallelujah Chorus." At some level she was conscious of his big hands and strong arms folding her close to his chest, but that delicious fact was overwhelmed by the shocking reality of his mouth on hers. If she'd known at fourteen what it was like to kiss Luke Marshall, she'd have gone into a nunnery when he'd dumped her.

Well, that wasn't fair, she thought hazily as his tongue gently eased between her lips and played with hers. Luke hadn't dumped her. She hadn't been his to be dumped. Some rational part of her brain tried to follow that train of thought, but it derailed when his lips moved to the sensitive skin beneath her ear.

He murmured against her throat, leaving little tingles of delight where his muttered words brushed her skin.

"You're beautiful, little Emily."

"I'm five-foot-nine," she croaked. "Not so little."

His mouth returned to hers, not quite so gentle this time. Her hands were clenched at his shoulders, gripping handfuls of starched cotton. He was devouring her, not a concept she had any personal experience with before tonight, but she recognized it in action.

His hand closed over her breast, and she cried out, genuinely shocked at the rush of pleasure the simple action evoked.

Her fingers trembled on his buttons, awkwardly tugging and straining at them until she could touch his chest. His chest. Sweet holy Hannah. Her fingernails raked his skin just for the sheer pleasure of it. She heard him groan, and she pressed closer, sliding her arms around his neck. She was kissing Luke Marshall. If it weren't so incredibly wonderful, it might have seemed surreal.

She could hear the roughness of his breathing, feel his heartbeat slamming in his chest. He smelled like warm, virile male. He tasted like everything she hadn't known she craved.

A tugboat pushing a barge on the river let out a loud, deep blast of its horn. Nearby ducks scattered in a flurry of raucous quacking. Emily and Luke jerked apart in unison and stared at each other in dismay.

Luke buttoned his shirt with fingers that were suspiciously unsteady. He cleared his throat. "Well, I guess repulsive won't be a problem."

Emily had been back in Nashville for three days before she heard a word from the definitely nonrepulsive Luke Marshall. She should be mad at him for making her wait, but if their kiss had rattled him even a fraction as much as it had her, it was no wonder he was taking his time about giving her an answer.

He'd taken her home rather abruptly at the end of their non-date evening. The atmosphere in the car on the way home had been tense and awkward. Ever the gentleman, he had walked her to the door. But there had been no good-night kiss. She refused to admit she was disappointed. If she started romanticizing that spontaneous kiss by the river, she'd be back where she started. Infatuated with Luke and unable to summon up even a tenth as much interest in any other man.

When her cell phone rang Wednesday afternoon, she had finished working out and was just stepping out of the shower at the gym. Luke must have heard something in her voice. How could he possibly know she was mostly nude? She tucked her towel more firmly beneath her arms, juggling the phone with damp hands.

"What's up?" she answered cheerfully, grateful for Caller ID.

"Why are you breathing funny?" he demanded.

She sighed. "I'm at the gym."

"Did I interrupt something?"

"I just got out of the shower."

There was dead silence on his end of the line, and her face turned red. Good lord, this was pathetic. She cleared her throat. "How are you, Luke?"

"You know how I am." The teasing note in his voice should have warned her. "I'm not repulsive. I'm thinking about putting it on my business cards."

And just that quickly she flashed back to the feel of his lips on her bare skin. Her pulse jumped and accelerated despite the cooldown she'd done after cardio. "Very funny, Marshall. Are you calling for a reason, or just to keep me standing here in a towel?"

She could almost hear him grin. "Not fair, little Emily. Now you're bringing back memories of all those *Penthouses.*"

She laughed softly in spite of herself, feeling the earth slide and shift beneath her feet. This was dangerous turf. "These are daytime minutes, Marshall. I use this phone for business."

"I thought I *was* your business, little Emily," he chided. "To the tune of ten grand."

She groaned. "Don't remind me." She looked in the mirror across the dressing room, and even from that distance could see the goofy grin on her face. She was beginning to regress to high school.

With an effort, she brought competent, professional Emily Drake back on the line. "Why are you calling, Luke?"

"Yes."

The bottom dropped out of her stomach. Her whole body trembled. "Yes. What does that mean?"

"It's an affirmative usually indicating agreement. I'm surprised you don't know the term."

His lawyer voice turned her on. She swallowed, wondering why the towel suddenly felt rough and scratchy against her breasts. "I want to be clear, Luke. Yes, what?"

He chuckled. "You want me to spell it out? On the phone? I'm pretty sure these cell connections aren't secure."

She closed her eyes, her thighs pressing together as a wave of heat settled deep in her belly. Her voice pleaded. "Yes, what?"

He sighed, and the sound carried clearly over the airwaves. It seemed to convey capitulation and anticipation in one heady cocktail. His voice dropped to a husky whisper. "Yes, Emily Drake," he said slowly. "I will most gladly have sex with you. Name the day and time."

And then he hung up on her.

It wasn't easy for a high-powered lawyer to clear his calendar for a long weekend, even when the reason was so damned tantalizing. Luke worked on autopilot, his usual urbane self on the outside, but inside a mass of hormonal, quasiadolescent, sex-obsessed uncertainty. What the hell was he doing? Brad would hunt him down and neuter him if he found out his buddy Luke was contemplating a weekend of no-holds-barred sex with little Emily.

Lawyer Luke took over, stating his case. Emily was a mature, grown woman who knew her own mind. She was free to sleep with whomever she chose. There was nothing weird or wrong or immoral about the four-year age difference between them. In the adult world, it was inconsequential.

So why did this whole idea still seem like one step away from a disaster? Perilously similar to the apple in the Garden of Eden— succulent, sweet, infinitely tempting, but with disastrous, long-reaching consequences.

He picked up his BlackBerry and punched in a series of numbers. No matter how much he avoided thinking about it, he ought to at least be man enough to admit what was really bothering him. He was damned insulted that Emily assumed sex with him would be ho-hum. He wanted to keep the adoration of the Emily who'd gazed at him with soulful, puppy-dog eyes. He wanted to have the Emily who fantasized about how wonderful he was. He sure as hell didn't want to be the man who finally convinced little Emily to move past her schoolgirl crush.

But maybe he'd won a few points with that kiss the other night. At least given her something to think about. It was kind of an egotistical thing to admit, but he liked the thought that she'd carried a torch for him all these years. He'd certainly never gotten over his affection for the sweet, funny girl who'd turned into such a beautiful, poised woman.

Dancing with her at Brad's wedding had been an eye-opener. He'd been swamped with a mixture of nostalgia and attraction that had caught him off guard. Chelsea had been his date for the wedding, for Pete's sake. And Luke had come within a hairbreadth of suggesting that he and Emily slip away for some quiet time to get reacquainted. He'd actually had a boner, though Lord knows he'd done his best to make sure she didn't notice.

Truth be told, his urgent response had shamed him. He hadn't wanted Emily to think he was a jerk. In hindsight, he really ought to have been concerned about Chelsea's reaction, but the truth was a bitch. Chelsea hadn't even been on his radar that night, and six months later he and Chelsea were history. When he thought about Emily from time to time in the days and weeks that followed, the memories were bittersweet. Brad had said she was dating a doctor at Vanderbilt. She'd sold the man his house. It hurt Luke to think about the possibility of little Emily sharing the doctor's house, so it had been easier to push her out of his mind.

And it had mostly worked. Then she bought him and paid for him and propositioned him and kissed him till he thought his head would explode. Now he was in uncharted territory, scared spitless, but feeling so damned alive he wanted to shout his good fortune from the rooftops.

Even his secretary had noticed and teased him about his mood. After that he'd done his best to quit acting like a moron. But by the time the Friday of Emily's planned *date* weekend rolled around, he was so pumped up on testosterone and gut-level excitement, he was one step away from turning into a babbling idiot. Presenting a nonchalant front would be a challenge.

She insisted on picking him up. She'd driven in from Nashville the night before and stayed at a hotel. He'd hinted at joining her there, but she'd refused, pleading exhaustion.

She pulled up in front of his condo at ten sharp, her black Mazda gleaming in the morning sun. He stepped outside, carrying a duffel and a garment bag. Emily had been very specific about the gear he was supposed to bring.

He thought about kissing her, just a friendly hello, but her eyes were guarded and when she slipped her sunglasses back on, he couldn't read her expression.

He sat back in the passenger seat, feeling his responsibilities slide away like mist in the wind. God, it was great to be taking time off. He was too young to be a buttoned-up tight-ass. He had his whole life ahead of him, and if he was lucky, he might have little Emily as well.

She drove with confidence, a small Cheshire cat smile tilting her lips. That little grin made him nuts. He wanted to know what she was thinking. She'd dressed casually in slim-fitting khakis and a short-sleeved cashmere sweater that was a soft peachy pink color.

They kept their conversation on light, impersonal topics as they drove. Their tastes in books, movies, and politics were similar, and it was easy to slide into a camaraderie that was comfortable and yet undergirded with a simmering layer of sexual awareness.

They stopped for lunch at a trendy hotel bistro in downtown Asheville, North Carolina. Emily had done her homework. The food was incredible.

He speared a forkful of baked trout smothered in some kind of mango salsa. "I could die a happy man eating this."

Emily shook her head. "Mom used to say having you as Brad's best friend doubled our food budget."

"Hey," he protested. "I wasn't that bad. Growing boys need a lot of calories. And my mom couldn't boil an egg."

Emily slapped his hand when he tried to filch the last of her squash casserole. "Back off, Marshall. And don't try getting sympathy from me. Your mom spoiled you rotten, even if carryout *was* her specialty."

Luke found room for a slice of apple pie and then pronounced himself full. He wasn't even offended when Emily insisted on paying the bill. This was her weekend. His turn would come.

Back in the car, he got around to wondering about their destination. Up until this very moment it hadn't seemed important. Anywhere with Emily would be a treat. His groin tightened, and he forced himself to focus on anything other than what he and Emily would be doing in a few hours.

He reached up to loosen his collar and remembered at the last minute that he wasn't wearing a tie. His jeans and sport shirt were comfortable and hopefully appropriate for the first leg of their adventure.

He picked up the map Emily had consulted earlier and scanned it. "Where is this place we're headed?"

She glanced sideways at him and reached in the console for a brochure. "Up in the mountains. Probably about forty-five minutes from here." She handed him the pamphlet.

Luke scanned it with interest. The Scimitar Hotel. Impressive. The black line drawing on the front showed a castlelike structure. He read in silence for a minute or two and then looked up, puzzled and a little concerned. "You had to sign an agreement of nondisclosure? What the hell for?"

She shrugged, not taking her eyes off the road. "Apparently the hotel caters to the rich, the famous, the powerful, and all combinations thereof. Privacy is their obsession and their expectation."

He shook his head. "But how can they possibly expect compliance? It can't be easy to enforce."

"Read the fine print. If you're caught divulging information, you are forever banned from returning to the Scimitar Hotel or any other of the Tennant properties around the world."

He snorted. "And that's a deterrent? Gimme a break. It's a hotel, not the Dalai Lama's inner sanctum. What could possibly be so great about a hotel?"

She reached down beside her seat and handed him a second brochure. "This might convince you."

He frowned in puzzlement and started to read. His eyes skimmed the first page and he flipped to the next one—fantasy suites . . . costumes . . . props . . . adults at play . . . privacy and discretion. He wondered if he was allergic to trout. His throat seemed to be closing up.

He kept reading, fascinated, incredulous—turned on. The description of each suite was comprehensive, explicit, and damned provocative. Finally he chanced a look at his companion. She had both hands on the steering wheel, and the little smile she'd worn in the morning had disappeared.

She was nibbling her lower lip. "Well, what do you think?"

"Pull over."

That got her attention. "What?" She frowned in confusion.

He repeated his request, uncomfortably aware that it sounded more like a command. "Pull over."

They were on a noninterstate four-lane road. Emily glanced in the rearview mirror and slowed gradually, steering the car off onto a wide shoulder. She shut off the ignition and turned to face him. "Are you sick?"

He released his seat belt and hers and pulled her bodily into his lap. Her knee hit the horn. His elbow smacked painfully into the windshield. He was shaky, horny, and so close to losing control, it scared him. They were in a public place in broad daylight, and all he could think about was that he had to taste her one more time.

He kissed her hard. She whimpered. "You're making me crazy, Emily. You know that, right?" His hands skated over her cashmere-covered curves. He could feel her nipples, tight little buds just begging to be licked. "Which one?" he muttered, returning to her mouth, moving over her sweet, apple-flavored lips.

Her eyes were closed. "Which what?" Her voice was slurred, her skin flushed and damp.

"Room," he ground out, shuddering when her tongue dueled with his. "Where are you taking me?"

Her hand went to his belt buckle and he pushed it away. They couldn't afford to get arrested, not with a whole incredible weekend ahead of them. She seemed to have lost the conversational thread, not that he could blame her. He was having trouble remembering his own name.

"Emily." He tried again. His fingers skated under the edge of her sweater. The skin at her midriff was smooth and warm. "What suite? You have to tell me. Tell me now."

Her lashes fluttered open. Why had he thought her eyes were plain brown? Up close he saw amber and gold mixed in with the chocolaty irises. Her pupils were dilated. She wet her lips with her tongue. "I thought about the jail cell," she murmured, nuzzling his neck. "You know . . . for revenge. I contemplated tying you up and making you beg for mercy, because you were so cruel to me."

He got even harder, if that was possible. "I'm sorry I hurt you, honey," he said, meaning every word of it. "You were beautiful and sweet and if you'd been even two years older, I might have considered it."

She pulled back abruptly, wincing when a piece of her hair tangled with one of his buttons. "Really?"

He freed her, his grin wry. "Really. You were very appealing, even as a fourteen-year-old. You were as much my friend as Brad was, but with you there was this pesky male-female dynamic going on."

Their breathing slowed and he helped her slide back into her seat. She flipped down the visor and fixed her hair and lipstick. He watched in silence, enjoying her quick, graceful movements.

Finally, she faced him again. Her expression was pensive. "Thank you for saying that," she said quietly. "It means a lot." Her eyes darkened. "When you said those things to me that afternoon, I was so humiliated . . . and hurt. And I missed you so much when you and Brad started college."

He took her hand, sliding his fingers over the delicate bones. He sighed. "If I'd been more mature I might have found a way to discourage you without being so harsh. But I felt something for you, and it scared me . . . so I lashed out. I've always regretted it." He leaned forward and kissed her gently. It was an apology and a promise. He'd never hurt her again.

Her lips clung to his, trembling. Her eyes shone with tears. Somewhere deep inside him he felt a click, as though things in his life that had been out of whack suddenly fell into place.

He released her reluctantly. "I guess we'd better go."

She nodded as she fastened her seat belt and started the engine.

After the car had eased back into traffic, he slid his sunglasses on and fastened his own seat belt. They drove in silence for at least five miles. Then his curiosity got the better of him again. "So you never did tell me, if not the jail cell, then what? Which one of those suites is going to be ours?"

The naughty smile was back. "I'll keep you guessing for now," she said. "But I promise you'll like it. You have my guarantee."

CHAPTER THREE

*E*mily was having serious second thoughts. This was supposed to be a onetime fling with the guy who'd been her high school crush. Luke was making it a little too personal. How was she supposed to find closure if he was going to kiss her like that? Perhaps she hadn't been clear about her objective.

They wound up a long, tree-shaded road. She turned off the air-conditioning and they both rolled down their windows. The smell of honeysuckle and warm earth hung heavy in the afternoon air. But the breeze was at least a dozen degrees cooler than it had been down in the valley.

When they rounded the last curve and the hotel came into view, she and Luke gasped in unison. The Scimitar was a massive stone edifice softened only by a profusion of flowering shrubs. Though it wasn't more than five years old, the building claimed the mountaintop with all the arrogance of a centuries-old fortress.

After surrendering her keys to a uniformed attendant, Emily walked beside Luke to the heavy oak doors that stood open wide. A black-garbed gentleman murmured a greeting and directed them to registration. The female employee who checked them in offered to summon a guide to show them the fantasy suites.

Emily declined nervously. "We'll take a look later," she said, not glancing at Luke. "I think right now we'd like to go to our room."

In a very brief flurry of activity they were escorted down a cor-ridor and into their luxurious quarters. Luke tipped the bellman who had followed them with their luggage, and the door closed, leaving Emily trapped in a hotel room with a man she had known her entire life. But the old familiar Luke had morphed into a man whose hotly intent gaze made her shiver. He leaned against the door with his hands in his pockets, his smile at once hungry and anticipatory.

She wet her lips with her tongue. "Want to unpack?"

Luke frowned slightly. "You're nervous. Why?"

Damn that lawyer perspicacity. She shrugged uneasily. "I don't do stuff like this."

He cocked his head, his eyes narrowed. "And . . . ?"

"And I'm not sure it's a good idea."

He sighed, crossing the room to stretch out on the bed. That didn't help her peace of mind at all. He tucked his hands behind his head, his smile taunting. "You're chickening out."

She flipped open her overnight case and pretended to be look-ing for something. "Maybe."

The groove in his cheek deepened, and his teeth flashed white in a smile that made her knees weak. "You've spent a hell of a lot of money to back out now, little Emily. I've never taken you for a quitter."

She pointed a toothbrush at him. "I can be impulsive. It gets me into trouble sometimes."

His grin was pure devilment. "And you think this will lead to trouble?" He paused and chuckled out loud. "I sure as hell hope so."

She smiled in spite of herself. "Behave, Marshall. I'm trying to be serious here. I may have been hasty in proposing this plan."

He held out a hand, and of their own free will, her traitorous feet took her to the bed. She perched nervously by his hip.

He sat up and played with her fingers. "Relax, Emily. We're friends. We enjoy each other's company. Why don't we let the weekend unfold and see what happens? I'll follow your lead."

She knew it was a bad sign when just the touch of his hand could send her stomach into a free fall. "Okay. I can live with that."

He smiled gently and tucked her hair behind her ear, his fingertips caressing the side of her neck and making her breath hitch. "Tell me something, Emily. If you're so intent on having ho-hum, forgettable sex, why did you bring us here? I'm pretty damn sure that people remember what happens in this place."

Trust Luke to zero in on the weak spot in her plan. She winced. "Well, one of the suites I read about seemed like the perfect place to exorcise my high school fantasies."

His eyebrows lifted. "Oh? Then why didn't we take the tour? I'd like to see it. And all the rest, if you want to know the truth."

"I wanted it to be a surprise," she admitted. "And we can always take the tour tomorrow. The suites are open for two or three hours every afternoon for guests to take a look."

"So what now?"

He was leaving the ball in her court.

She stood up. "Let's take a hike."

Luke loved the outdoors, and spending a lazy summer afternoon with a beautiful woman was no hardship at all. But he was a little surprised when Emily procured a trail map from the front desk and set off like a woman on a mission. Emily, at least the Emily he thought he knew, was not an athlete. She kept herself in shape, but according to Brad, she was more champagne and room service than bugs and sweat.

The hotel staff had provided a small pack, bottled water, and trail mix to snack on if they got hungry. Emily added a Hershey's bar from her own stash. Luke followed her down the wooded trail, enjoying the view of her curvy backside in snug khaki shorts. Her long legs were slim and muscular, and she was walking at a good clip. Maybe old Brad didn't know his sister as well as he thought.

After a couple of miles, the trail began to climb steeply. They stopped for water and to catch their breath. The destination ahead was an overlook that was supposed to provide a spectacular view of the countryside.

Emily was unusually quiet, perhaps because she needed her air for breathing. Luke was accustomed to hiking, and the elevation gain was challenging but not anything out of the ordinary. When they finally reached the summit, the trail opened into a small clearing. The hillside dropped away at their feet, revealing the valley below, and in the distance, ridge after ridge of beautiful, tree-covered mountains.

Emily consulted the map and pointed. "It says that peak over there is Cold Mountain."

"Like the movie and the book?"

"I guess so."

The air was hazy with afternoon heat, but the vista was incredible. They perched on a convenient flat-topped boulder and sat in silence. Overhead, a hawk glided on the wind currents shooting up the side of the mountain.

He leaned back on his hands and absorbed the moment. Emily's profile was serene, the little half smile he was beginning to know so well tilting the corners of her mouth. He played with a damp curl at her neck. "I could get used to this. Can you imagine a house with this view?"

She nodded. "It's so peaceful."

He stroked her arm, feeling her sun-warmed skin. "We don't have to go through with your plan."

She turned abruptly. "You don't want to?" Her expression was suddenly anxious.

"*I* want to," he admitted. "But what if this changes things between us? What if it turns out to be more than we bargained for? I'm not sure I can have sex with you and keep feelings out of the equation."

A new flush, this one not heat related, colored her cheeks. She gazed out across the landscape. "If anything was going to develop between us romantically, it would have happened long before now."

"Can you be so sure about that? Maybe our timing has been wrong. Maybe we weren't ready." As he said the words, he realized the truth in them. Here . . . now . . . being with Emily seemed right. Perhaps he couldn't explain it as clearly as he felt it, but it was true.

She turned back to face him, her eyes troubled. "Don't make this more than it is, Luke. I see this as an ending, not a beginning."

A lump settled in his stomach, but he didn't protest. Maybe Emily was kidding herself. Or maybe he was. Time would tell.

He cupped her cheek with his hand, his thumb stroking her chin. "In that case, I plan to go out with a bang."

She winced theatrically. "Please tell me you didn't mean that the way it came out."

He chuckled. "Sorry. That sounded better in my head." He brushed a smudge of dirt from her cheek. He studied her intently, trying to remember the young girl she had been. "You're beautiful, Emily, inside and out." His voice was husky with a wave of emotion that surprised him. He'd never been a sentimental kind of man, but suddenly he was overwhelmed with memories. Memories of a sweet, serious young woman who had listened to every word he had to say as though he were the smartest and most interesting man in the world.

At eighteen he had accepted her adoration as his due. Now, at thirty-three, he wished he hadn't taken her girlish devotion so lightly.

He kissed her, telling himself that he had imagined all the bells and whistles earlier. Her slender arms were around his neck now, her soft breasts pressed against his chest. She was trembling. He explored her mouth lazily, enjoying the slow, gradual build to arousal. The deepening sense of expectation. Holding Emily felt like coming home.

Tenderness slipped into urgency with shocking swiftness. It

was his turn to shake. Sex never felt like this. Sex, in his experience, didn't have this edge of desperation. Was he afraid she would change her mind? Or was he afraid this trip down memory lane was going to leave him bruised and battered?

He kissed her hungrily, loving the little sounds she made, loving the feel of her beneath his fingertips. She was so responsive, it made his head reel with dizziness. He slid a hand beneath her shirt, tracing her ribs and touching her breast through her silky bra. She moaned. If the goal of this exercise was to be forgettable, they were both in trouble.

He stretched out awkwardly on the rock and pulled her on top of him. Smooth or not, the boulder was unyielding and damned uncomfortable. But when Emily nibbled from his ear down to his collarbone, he could have been reclining on a bed of nails and he wouldn't have noticed.

Her hair tickled his chin. He gripped her hips with both hands and tried to remember the last time he'd had sex outdoors. This was nuts.

He shuddered when she wiggled, causing her lower body to meld with his in interesting ways. He tried to find his voice. "Emily . . ."

She murmured something indecipherable and shifted, banging her knee on the rock. "Ouch."

Her disgruntled expression made him grin, despite the ache in his groin. "We could take this somewhere more comfortable," he suggested, wondering if he could walk back with a boner as hard as the granite beneath him.

She shifted to one side and shrieked, as suddenly, without warning, she tumbled over the edge of the rock.

For one long, agonizing, panicked second, his heart stopped, until he saw that the drop was no more than four feet. Relief made him light-headed. Emily was already picking herself up.

He slid down the small incline to join her. "Are you okay, honey?" She had a small trickle of blood on her forearm where a bush had scraped her and a rapidly purpling bruise on her shin, but those were minor. She winced as she tried to put weight on her foot. "I think I twisted my ankle when I landed."

He knelt at her feet. Her left ankle was already showing signs of swelling. When he pressed gently, she yelped.

He released her and stood up, shaking his head. "It might even be broken. We've got to get you back."

It took them several minutes to scramble up and though the underbrush at the side of the huge boulder. When they were finally on top once again, Emily was pale and breathless.

She tried a few tentative painful steps with his help.

He shook his head, reading her discomfort clearly. "You'll have to ride piggyback. There's no other choice. It's either that or leave you here while I go for help, and I'm not willing to do that."

Emily protested. "I'm too heavy. It's ridiculous."

"I've had you on top of me," he grinned, trying to coax a smile. "You're a featherweight."

She gave in reluctantly, and when he had her settled comfortably on his back, he stood up slowly and headed down the hillside.

Emily was enjoying an entirely adult fantasy. Though she had dreamed about Luke on and off for years, this particular scenario was a new one. Her legs were wrapped around his taut waist, and his hands were supporting her thighs. Her . . . well . . . you know, was pressed against his back, and every bump and jiggle produced some very interesting results.

Luke seemed to be breathing normally, and even though she expected him to stop any minute and take a break, he strode on, not appearing winded in the least. His strength and stamina were arousing, especially if she allowed herself to think about the night to come.

By the time they made it back to the hotel, they were both sweaty and tired. One of the staff trained in first aid eased off her boot and took a look. He professed it to be a sprain, with the proviso that they should get the ankle x-rayed on Monday.

Back in their room, Emily claimed first shower. Luke helped her take off her remaining boot and turned on the water, adjusting the temperature. She saw the speculation on his face and immediately nipped that one in the bud. "I am perfectly capable of undressing myself," she stated emphatically.

He looked disappointed. "Well, don't lock the door."

The hot water felt blissful. Balancing on one foot was a challenge, but she managed, even to the point of washing her hair. When she was finished, she put on one of the hotel's fluffy robes and sat on a little vanity bench to dry her hair.

She studied her face in the mirror. Her eyes were bright, and her mouth couldn't stop smiling. She looked happy and excited all at the same time. But it was time to put an end to her self-deception. She sobered, realizing that she had skated way out on thin ice. She didn't want to get past Luke Marshall and move on with her life. She was ready to fall in love with him all over again.

Luke flipped back the bedcovers and propped pillows against the headboard. He filled a plastic bag with ice and fastened it tightly, wrapping the whole thing in a towel. By the time Emily emerged from the bathroom, he had her little nest all ready. Before she could cross the room, he scooped her up and carried her to the bed, inhaling the now familiar scent of her light floral perfume.

She didn't protest, and with surprising docility, allowed him to tuck her beneath the covers and carefully drape the ice bag over her ankle. As he straightened, he realized that the lapels of her robe had gaped open. All that creamy cleavage had a mesmerizing effect on his libido. He turned away abruptly, reaching for the remote. "Relax. Get some rest. I'll clean up and maybe we can order room service."

"Not a chance."

He looked at her in confusion. Thankfully, she had covered up temptation. "What do you mean?"

"I've had to forgo the idea of dancing with you, but the chef is Cordon Bleu trained. I want the full dining experience from appetizer to dessert, even if I have to hobble up and down the halls."

"Duly noted," he said with a grin. For someone so slender, the lady was serious about her food. She must burn it off with nervous energy.

Thinking about Emily's energy took his thoughts down an unwise path, so he escaped into the bathroom. He probably needed a cold shower, but his aching muscles opted for blistering heat. He tipped his head back and let the spray pound his face and shoulders. With his eyes closed, images of Emily danced across his mental video screen. Her gamine smile, the little thrust of her chin when she was determined. The lush curves of her breasts.

His hand drifted to his cock, stroking it absentmindedly. He hoped the night ahead was going in a certain direction, but if Emily was getting cold feet, he wouldn't push her. He'd missed too many other opportunities. This time he was going to do things right. It might be his last chance.

They dined on baked chicken stuffed with spinach and feta cheese. Emily, naturally gregarious, chatted with the waiter and the wine steward as though they were old friends. Luke studied the other men's faces. They were charmed, and no wonder. Emily Drake was a fascinating woman.

He saw the wistfulness in her eyes as she watched the couples dancing. He reached across the table and touched her hand. "Maybe tomorrow night, Emily. Your ankle is already doing better. The swelling has really gone down, and it's possible the sprain isn't as bad as we first thought."

Her smile was wry. "I hope you're right. I love to dance."

Luke wasn't entirely comfortable on the dance floor. Few men of his acquaintance were. But the thought of holding Emily in his arms and moving to the unabashedly romantic music held definite appeal.

He leaned back in his chair. "So tell me about these unimpressive men you've been dating."

She blinked. "Where did that come from?"

He shrugged. "I'm curious. Why didn't the doctor measure up?"

Her eyes narrowed. "How do you know about him?" Then she huffed. "Brad. My brother has a big mouth."

"He loves you. He wants you to be happy. So I'm asking. Why not the doctor? Sounds like he looked good on paper."

She looked away for a moment, her expression pensive. Then she sighed. "That's just it. He should have been perfect. He was intelligent, handsome, kind, considerate."

"Sounds like a damned Boy Scout."

She frowned. "He was a great guy."

"But?"

"But there was no spark. He was a cerebral kind of guy, and I guess I'm more shallow than I thought. Anytime he was quiet when we were together, I had this weird feeling he was contemplating cures for terrible diseases. And there I was wondering what to wear to the hospital fund-raiser."

He chuckled. "So the doc wasn't the right one. Who else failed the test?"

She shook her head. "That's enough about my dismal love life. Believe me, it's not that interesting."

They lingered over dessert and coffee. He'd promised to let Emily call the shots, and he wondered what she was thinking. She was wearing the dress she'd had on the first time he kissed her by the river. He was pretty sure he could slip the straps from her shoulders and the whole thing would slide to the floor.

He explored that tantalizing possibility for several minutes until his body's urgent response reminded him that the evening's outcome was still up in the air. He'd better not get his hopes (or anything else) up if he wanted to keep his sanity.

It was after ten when Emily indicated she was ready to call it a night. His heart started pounding an uneven rhythm in his chest. He supported her as they made their way back to the room. She was able to put some weight on the foot now, which was a good sign.

Once inside their door, he leaned against it and watched Emily grow more nervous by increments. She was pacing from one side of the room to the other, talking a mile a minute, stream-of-consciousness stuff that required no response from him. After five minutes of that he took pity on her.

"Emily . . . honey . . . sit down and rest your foot."

She looked at him blankly and then reluctantly settled on a chaise lounge upholstered in mauve embroidered brocade. He joined her, tucking her legs to one side so he could sit. He lifted her ankles and settled them in his lap. Her dark eyes were wary, and even though she reclined at his urging, her posture was not even close to relaxed.

He ran a thumb up the length of one calf. "You brought me here to have sex, Emily. But if you've changed your mind, it's okay."

Her eyelashes flickered and his heart sank. But a guy didn't die from sexual disappointment. He'd just have to suck it up and be a man.

Her expression, usually an open book, was indecipherable. He turned his attention to her other leg, measuring its silky length with firm fingertips. Her eyes closed, and she slumped deeper into the chair cushions.

Her knees were next to receive his homage. Whoever said knees were unattractive had clearly never seen Emily's. He leaned forward and brushed a light kiss on one kneecap and then the other. Emily moaned.

Encouraged by her compliance, he moved higher, his thumbs grazing the insides of her legs. The dress was in his way, so he pushed it up, baring her to the tops of her thighs.

He changed positions, shifting until he half reclined beside her. He bent and kissed the path his thumbs had recently traced. When his nose bumped the hem of her dress, he hesitated. Emily's hands settled in his hair, her plea crystal clear. He groaned and shoved the silky fabric to her waist, revealing minute black silk thong panties.

At the base of the inverted triangle of fabric, a tiny rhinestone heart glittered. He pressed gently on the little decoration with his thumb, scooting it back and forth until he felt her clitoris. Emily shivered, and her teeth dug into her bottom lip.

He eased two fingers beneath the panties and entered her slick warmth, all the while rubbing the heart at the center of things. Emily's breathing grew rapid and she panted in shallow gasps. She clutched the arms of the chair, her fingers gripping the fabric with white knuckles.

He stilled his hand. Emily cried out, arching her back as she sought relief. He bent his head and tongued the heart, wetting the thin silk and tasting her arousal. He probed once, twice, and Emily came with a little choked sigh.

He slid all the way down beside her and spooned her against his chest, holding her as she recovered. She was trembling, and he felt such a rush of tenderness, it almost overwhelmed him. He pulled her dress back into place and nuzzled her neck, inhaling the faint scent of her perfume.

Then he bit gently on her earlobe. "You're amazing," he muttered, his throat tight.

She maneuvered onto her back, no small feat, given the narrow confines of the chaise. Her eyes searched his, her cheeks flushed. "I want you, Luke," she whispered. "Very, very badly."

He hovered over her on one elbow, his other hand resting on her stomach. He swallowed and searched for the right words. "You have me, Emily. My whole body is one big ache. You make me crazy. But for me it can't be just sex. Not with you. I'm sorry."

Her eyes grew wider still. "What do you mean?"

He kissed her, lingering and lengthening the kiss until every muscle in his body screamed for release. He pulled back, breathing hard. "You've always had a special place in my heart. I can't treat this like a one-night-stand. It's not really my style anyway, and certainly not with you. You matter to me, honey."

Her eyes glittered with unshed tears, and her lower lip trembled. "You're not making this easy," she murmured, stroking his chin with her fingertip.

He trapped the finger in his mouth and nipped it with his teeth. "None of the good things in my life have come easily, Emily."

"And I'm a good thing?" she asked with a tiny smile.

"A very good thing," he vowed. "So what do you say? Do you still want me under those conditions?"

Her three-second pause seemed like an eternity. Finally, she nodded. "Yes, Luke," she said softly, looking at him the way a woman looks at a prospective lover. "I do want you."

Her confession seemed to take him by surprise, though she couldn't imagine why. He reacted visibly, his body jerking slightly as though he had received an electric shock. Surely he didn't think she would change her mind now. Not when he had just reduced her to a mass of quivering nerves with his creative, exploratory caresses. This was a man who knew his way around a woman's body.

She couldn't decide whether to be jealous or glad.

He took her hand and pulled her to her feet, his expression fierce. "This chaise thing is probably supposed to be romantic," he muttered. "But I'd like to have a little more room to maneuver for the next round."

The raw intent on his face made her knees quiver. She followed him blindly, holding on to his hand with a death grip. His large frame exuded urgency, and seeing his arousal made something inside her go all soft and yielding.

He stopped beside the bed. "Are you on the pill?"

"Yes," she whispered, wondering how he managed to stay focused when she was falling apart.

He cupped her face in his hands. His smoky gray eyes glittered with emotion. "I've never made love to a woman without a condom,

but I want to with you. I want to feel you, Emily, in the most intimate way. You can trust me. I'd never be careless with your safety."

"I know that," she said shakily, feeling as if everything inside
her was melting.

His fingers toyed with the narrow strap of her dress and slid it
down her arm until it was trapped at her elbow. Then he repeated
that languid, painstakingly slow motion on the opposite side.
Ever so gently, he pressed her hands to her hips and with his
thumbs peeled the dress an inch at a time down her body until it
dropped to the floor. He supported her as she stepped out of the
small puddle of black fabric.

For long seconds, his gaze was rapt as it skated from her face
to her bare breasts to the tiny covering below her hips. "God,
you're perfect."

She crossed her arms over her chest, feeling vulnerable . . . exposed. "You're overdressed, Marshall," she said, striving for a hu-
morous tone but sounding more breathless than amused. She
slipped off his tux jacket and started in on his studs. He stood
perfectly still, only the rapid rise and fall of his chest betraying
his state of mind.

She dispensed with his bow tie, unfastened his cuff links, and
with a quick exhalation of breath, pulled his shirttail loose and
tugged off his shirt. All that smoothly muscled tanned skin
blinded her for a moment. A narrow line of dark hair arrowed
from his collarbone to his belt. When she lost her nerve, Luke
impatiently finished the task, kicking off his shoes and socks and
stripping off his pants and shorts.

Her breath lodged in her throat. His penis reared proud and
thick from a nest of hair at his groin. Her hands itched to stroke
it, but she was paralyzed by sudden shyness, flashing back to her
younger self, who had idolized this man.

But she was a grown woman now. She had experience in the
bedroom . . . maybe not a lot, but enough to hold her own. She
lifted her chin. "It's a good thing you were clothed at that auction.

If those women had seen you like this, my ten-thousand-dollar bid would never have held."

His cheeks reddened endearingly. He pulled her close. "I was damned glad you bought me. The thought of going out with a stranger gave me the heebie-jeebies. Pamela is going to owe me for that one."

"Even now?" she teased, rubbing her cheek on his chest.

He chuckled, his hands cupping her butt. "I'll get back to you on that. I have a sneaking suspicion I'm going to owe her."

The feel of his heavy erection against her lower abdomen was eroding her patience. He scooped her up suddenly, flipped back the covers, and deposited her on the soft, cool sheets. She'd expected him to get right to business, since he'd already generously sent her to the moon and back. But apparently Luke Marshall had infinite stores of patience.

He flipped her to her stomach, straddled her waist, and rubbed her from neck to bottom, his big hands working her tense muscles until she was nothing more than a puddle of longing. Despite her off-the-charts orgasm not twenty minutes before, her skin was already humming with heat, and need built steadily as his touch grew more bold. He eased her over and onto her back.

A lock of his hair tumbled over his forehead, and he no longer looked like the polished, debonair attorney. He looked hungry . . . determined . . . predatory. He settled between her legs. Every inch of skin where his body touched hers felt painfully sensitive. She flinched involuntarily, and of course, he noticed.

He frowned, the cords in his neck standing out. "Emily?" It was a hoarse, incredulous question.

She wet her lips. Panic threatened. After this they could never go back. "Does this seem weird to you?" she asked, craving reassurance.

He kissed her forehead, her eyelids, and finally her lips. She could see the control he was exerting in the line of his jaw when he pulled back. "Not weird at all," he muttered. "It feels like the most right thing I've ever done." He paused, and a pained look crossed his face. "But if you aren't okay with this, tell me now."

His cock pressed hard and heavy at her opening, and she tried to catch her breath. This was supposed to be light and fun and temporary. She wanted to cry and laugh at the same time. No adolescent fantasy had prepared her for the feel of Luke's big male body ready to enter hers.

"You don't think we'll have regrets?" It was a moot point with his cock already teasing her moist folds.

He groaned from deep in his chest. "Please, Emily," he grated, his whole body shaking. "Yes or no?"

She tilted her hips and gasped as he slid forward an inch. "Yes," she whispered. "Yes . . . yes . . . yes."

CHAPTER FOUR

*L*uke pressed forward slowly, feeling her slick warmth envelop him like an erotic glove. It wasn't an easy fit. She was tight, and he had to thrust and withdraw several times until she could take all of him. When he was buried to the hilt, he rested his forehead against hers and struggled for control.

The feel of her, without a rubber, had every nerve cell in his body tensed for an imminent explosion. He was sweating, trembling. He dragged in some air and tried to focus on her face. "Emily? Talk to me, hon."

"Now?" Her voice was slurred, her eyes closed, her lips parted. She wiggled her hips, silently demanding that he continue.

Her unspoken eagerness reassured him. He began to move, trying for a slow, steady rhythm, but was sabotaged by the feel of her long, slender legs wrapped around his back. He thrust hard, wringing a cry from her throat. He shuddered, trying to hold on, but riding bareback did him in. With a hoarse shout, he pounded into her over and over again, mindless, driven by the depth of his hunger.

He felt her vaginal muscles tighten around him, and his orgasm ripped through him with tidal-wave force as he shot his release deep inside her.

* * *

He roused sometime later to the sound of Emily in the bathroom. When she rejoined him in the bed, he reached for her, his cock already full and ready. He spread her legs and entered her slowly, this time finding it easier and at the same time more agonizingly sweet.

Emily whimpered. He slid a hand between them to stroke her intimately. It was only a matter of minutes before she cried out her release, and despite his earlier orgasm, he wasn't able to delay his own climax for long. Knowing she had peaked allowed him to give in to the gnawing, driving hunger. He moaned and thrust one last time, and soon darkness overtook him.

He had her twice more before morning. In both instances, she met his overtures eagerly, passionately. In fact, the second time, she was the one to wake him, climbing on top and guiding him into her welcoming body without apology. It might have seemed like a dream were it not for the smell of sex in the air and the very real feel of her body tangled with his in the twisted sheets.

It was no surprise that the sun was high in the sky when they finally surfaced. Groggy with exhaustion, but perfectly aware of every incredible moment from the night before, he nuzzled her throat and then slipped between the covers to lick her nipples. But at that precise moment, some sixth sense picked up on her uneasiness. It was one thing to go crazy in the cocoon of darkness, but he knew Emily well enough to suspect that she was unsure how to handle the morning after.

Despite the tantalizing possibility of round five, and he was truly amazed that such a thing was a physical possibility, he dragged himself out of bed, yawning and stretching. He pulled on tennis shoes, shorts, and a T-shirt. "I think I'll go for a run and let you have first crack at the bathroom."

The sheer relief on her face almost made him laugh out loud, but he bit down hard on his lip and kept his expression casual. "Back in a little while."

Emily pulled the blanket to her chin and felt her body begin to tremble from her toes to the top of her head. She'd had sex with Luke Marshall. Well, no . . . that wasn't quite it. No three-letter word was sufficient to describe the cataclysmic, utterly abandoned, sexual frenzy they'd indulged in.

Luke hadn't just had sex with her . . . he'd laid claim to her, body and soul. He'd stamped his mark on her so indelibly, so incredibly, she wasn't sure she'd ever be just Emily again. It scared the hell out of her.

She glanced at the clock on the bedside table. Noon? Good lord. She scrambled out of bed, wincing in disbelief at the naked woman in the mirror. Her hair was a rat's nest, and there were bite marks on her neck. Her nipples were erect, almost swollen, and the familiar contours of her mouth were puffy and red. She didn't recognize the reflection at all.

Grabbing jeans, clean underwear, and a lilac T-shirt out of her suitcase, she dashed for the relative safety of the bathroom, locked the door, and turned on the shower. Thankfully, her ankle barely gave a twinge of discomfort.

She stood under the hot, pelting spray, soaped her tender breasts, and washed between her legs with a shudder of remembrance. Luke had used his hands, his mouth, and his unflagging penis to drive her insane. She'd lost count of the orgasms. One had seemed to blend into the next. Even this morning, as glad as she had been to see him leave the room so she could recover, a part of her had been disappointed that they weren't going to have sex again.

She'd become a nymphomaniac . . .

Forty-five minutes later, the woman in the mirror once again resembled the Emily Drake she knew. When Luke returned from his run, sweaty and gorgeous, she was able to greet him with equanimity.

He stripped off his shirt and grinned. "You look nice."

That simple compliment weakened her knees. She smiled, loving his easy good humor. "Hurry up, Luke. I'm starving."

He gave her a quick kiss. "I know. I know . . . you missed breakfast. So sue me. Who knew you were so locked in to three meals a day?"

She tidied up the room and listened to the shower running, imagining him sleek and wet, soapy . . . hard. She dropped a small glass tumbler. It fell harmlessly on the soft carpet, and sheepishly, she retrieved it. Somehow she had to get herself newly ravenous libido under control.

They were . . . careful . . . with each other that afternoon. After lunch, Luke suggested tennis, and she agreed with alacrity. She ran and lobbed and stretched for returns, stopping only when her ankle began to protest.

Luke was chagrined. "I'm so sorry. I wasn't even thinking. Why didn't you say something?"

She walked around the net to where he stood and reached up with her towel to wipe the sweat from his forehead. She liked touching him. This close, her body reacted predictably, tingling, tightening, softening in places that preserved vivid mental pictures of the night before. "I didn't think about my ankle either. Someone had my mind on other things."

His eyes widened, and a pulse beat in his neck. It was the first overtly sexual remark either of them had made all day. He cleared his throat. "I see."

She rose on her tiptoes to capture his lips. They were firm and warm and pleasingly familiar. "I'm not complaining. I want to be clear about that."

His tongue dueled lazily with hers. "Good. I hope to be able to distract you again very soon."

She broke the kiss reluctantly. Luke wasn't smiling, but deep in his eyes she thought she detected a twinkle. She picked up her racket. "Want to tour those suites now?"

Luke followed Emily and their guide from one fantasy suite to the next with his mouth dry, his heart pounding, and his sex uncomfortably heavy in his jeans. Each room was more suggestive than the last. An elevator, an opium den, a saloon, a doctor's office . . . and that was only the beginning. Someone had put a great deal of time and thought into preparing the ultimate adult fantasy experience.

When their guide finally left them, Luke pulled Emily aside in the hallway. "Tell me, please . . . the suspense is killing me. Which room is ours?"

She patted his cheek, her face full of mischief. "Patience, my horny barrister. You'll see right after dinner. I made an early reservation, because our time slot in the suite is eight till eleven."

Luke stumbled through the next few hours in a fog of arousal. When they cleaned up and changed for dinner, he put on his tux again, heartily glad that men weren't required to think too hard about wardrobe choices.

Emily's halter-top dress tested his control. It was made of some satiny kind of fabric that caught the light and emphasized every curve of her body. The color—sunshine yellow—made her skin glow.

He never even knew what he was eating this time. He chewed and swallowed and made conversation on autopilot, unable to drag his thoughts away from the fantasy suites. And as stimulating as it was to see each one of those fantastic rooms and imagine the possibilities, it was even more arousing to contemplate Emily's choice and to wonder where and when he'd be able to make love to her next.

Despite the fact that her ankle had swelled a bit, he couldn't resist the pleading look in her eyes when people began to dance.

He led her out onto the floor and tucked her close to his chest. He could almost be content with just holding her . . . almost, but not quite.

They moved with the music, their bodies in perfect sync. His fingers explored the bare skin at her back, tracing her spine and holding her closer when she shivered. He bent to whisper in her ear. "Cold?"

She shook her head. "No."

She gave no further explanation, and he didn't ask. They were each remembering . . . waiting . . . enjoying the provocative aura of anticipation.

After dinner, they returned to their room and changed back into casual clothes. When it was time, they walked side by side to the entertainment corridor, as it was called. Emily stopped in front of suite eight, opened her purse, and extracted a key. She glanced up at him in the dim hallway. "Ready?"

He nodded. "I was born ready, sweetheart. Lead the way." Standing in the hallway, all the doors looked the same, and he couldn't remember which suite they were about to enter.

Emily unlocked the door and he followed her inside. He glanced around with a mixture of wariness and interest. She'd surprised him again.

The room was narrow and deep. The walls were covered with some kind of black fabric. At the far end of the room, a movie screen had been made to resemble an outdoor drive-in theater. Images flickered there, enough to seem realistic without being distracting. A sound system, no doubt state-of-the-art, was responsible for the hum of cicadas and the steady beeping of tree frogs. A light breeze stirred the air. He could swear he smelled honeysuckle.

At the center of the room, directly in front of them was a car, an honest to God, vintage convertible, turquoise and beige with a cream leather interior. The top was down. Popcorn, candy, and soft drinks on a nearby refreshment stand completed the scene.

He glanced at his silent partner.

She shifted from one foot to another. "I'm going to change." She waved a hand at one of the screens that closed off a corner alcove. "Your jeans and shirt are fine, unless you want to wear something else."

He let out a raspy laugh. "I'm not planning on spending long in my clothes sweetheart, so it's immaterial."

He watched her disappear behind the screen, and he decided to explore the car. He wasn't knowledgeable enough to pinpoint dates, but it looked like it might be a late-fifties model. He opened the driver's door and sat down, marveling at the roomy interior. These things were like tanks.

He fiddled with the radio and found a track of oldies, mostly love songs and mournful ballads. Nothing sharp and catchy to break the mood.

He had his back to the corner where Emily was changing, so he didn't see her when she first stepped out. Some small noise made him turn his head. He sucked in a breath. Now he knew why Emily had picked this particular suite. They were going to revisit high school. Obviously a few decades earlier than reality warranted, but they could improvise.

She stood hesitantly, waiting for him to comment. Her costume was clichéd but cute. A white cheerleading sweater with a big red *S* on the front topped a flirty pleated crimson skirt. Her bare legs looked about a million miles long, and her bobby socks and saddle oxfords rounded out the provocative picture.

He got out of the car and stood watching her, his hands on his hips. "Nice outfit, Emily. But just so you know, in this fantasy, you're seventeen, not a day younger. I'm not into jailbait scenarios."

She grinned. "Duly noted."

He rocked back on his heels. "Where are your pom-poms?"

She shrugged. "They're kind of big. I left them at home, 'cause I didn't want them to get in our way."

He walked closer. "I see." Her sweater had a deep V neck. He ran his finger from her throat to her cleavage. Then he shook his head. "No bra? Naughty, Miss Drake. I might have to report you to the cheerleading sponsor."

She pouted. "I dressed this way for you. I thought you'd like it."

He flipped the hem of her skirt. "I'd like it better if you went to the movies with me."

She tilted her head with a coy smile. "I have a curfew."

He ruffled her hair. "I'll watch the time."

He took her hand and led her to the car, opening her door with a gentlemanly flourish. Then he rounded the vehicle and jumped in behind the wheel. When Emily laughed, he smiled sheepishly. "I've always wanted to do that."

A switch on the dashboard of the car dimmed the lights in the room and made the illusion of being outdoors even more believable. He turned sideways on the seat and looked at his companion. She sat primly, her hands folded in her lap, her knees together. He sighed, feeling like a lucky man. This was going to be fun.

He scooted toward the middle of the bench seat and slipped an arm behind her. "I'm going to miss you when I go off to school this fall." He kissed her neck just below her ear.

She sighed. "I know. And you'll be so far away. With all those other girls." Her voice was the perfect blend of pouting and a demand for reassurance.

He played with the clasp of her necklace at the nape of her neck. "I'll be concentrating on my schoolwork. I won't even notice other girls."

Her eyes blinked rapidly, as though she were about to cry. "I could go with you. We could get married and have an apartment."

He frowned. "Don't be silly. You still have a year of school to finish."

She lifted her chin, haughty dignity personified. "Don't call me silly, Luke. I'm a grown woman, and I can finish high school anywhere."

"With strangers? You'd miss your prom and your senior cheerleading season. You're the captain, Emily."

She put her hand on his thigh. "Those are childish things. They don't matter. All that's important to me is being with you."

Luke hesitated, wondering where the real Emily intersected with this little tease. He cleared his throat. "I'll wait for you."

"A year is an eternity," she cried. "And even though you say that, it won't be easy with you there and me here. You'll change your mind."

He frowned. "You don't have much faith in us . . . or in me. Not if you think I'm that fickle."

Her fingers inched closer to his crotch. "I know how guys are. You have needs. I want to be the one to satisfy those needs."

Her low, husky voice made the hair on the back of his neck stand up. He swallowed a gulp of air. "Nice girls don't talk about stuff like that."

This time her hand settled over his groin. His cock jumped and twitched. She curled into his embrace. "Maybe I'm not a nice girl."

Her free hand stroked his chest through his shirt. He tried to remember the part he was supposed to be playing. "I respect you, Emily. Too much to mess up your life. You have to let me go."

"I can't," she wailed, burrowing her head in his shoulder. "I'll die without you. It will be awful."

He patted her hair. "We can write letters," he said weakly, feeling the warmth of her fingers burn through his jeans.

She sniffed. "That'll last for a week or so." Her fingers played with the tab on his zipper. "Think about it, Luke. Coming home to me after a long day of school. A hot meal. Sex anytime you want it. I could make your life really sweet. All the other guys would be jealous."

He batted her hand away from his pants. "I'm eighteen, Emily. I want a chance to be out on my own. A guy deserves that. Heck, you deserve that. We're too young to be thinking about settling down. There's plenty of time for that later."

She had retreated to her corner of the seat, looking glum. She crossed her legs, and the fluffy little skirt rode up her thighs.

He shook his head. "How 'bout some popcorn and a drink?"

She scowled. "I can't be placated with snack food, Luke. Don't treat me like a child."

"Well, you sure are acting like one," he snapped. He opened the car door to get out, not wanting to press his luck twice in one evening, and went to the refreshment stand to get a bag of popcorn and a soft drink. Back in the car, he offered Emily the popcorn. She took some, still scowling, and they ate in silence. He took a swig from the bottle, and offered that as well.

When they had finished, he disposed of the trash and tugged her to his side. "The movie's about to start, sweetheart. "Come here and let me hold you."

They watched the flickering images on the screen for several minutes until Emily finally spoke again. "So you don't want to get married."

"No, honey, I don't."

"Because you want to go out with other girls."

He sighed. "Maybe I will. But it won't be serious. I love you, Emily, and if you feel the same thing about me, you'll be willing to wait. If our love is real and deep, it will last. You know I'm right."

She propped her feet on the dashboard, her face pensive. "Then I have one request. If I don't hassle you anymore about leaving, or getting married, or other girls, or any of that stuff, will you do something for me?"

He hugged her close. "Of course I will."

"I want you to take my virginity before you go."

Emily felt him jerk in shock as he processed her words. And it gave her a fierce sense of satisfaction to know she could throw the mighty Luke Marshall off balance, even temporarily, and even if this was an entirely fictitious scenario.

He'd gone perfectly still, and she could almost see the little wheels in his brain turning as he debated his response.

She didn't plan to make it easy for him to say no. She reached under her skirt and pulled her panties down her legs. A moment later they disappeared over the side of the car. She ran her hands up and down her thighs. "I've heard it's wonderful," she whispered. "Sex, I mean."

He was breathing hard. "You're too young."

"Of course I'm not. Women used to be married and had babies at my age. I'm practically over the hill."

He ran a hand through his hair and rubbed the bridge of his nose. "Emily, honey, I can't take your virginity and then leave. That would make me the worst kind of scum. You're special."

"I'd be *giving* it to you," she insisted. "And there's nothing wrong with that. I don't want you to forget me."

"I won't forget you, I swear, Emily."

"And I'll never forget you," she whispered huskily. "You're a guy who sticks in a girl's mind. And that's why I want you to be my first."

She stretched her legs across his lap. He looked very nervous. She licked her lips, resting her forehead against his shoulder. "Touch me, Luke. I want to feel your hands on my bare skin." She lifted her head and kissed him, curling an arm around his neck.

She felt him shudder. Beneath her legs, the proof of his desire was unmistakable. Slowly, he slid his hands under the hem of her sweater and cupped her breasts. The nipples pebbled immediately, and he tugged on them gently, sending streaks of fire straight to her womb.

She groaned and leaned back against the seat. He shoved the sweater as high as it would go and bent his head to suckle her breast.

The sensation was incredible. "Luke . . ." She wasn't sure what she meant to say, but he switched to the other breast and she lost her train of thought.

He muttered endearments, his voice muffled against her skin. "You're perfect, Emily. So warm . . . so soft."

His tongue found her navel, the tickling caress making her squirm. "I'm warm other places, too," she panted. She grabbed one of his wrists and guided it under her skirt.

He put on a convincing show of reluctance. His hand stilled on her thigh, his large frame tense. "Petting is one thing, honey. But we can't do this. You'll regret it and so will I."

"Don't reject me, Luke," she pleaded. "Don't say I'm too young or that you're leaving. Don't break my heart. I want to have this one night to remember." She moved his hand an inch higher, and his fingers brushed her most intimate flesh.

She whimpered.

He groaned. "I'll touch you here, honey," he muttered, his voice rough. "But that's as far as we're going." Slowly, tentatively, he explored the moist, velvety lips of her sex. Her legs parted. His hand grew bolder. An eighteen-year-old might not have known how to give pleasure, but Luke was no callow youth. He stroked her firmly, precisely at the point where every pulse of heat collected and burned.

She twisted on the seat, seeking relief. She wanted Luke inside her, deep and heavy, making her complete. But he was still completely dressed. She tried to stop his hand. "No," she muttered. "Not like this. I want *you*."

He ignored her protests, his arm heavy across her abdomen, trapping her between his body and the seat. He lowered his head and kissed her tenderly. "Relax, Emily. Let me do this for you."

His kiss, so gentle she wanted to weep, lowered her defenses and sent her over the edge. The orgasm was an easy, rolling crest that melted into pure pleasure, leaving her weak and boneless.

Afterwards, he cuddled her, kissing her forehead, her cheeks, her throat.

She resented his control. "Don't patronize me, Luke. I want more than that from you. I want it all."

"And what if I *don't* want that?"

"Your body doesn't lie." She squeezed his length through his jeans. "You're dying to have me."

He covered her hand with his, pressing down. He was trembling, and she knew his capitulation was only a matter of time. She touched the top button at his throat, smugly happy when he didn't try to stop her from unfastening it. "I love your chest," she muttered, moving down one by one. She freed the buttons at his wrists, and with his help, removed the shirt entirely.

She traced the muscles in his abdomen, and then once again, she toyed with his zipper. She lowered the gold tab an inch, then two, then all the way. "You're all tensed up, Luke. I can make it feel better."

She opened his belt and the snap at his waist, folding back the sides of his pants to reveal snug navy briefs. His erection strained the fabric, a damp spot indicating his eagerness.

Carefully, she lifted him free of the confining cloth, cupping him in both hands and pressing kisses along his silky length. Luke twisted restlessly, and his elbow hit the car horn. The sound reverberated in the small room.

He took her hand, panting. "Backseat . . . more room."

"What if someone sees us?"

"It's dark . . . don't worry."

He helped her over first, his hands cupping and fondling her bare butt as she crawled to the rear of the car. She'd barely had time to settle onto her back, when he loomed over the seat, sliding clumsily to join her, still hampered by his tight jeans.

He found her mouth, his tongue sliding deep, mimicking the act of possession. Her heart was slamming in her chest, and she felt as jittery as if it really were going to be her first time. He braced himself on one arm, stroking her breast over and over, his thumbnail scraping her nipple. Her thighs clenched, and she wanted to scream at him to hurry, but she'd lost the ability to speak.

He sat back on his haunches and lifted her to a sitting position. "Raise your arms," he said, his voice rough and low.

She obeyed instantly, momentarily blinded when the sweater bunched around her face before being freed. His big hands began mapping her torso, exploring every hill and valley like the most dedicated of surveyors.

He found the zipper at the side of her skirt and released it, then tugged her last remaining garment up and over her head. He sat completely still for maybe half a minute before pulling her into his arms. And then he hugged her. Nothing more. His big strong arms wrapped around her back, and her breasts nestled against his broad, warm chest. For the first time that evening, she really felt like crying. The tenderness threatened to do her in.

Finally, he lowered her once again to the seat. She shivered when the cool leather chilled her skin. He shoved his jeans to his knees. Even in the dim light, his erection looked huge, rearing proudly against his abdomen.

He spread her legs. One of her feet rested on the floor of the car, the other was propped along the edge of the backseat. He settled awkwardly between her legs. She felt the blunt head of his penis probe at her opening. Before she could anticipate his next move, he was sliding back and forth with his cock, deliberately rubbing her aching clitoris.

"I'm ready, Luke . . . really." She was begging and she didn't care.

"I don't want to hurt you," he ground out, breathless, shaking.

"You won't . . . or not much. I don't care, dammit. Take me, Luke . . . please, before I shatter into a million pieces."

Once again he positioned himself to enter her. He leaned down to kiss her. "Tell me if I should stop." He pushed gently, stretching her, filling her. If it had really been her first time, their coming together would have been a challenge. But she wasn't an untried virgin. Already she knew the feel of his body. Already she craved the fullness, the heat, the friction.

His body was hot against hers. She put her arms around his

neck, pulling him closer. His hips flexed as he surged deeper. She felt surrounded, engulfed, totally swallowed up in what was happening. She never wanted him to stop. She wanted to stay here forever, in this world where Luke Marshall finally showed his love to little Emily Drake.

But despite their game, the emotions she was feeling were painfully adult. Luke had actually said he loved her, but he was playing a part, getting into the character she'd demanded he become.

He slowed his movements, his arms braced as he looked down at her. "Where'd you go, Emily?" he rasped. "I could swear we were on the same page, but then I lost you."

She tried to smile. "I'm right here."

He frowned, his whole body tensed. "Is that cheerleader Emily talking or the real Emily?"

She touched her fingers to his mouth, caressing his lips. "Who would you rather have?" It wasn't a fair question given their little fantasy play, but she was getting desperate.

His eyes were hot, his cheeks flushed. The tendons in his arms stood out in relief. His jaw clenched. "I want the fabulous woman who bought and paid for me," he said, breathing hoarsely. "The woman who blew my mind last night."

Tears wet her lashes, and her eyes stung. Her chest was tight. "Yes." That single syllable was all she could force from her throat.

He must have been convinced by what he saw in her face. He groaned, pumping his hips, making her vision go blurry. "God, Emily," he ground out. "I can't get enough of you."

And after that there was no more talking . . . no more second-guessing. Only feeling and yearning and the splintering of a million tiny stars.

They stumbled back to their room at eleven, showered together, and tumbled into bed. Luke slept instantly, deeply. Emily lay awake, dry-eyed, wondering how she had managed to screw up her life so completely.

CHAPTER FIVE

*L*uke rolled over and reached for Emily, frowning when he found nothing but empty sheets. He rose on one elbow, rubbing his eyes with the heel of his hand, and glanced toward the bathroom. No light shone from beneath the door. The first gray streaks of dawn were illuminating the room, so maybe she didn't need a light.

He listened intently. But the gentle steady hum of the air-conditioning unit effectively masked any noise she might be making. And even as he acknowledged that mundane fact, the weight of dread settled in his stomach.

He tossed back the covers and stood up, stretching and yawning. Keeping up with Emily might require a few extra trips to the gym, or at the very least some power naps. He reached for his watch on the bedside table, and his hand froze. A small white envelope rested against a half-empty water glass.

He had trouble fastening his watchband because his hand was shaking. He glanced at the time. Ten thirty. Not as late as yesterday. He walked into the bathroom, not really surprised to find it empty. After he showered and shaved, he dressed and was ready to go.

Some small stunned corner of his mind registered the fact that every last trace of Emily Drake had disappeared from the room.

He tucked his shaving kit into his overnight bag. Then he took care of hanging his clothes in the garment bag. He placed both pieces of luggage by the door. Checkout was at noon.

When he couldn't postpone it any longer, he picked up the envelope. His name was written in feminine scrawl on the front. He freed the flap and extricated the single sheet of hotel stationery. Blindly, he stared at it. And then he started to read.

Dear Luke:

You are a dear and wonderful man for allowing me to fulfill my silly fantasies. I know you are probably angry right now, but I simply didn't know how to face you this morning. I couldn't have asked for a better partner this weekend. You made everything so much fun. I guess I was way off base on that "forgettable" thing. I will always remember our time at the Scimitar.

I am so glad we have been friends all these years, and I hope that connection will remain. You have always been a special part of my life. We settled some things for me this weekend, and I am grateful. Thank you for your tenderness, your generosity, and your amazing creativity. I have arranged for a rental car to be delivered at noon.

Fondly,
Emily

He crushed the paper in his fist as pain slammed into him, a searing, nauseating hurt that went bone deep. Fondly? God, he was a fool. He'd given everything to Emily Drake, and she'd used him like a damned lab rat.

Just when he'd begun to wonder if he and Emily had a shot at something more than a weekend fling, she'd pulled the rug out from under him. He was nothing to her but a means to an end. She wasn't infatuated with him. She wasn't in love with him. She was moving on.

And he was an idiot to think that auld lang syne was a basis for some romantic scenario where Emily Drake still thought Luke Marshall hung the moon. He was nobody's knight in shining armor, least of all hers.

Emily pulled up a recent listing on her computer. Five bedrooms and an acre and a half of land. This might be exactly what the Walkers were looking for.

She glanced out the window. It was raining again. June had been a wet month, not the best time for prospective buyers to look at houses.

She needed to stop for groceries on the way home. She spun her chair back around. The stack of mail on her desk was growing. She tossed the ones she knew were junk mail. The next one looked personal. Sometimes she used her work address for correspondence because she lived alone and didn't want her private information plastered everywhere.

She opened the envelope and began to read the brief letter. It was a thank-you and a form from Children's Hospital for tax purposes. *We appreciate your recent donation of ten thousand dollars. In accordance with IRS regulations, this is to acknowledge that no concrete goods or services were provided in exchange for this gift.*

A tiny hysterical giggle escaped her. No goods or services? Clearly the IRS didn't care that Emily had paid a man ten grand for sex. Maybe if they'd been in Vegas . . . but in North Carolina, probably not.

Her chest tightened and her stomach clenched. She blinked rapidly against hot tears. Dammit. She'd been doing a fair job of compartmentalizing her brain. If she didn't allow herself to think about last weekend, she could avoid the pain that hovered just outside conscious thought. Stupid letter . . .

With trembling hands, she gathered her keys and pocketbook. She would go home and hide out. Try to forget what an idiot she'd been. And somehow she'd come up with a plan for the future. A future she no longer cared about at all.

Four days and nights of chick-flick DVDs, deep-dish pizza, and chocolate-chip cookie dough were usually enough to smooth out the rough edges of even the most devastating crisis. But who knew that when it came to true love, a girl's tried-and-true standby remedies would be worse than useless?

On Saturday morning when she woke up at the ungodly hour of six a.m. and stood on the scales, she'd gained two pounds, her hair was lank and dull, and her fingernails were a ragged mess.

She stared at herself in the mirror. She was a coward and a wimp. She should have stayed and brazened it out. What if there was a slim chance that Luke had fallen in love with her? Ha! Fat chance. *She'd* been the one to approach him after five years of no contact whatsoever. *She'd* been the one to embarrass him with a ten-thousand-dollar bid at a public auction. *She'd* been the one to ask for sex. And *she* was the one with the pathetic crush . . . and if you wanted to call a spade a spade, she might as well admit that crush was a misnomer. She was head over heels, sick at her stomach, completely and irrevocably in love with Luke Marshall.

Luke knew how she felt about him years ago and had never evinced the slightest interest in having a relationship with her other than their recent sexual escapades. If she had stayed, she would only have embarrassed them both. Even though he said it wasn't a one-night-stand, spectacular sex between consenting adults was not a free pass to matrimony. Luke was a virile, healthy, sexual man, and he was fond of her and her family. Oh God, why did that admission have to hurt so much?

She looked in the mirror one last time, disgusted with what she saw. So she'd made a mistake . . . a world-class, knock-the-feet-out-from-under-you mistake. But maybe self-awareness was a good thing. Now she knew. Luke would always be the man for her. She might never be able to get over him.

But there was more to life than romance, and she owed it to herself to pick up the pieces and make a new beginning.

A short time later she was dressed, clearheaded, and able to think of Luke without crying. She headed for the realty company offices, unwilling to spend another minute at home hosting her own private pity party.

Even the most gung-ho of her coworkers weren't around this early on a weekend, thank God. She'd begin her twelve-step program in private. It wasn't much, but it was a start. Cleaning out the communal refrigerator seemed like a cathartic way to approach her new recovery plan.

She had dumped all the old jars of salad dressing and out-of-date yogurt into the garbage and was getting ready to wipe out the shelves when the doorbell rang. She sighed. Probably one of the neighborhood kids selling magazines to fund their summer gymnastics competition. Although why any of them would be out and about this early was a mystery.

She wiped her damp hands on a dish towel and walked to the front door, opening it with a smile. But her smile faltered when she registered the identity of her visitor. "Luke. What are you doing here?"

He jammed his fists into his pockets, not really sure if he wanted to kiss her or strangle her. He was so still so angry, even after six days, and damned if he wanted to let her see how much she had hurt him.

Her face had gone completely pale when she saw him. She gripped the doorframe with one hand as though she might shut it in his face. He moved past her, forcing her to close the door and follow him.

He settled into a comfortable chair and looked around with interest. The reception area was small but elegant. He stared at her without smiling. "I want you to come with me, Emily . . . preferably now. I've got everything you need in the car."

Her hands were at her waist, twisting and fidgeting. He saw her swallow hard. "What for?"

He scowled. "Let's just call it evening the score. Get your purse or sweater or whatever." He looked at his watch and then back at her.

With an inarticulate protest, she disappeared down the hall. He got to his feet and paced. His skin felt tight. His gut cramped. He wasn't accustomed to making decisions in the heat of the moment, but he hadn't been able to calm down long enough for clear thought.

He was riding on his emotions, and it was an uncomfortable experience for a man who was accustomed to cool, rational evaluation.

When she returned, he ushered her out to the car. Emily was suspiciously quiet, and she looked anxious. Good. She deserved to suffer a little bit.

But her curiosity finally got the better of her. "Where are we going, Luke? You haven't said a word."

He gave her one quick frowning glance and returned his attention to the road. "Trust me, Emily, I'm so ticked with you at the moment, I wouldn't push it."

The tone of his voice must have convinced her. She sat back in her seat, and dead silence reigned in the vehicle for the next half hour.

But when he pulled into the airport parking garage, she snapped. "This is ridiculous. Quit being so damned mysterious."

He pulled into a space and shut off the car. "You owe me a date," he said flatly, struggling to keep his temper from boiling over.

"What?" Her brow creased in confusion.

"You owe me a date. The bachelors were supposed to plan the second date. Remember?"

She winced. "Well, I didn't think under the circumstances—"

He cut her off with a slice of his hand in the air. "You didn't think, period. You treated me like shit last weekend, Emily. If a man had done what you did, he'd be called a really nasty name."

Her face went even whiter, her lips trembling. "I was afraid I had embarrassed you," she whispered unsteadily. "I was trying to give you a graceful way out."

He slammed his fist on the steering wheel. "I even told you up front I couldn't be blasé about having sex with you. I told you that you meant something to me, but clearly, I was nothing more than a convenient prick as far as you were concerned. I hope you got your money's worth."

She was crying now, big, fat, silent tears that rolled down her cheeks and dripped from her chin. "I'm sorry."

He ground his teeth together before he could say anything more. A simple apology wasn't what he wanted to hear. "Let's go."

After that, he might as well have been traveling with a mute. She dried her eyes, and now her expression was blank. They checked in, boarded, and settled into seats opposite the aisle from each other on a small commuter jet.

After takeoff, the flight attendant offered soft drinks. Emily declined. Luke asked for a club soda.

They landed at the Asheville airport at two o'clock. He picked up their rental car, and in less than an hour they were on the road back to the Scimitar. Emily sat as far away from him as possible in the front seat of the roomy Lincoln.

They arrived and went through the now familiar registration process. When the bellman escorted them to their room and left, Luke found himself alone with Emily and not knowing what the hell he was going to say. He'd cruised through the week on anger and adrenaline, and now that he had her here, at the scene of the crime so to speak, he wasn't at all sure how to proceed.

She gazed anywhere but at him. She looked miserable . . . defeated.

He crossed his arms over his chest, trying to fan the flames of his righteous indignation, but he wasn't interested in revenge. He wanted to know if he and Emily had a chance to start something important. He should be trying to talk to her, using rational conversation to clear up their murky relationship. But now that she was here with him, all he could think about was how much he wanted to see her nude on that bed. He had asked for the same room. Everything was identical to last weekend except for the state of mind of the participants.

"Oh, hell." He raked a hand through his hair. "You look like you've lost your best friend."

Emily winced. She hoped that wasn't true. He was so angry, and he had every right to be. She'd known he would be royally pissed off by her abrupt departure, but he was more than that . . . he was hurt. She could see it in his eyes, and it cut her to the bone. Luke was right. She had treated him terribly. And as personally painful and humiliating as it might be for her to tell him how she felt, he deserved to know the truth. She owed him that much. But later, much later . . . when she had gathered her courage and when he was in a more amenable mood.

She went to him, her eyes contrite. "I was a fool," she whispered, circling his waist with her arms and resting her head on his shoulder. "I plead temporary insanity. And I'm sorry, Luke, really sorry. Please say you forgive me." She felt a deep breath shudder from his body, and beneath her cheek, his tense muscles relaxed.

"Thank you for coming with me," he muttered. "Kidnapping isn't really my style."

"But you do it so well," she teased.

He pulled back to look searchingly at her face. "So you're willing to give this another try? I brought you here so we can write a different ending to this fantasy. The last one sucked."

She nodded solemnly. "I am. And I promise not to do a disappearing act this time."

Dinner was silent and a little awkward. She might have been chewing sawdust, as much of her entrée as she actually tasted. He appeared to have accepted her apology at face value, but she couldn't read his pensive expression.

She finished a second glass of wine and reached for the bottle. Her nerves were ragged, and the uncertainty about what Luke had planned for the night ahead was pure torture.

He reached a hand across the table and stopped her, moving the bottle out of reach. His eyes were pewter, his expression veiled. "You don't need that, Emily."

She heard humor in his voice and sank back in her chair, nonplussed. She had no choice but to follow his lead. She was awash in a sea of confusion, regret, and guilt.

Luke settled the bill and they went back to their room. He took off his jacket. "I have a suite booked for eight. Do you want to change clothes?"

His voice was matter-of-fact. Emily shivered. She didn't respond verbally, but she grabbed some things and disappeared into the bathroom. She wanted to lock the door, but she was afraid he would hear the click, and she didn't want to do anything else to revive his anger.

At five till eight they walked in silence to the entertainment corridor. Luke stopped in front of suite fourteen. It was at the far end of the hall in an alcove. She hadn't really noticed it on their earlier tour.

He opened the door and led her into an artist's garret. The ceiling sloped on either side of the room, and the dormer windows appeared to look down onto some mythical street below. The ambience was unmistakably French . . . beaded lampshades, silk draperies, a trompe l'oiel table. A beret and jacket tossed carelessly on a chair and a crude glass jar filled with daffodils suggested Paris in the spring.

The lighting was indirect, leaving shadows on the wall and dimly lit corners. A single bed against one wall had tumbled covers as though the creative urge struck its owner quite suddenly.

She stood hesitantly while Luke set flame to a single fat burgundy candle in a crystal dish. He disposed of the match and then reached behind a painted silk screen and removed a

black lace negligee so fine it seemed stitched together of cob-
webs.

He held it out to her. "Please take off your clothes, Emily."

She started to tremble, and he must have noticed, because she
could swear his eyes softened just the tiniest bit. He cocked his
head, his hands in his pockets. His steady gaze made her feel
nude already, reminded her that he had already seen and touched
and made love to every inch of her body.

She took the piece of clothing with numb hands. He brushed
her cheek with the backs of his fingers. "You needn't be nervous,
Emily," he said, his voice husky. "I'd slit my throat before I'd ever
hurt you."

She nodded slowly. "I know."

He turned his back and moved away from her. She stepped behind the screen and changed with clumsy hands and breathless
haste. There was no mirror, so she was unable to gauge how she
looked. Until she saw his face and saw the raw flare of hunger he
was unable to suppress.

He led her to a low leather bench at the foot of the bed. The
kind of spot where you might put on your shoes in the morning.
He pulled the bench into the center of the room and indicated for
her to lie down on it. She obeyed awkwardly. It was not all that
long, and her feet rested on the floor. When she reclined, the
gown fell open, held in place by only a couple of ties between her
breasts. She tried to pull it over her legs and stomach, but Luke's
terse command stopped her in midmotion.

"Leave it," he said, his voice unsteady.

The leather stool was cool against her hot skin, the thin piece
of nightwear no more than a wispy layer of protection. She lay
perfectly still, her hands clasped at her waist.

Luke crossed to an armoire and opened a drawer. He extracted
a handful of rainbow-colored chiffon scarves. Crimson, tangerine,
emerald, and turquoise. They fluttered in his palm like butter-
flies.

He knelt beside her, his eyes quizzical. "Will you let me tie you up, Emily? Be honest. If the idea upsets you, I want you to tell me."

She looked up at him, her heart giving little jumpy, fluttery beats. "It doesn't upset me," she whispered. He took one of her hands, pulling it toward the floor. With deft movements, he tied her wrist to the leg of the bench. He repeated the motion with her other hand and then moved to her feet. Each ankle was bound securely to a smooth wooden leg. In order to immobilize her legs, he had to spread her knees apart, leaving her completely open to his gaze.

She closed her eyes, her heart in her throat. Moisture pearled between her thighs, and sharp longing set up an urgent rhythm in her womb. She could hear faint noises as he moved around the room.

Once, when she was brave enough to peek, she saw that he had undressed except for his trousers. His bare feet made soft brushing sounds on the weathered plank floor. His broad chest gleamed in the candlelight.

When he came toward the bench a second time, her heart jumped and her hands pulled instinctively against their restraints.

Even with her eyes squeezed shut, she could sense him standing over her, his giant wavering shadow covering her like a caress. She thought she heard him sigh. Her nipples tightened, and her skin erupted in gooseflesh.

He knelt beside her, placing the flat of his hand on her belly. "Open your eyes, Emily. I want you to watch me."

She obeyed with difficulty. She felt drugged with passion, weak and dizzy. At this moment she was his puppet, his slave. And a willing slave, at that.

He held a small jar in one hand. The writing on the label was foreign. He unscrewed the lid and tossed it aside. Then he reached for a slim leather case and opened it. Inside were paintbrushes, the expensive kind professional artists used. He stared intently at the collection and finally selected one with a long slender handle and thick, soft sable fibers.

Her breath lodged in her throat. Her mouth was dry.

He dipped the end of the brush in the jar and swirled it around. Wiping the excess on the side, he lifted the brush toward her breasts.

"What is it?" Her voice was little more than a thread of sound.

His eyes were hooded, his mouth curved in a sensual smile. "Eucalyptus oil."

He touched the brush to her left nipple and she jerked involuntarily.

He scowled. "Be still." It was an order, and she obeyed, her fingers digging into the bench legs.

He painted a small circle around her aureole and then a larger one farther out. Every few brushstrokes he returned to the nipple, giving it layer after layer of glistening oil until it gleamed against her pale skin.

On the other breast he sketched what felt like a chain of tiny flowers, and she remembered with some incredulity that he had been a natural artist in school, often designing banners for sporting events.

When he finished with her breasts, he formed a jagged line to her navel, and turned her belly button into a star. The brush arced down to her mound, where he stopped just short of her damp curls.

He set the jar of oil and the large brush aside and consulted the case once again. This time the brush he picked up was small, the bristles nothing more than a narrow point. It was the type a professional artist might use for intricate detail work. Luke's large hands seemed incongruous against the delicate stem of the brush.

He bent closer. His breath tickled her aching sex. Carefully, dextrously, he twirled the tiny brush in the hair at her opening. Every touch of his fingers was agony. Arousal grew and expanded until she writhed with the need for release, but he seemed oblivious to her torment. He used the bristles for several minutes in random patterns and then reversed the brush to drag the polished wooden handle back and forth through her curls. She closed her eyes against the provocative sight of her lover treating her body like a canvas.

She prayed for the firm touch that would give her release. It never came. After a time, he abandoned the brush and poured oil into his palms. Slick, scented oil that turned her flesh into a glistening, pearly sheen and made every nerve cell beneath her skin quiver and burn. He touched her from her throat to the arches of her feet. His big hands were firm and caressing against her flesh.

Finally, when she thought he was surely finished, he reached for the jar one more time. Her forehead wrinkled in confusion. What was left to paint?

He reached toward her, and she shrieked when she realized his intent. "No," she moaned desperately, trying to free herself. "I can't bear it, Luke. No."

He was pitiless, his eyes midnight dark, his jaw stubborn. "Relax, Emily. Let yourself feel . . . embrace the fantasy." And then he touched her.

Her back arched off the bench and a strangled groan stuck in her throat. Gently he parted one delicate fold of skin and began to paint. Each delicate brushstroke was like a jolt of electricity. She quivered in his grasp. She begged, she pleaded.

Once, the tip of the brush came so near her clitoris, she forgot to breathe for several long seconds. Her teeth sank deep into her bottom lip, and the muscles in her center clenched in a vain effort to reach an unattainable peak.

By the time he finished embellishing every crevice of her pink, warm femininity, she was almost incoherent. He'd kept her poised on the painful edge of arousal for an eternity. He actually found a mirror and held it up so she could admire his handiwork. A hot, crimson flush covered her from head to toe as she gazed at her wanton image. She licked her lips, her throat parched.

"Please, Luke . . ." She whimpered the faint request with no real belief that he would release her.

A third time he picked up the case of brushes, extracting the largest one. The handle was shiny red, the brush end, perhaps a half inch wide and an inch long. This time he didn't reach for the oil. He knelt at the foot of the bench between her knees. Then, with the brush poised over her clitoris, he began his inquisition.

A fleeting, barely perceptible brushstroke. "Why did you leave me last weekend, Emily?" She lifted her hips in vain but the brush disappeared. "I was afraid."

The brush returned, dancing over the little spot so hungry for his touch. "Afraid of me?"

"No."

"Then what?"

"Afraid you would feel sorry for me."

"And why would you think that?"

She was mute. In her heart she had promised him the truth. But it was so hard to admit.

He sat back on his haunches, taking the brush with him. She stifled a sob.

He stared at her in silence. "Did I disappoint you?" he asked quietly, his eyes unguarded for a split second, revealing surprising vulnerability.

"No, oh no," she cried. "You were amazing."

"But you left. You were done with me."

"No."

"Yes, Emily," he ground out, his voice implacable. "I woke up and you were gone. You left a note . . . a goddamned note."

His eyes flashed fire. He came closer with the brush. He flicked her most sensitive spot with two firm brushstrokes. Spots of light danced behind her eyelids. She panted.

He leaned near her ear, his breath hot on her cheek. "Tell me why." Another brushstroke and then nothing. Her mind scattered in a million different directions. All she had to do was tell him the truth, and sweet release would be hers, but at what cost?

A lie . . . she thought hazily. Maybe a lie. No . . . that was wrong. This was Luke. She couldn't do that to him. She wouldn't do that to him.

The brush played with her now, swirling and stroking, sending her closer to what she craved.

Her continued silence must have tried his patience. He zeroed in on her clitoris, flicking it carelessly, then working it back and forth with the diabolical brush. Higher and higher she climbed, reaching, aching, almost there . . . she was almost there.

And he stopped. Her eyelids fluttered open, her vision hazy, her thought processes in shambles.

His smile sent chills racing down her spine. "I can play this game forever, Emily. I lied earlier. We have this suite all night. Tell me. Why did you leave?"

Her willpower was in shreds, her sense of self-preservation obliterated. She gazed at him tiredly, her muscles quivering. "Because I love you, Luke. And I couldn't bear to see pity in your eyes."

Shock flashed across his face, and he paled beneath his tan. He dropped the brush, and his hands fumbled to untie her feet and wrists. When she was free, he lifted her into his arms and carried her to the bed. She curled into his chest, exhausted.

He pulled back the faded cotton quilt and laid her on the narrow mattress, lying down beside her and tenderly brushing the hair from her face. His eyes were filled with wonder and something else, something so incredible she was afraid even to think it might be true. He kissed her, a long, slow, drugging kiss. A kiss that was equal parts tenderness and passion.

Finally, he rose onto an elbow and traced her breast with a fingertip, the expression in his gaze shielded by his thick lashes. "No artist ever had a more lovely canvas," he muttered.

She wrapped her arms around his neck. "I'm sorry about last weekend, Luke. Really I am. I didn't mean to hurt you."

His lips twisted in a crooked smile of self-derision. "I fell in love with you, Emily. I even told you so, but you walked out."

Her eyes widened. "In the convertible? I thought you were playing a part. I figured it was part of the game."

He kissed her chin. "I was dead serious. I decided by sliding it in that way, I could gauge your reaction . . . see how you felt about me. But it backfired. I woke up the next morning and you were gone."

She rubbed the stubble on his cheek. "People don't fall in love in three days, Luke."

He chuckled, his expression rueful. "I think I've been falling in love with you for twenty-nine years."

She melted inside. What a sappy thing to say . . . and so romantic it almost made her weep. She stiffened her backbone. "I didn't see you for five years, Luke. If I hadn't contacted you, we'd still be long-distance, once-in-a-while friends."

He traced a line to her navel, making her pulse jump. "Can I tell you something?"

She nodded, concentrating on the feel of his fingers on her skin.

He sighed. "At Brad's wedding I nearly asked you out."

Her eyes narrowed. "You were in a relationship with Chelsea."

"And you lived in Nashville. So what? I'm telling you how I felt. Seeing you all grown up and beautiful hit me like a punch to the gut. You were luminous. I wanted you all to myself. But I let the moment pass, and I've regretted it ever since. Just like I regretted breaking the heart of a fourteen-year-old girl. You've been in and out of my life for years, and somehow I never got it right. Last weekend everything fell into place. Or so I thought."

She winced. "I told myself I wanted that one weekend to get you out of my system, but I was lying. I knew almost from the first moment you stepped out on the catwalk that I was tired of wondering what might have happened between us. I wanted to know once and for all."

He brushed her clitoris with his thumb and grinned when her eyes fluttered shut. Quickly, he removed his trousers, rolled to his back, and pulled her on top of him. "And tell me, Ms. Drake . . . what do you know?"

He positioned his erection to enter her. She tried to join their bodies, but his hands were firm and strong on her hips. "What do you know?" he grunted, his jaw clenched.

She sighed long and low, feeling the delicious truth slide through her veins like champagne. "I love you. You love me. This is our time."

He lowered her slowly, groaning from deep in his chest when they fit together like longtime lovers. "You're mine, little Emily. From this day forward."

And finally, at long last, he sent her to the stars.